# The Dead of Phuket

# The Dead of Phuket

a Detective Sergeant Nick Foster novel

## Ian Fereday

First published July 2022
Published by Ian Fereday

ISBN 9786165932899

In memory of my dad

# Chapter 1

The young woman didn't need to consult her phone to know she was on schedule to arrive at work precisely two or three minutes ahead of the required start time of nine o'clock. She was quite certain she had either OCD or was a little bit autistic because the idea of arriving late anywhere filled her with terrible anxiety, sometimes to the point that she was physically sick. She had no idea how autism was measured scientifically, but if the spectrum was from one to a hundred, she guessed she would at least be somewhere in single digits.

These were the familiar kind of rambling thoughts going through her mind as she exited the lift of her apartment building with a number of fellow commuters to make her way to the call centre she worked at, on the last workday of the week.

1

She left the building at the front door and turned right, feeling the heat of the sun on her face and narrowing her eyes at the sudden flash of bright morning sunlight. Following the footpath around the edge of the building that would take her to the entrance to the underground station, the noise of the early morning commuter traffic got louder as she went. Her thoughts became more focussed and turned to the weekend and planned meet-up with girlfriends on Saturday afternoon for shopping and a meal. Sunday was free for a leisurely lie-in before dealing with all the household chores she put off through the week.

The soft thud behind her could barely be heard, but the screams that immediately followed got her attention and she instinctively stopped and turned round to see what was causing the fuss. There was a crumpled mess on the floor just a couple of paces away, exactly where she had walked only two or three moments ago, and for just a second she couldn't grasp how it could possibly be there now when it hadn't been there before.

In those few moments, her brain helpfully assembled the jumble into the smashed body of a man who had clearly just fallen from a great height and landed head-first. Realising this, she promptly joined in the continuing chorus of screams.

Her next thought was that she was going to be very, very late for work and the stomach-churning began in earnest.

2

# Chapter 2

**London, 06:20 a.m., Monday, 4th October 2021**

The truck passed through customs at the channel tunnel into the UK without a hitch. Its paperwork was in order, the Border Force heartbeat detector did not pick up any human passengers on board and the sniffer dogs didn't alert their handlers to anything untoward.

As it exited the terminal to join the motorway heading north, the Executive Officer on duty dialled a number he'd recently saved in his mobile phone to pass on the information.

"Detective Sergeant Foster, go ahead," came the immediate response.

"Target vehicle whisky tango seven zero, oscar victor tango has departed the terminal. I can confirm it's as briefed; driver only, no cab passenger, it's a blue DAF XF tractor unit hauling a full-size container.

Container is sealed and nothing was found during our standard checks." The officer spoke precisely and clearly, passing on no more or less information than was required.

"Thanks XO, our team is in place. Again, thanks for your assistance."

"I look forward to seeing it on the news later. Good luck," he finished and hung up.

Detective Sergeant Nick Foster was in the rear passenger seat of a parked, unmarked, dark blue police BMW 5-series at that moment, with his boss to his right and two armed constables sitting up front. With the truck having two potential routes it could take from the tunnel terminal to join the M25 London orbital, they had been sitting in a service station car park between the two possible junctions since 5:00 a.m. and, as planned, they would wait until the truck's route was confirmed before joining the tracking team.

His phone rang again right away and he answered on the first ring, having noted the caller ID.

"Foster, go ahead Bravo One."

"Target is on the M20, heading northwest. We have two vehicles behind and two ahead," Bravo One reported.

"Understood, moving now," Nick replied and hung up the call.

"He's on the M20, so he's about an hour away. Let's head down to the Farningham junction to meet them," he instructed the driver. With a silent nod, the driver started the engine and manoeuvred the BMW out of the car park to join the M25 south.

**07:45 a.m., Monday, 4th October 2021**

Although the day had started out fine, it had begun to drizzle and turned the sky a dirty steel grey. Visibility was reduced, but the truck had been shadowed the length of the motorway by the four unmarked cars, joined the M25 orbital and was now in the leftmost lane entering the Dartford tunnel under the Thames.

Nick's driver had quickly caught up with the truck after it passed them, then matched the truck's speed to follow at a distance. Two cars were still ahead and the other two were behind Nick's command car.

"Do we have a 'go', sir?" Nick asked his boss, who had remained quiet throughout the long wait. He'd been sitting unmoving with his hands in his overcoat pockets for so long, Nick thought he'd been napping.

"It's your shout, sergeant," was all he answered without a trace of a smile, although Nick knew he was in a good mood. Just like him, his boss lived for this moment, catching criminals in the act, bang to rights.

Nick picked up the radio and pressed the transmit button "We're a Go, Go, Go the other side of the crossing, just before the slip road. Bravo One and Three slow up ahead of the truck, Two and Four close up behind and command will take the driver's door."

Four quick double-clicks of the radio came back as acknowledgement from each of the cars. Nick sat up straight in his seat and unclipped his seatbelt in readiness. The officer in the front passenger seat

5

checked his own and his colleague's weapons, stowed them in the footwell in front of him, then unclipped both front seatbelts.

The truck was still travelling at a steady fifty miles per hour when it reappeared above ground from the tunnel, and Nick could see that all the cars had repositioned to close in on it. As the junction markers began counting down at the side of the road, he saw Bravo One begin to gently slow directly in front of the truck. Bravo Two was ahead and to the truck's right, preventing him from changing lanes. The truck driver flashed his headlights and gave a single blast of his horn, clearly frustrated at being held up.

Nick was nervous now and hoped the driver got angry rather than suspicious. They needed the truck stopped and under control before the driver could make a phone call. If he got out a warning, there would be no way to catch any others involved, and they were today's real target.

Within seconds, Bravo One had braked to a halt and the truck had no choice but to do likewise. Nick's driver had made sure they were in the lane to the right of the cab and skidded to a halt next to the driver's door. All five cars now had their blue lights flashing. Nick and the front seat officer already had their doors open and jumped out in unison. The officer took a few quick steps to the front of the truck where the driver could see him and pointed his weapon.

"Armed police! Show me your hands!" he shouted and repeated it. The driver looked terrified but his hands didn't appear.

Nick leaped onto the driver's side footplate and pulled the door open. The driver's eyes were glued to the armed officer and the ugly black weapon pointing at him, but his fingers were desperately searching the steering wheel for the phone dial buttons. Nick grabbed both the man's wrists and wrenched his hands away from the wheel before he could make a call.

The two armed officers quickly joined him to cuff the driver and as Nick climbed back down he saw his boss leaning against the car door with his hands in his pockets and the slightest trace of a smile on his face.

### 09:10 a.m., Monday, 4th October 2021

With the driver in custody and the trailer removed to be opened and inspected, Bravo Two had taken over driving the truck and the team were once again headed north on the M25. The truck driver had willingly provided his destination, claiming no knowledge of anything illegal about the cargo. There had been a short delay while they waited for the prearranged second trailer with an empty container to arrive and be hitched, but they soon reached the exit that would take them directly to an industrial estate. As instructed by the now arrested driver, once Nick saw a signpost to the estate he sent a text to a number already saved in the driver's seized phone; 'five minutes out'.

Two of the unmarked cars went ahead into the estate and pulled up some distance past a warehouse with a sign proclaiming *Johnson Import & Export*. The roller shutter door began sliding up as the truck pulled in front of the building and a man appeared to wave it straight inside. As agreed, Bravo Two turned the truck towards the waiting entrance but stopped outside and kept the engine running, by which time all five unmarked vehicles were within yards of the warehouse.

The front seat officer in Nick's car fired up the lights that indicated it was a police vehicle and the driver drove straight inside, screeching to a halt in the middle of the large empty space intended for the truck. There were four men immediately visible, and they all started running toward the back of the warehouse, where Nick guessed they had a rear entrance and a car waiting. Just at that moment, the officers from the first two police vehicles came in through the back door with weapons ready. The four men stopped in their tracks and raised their hands.

The two officers from Nick's vehicle joined their team to secure the building, complete the arrests and search for anyone else on the premises. Once they were satisfied there was no one else in the building besides the four now in custody, Nick walked to the open roller door to call the team with the container for an update, passing folding tables covered in food and water bottles as he went.

"Sorry for the delay, sarge. We had to get a forklift once we opened it up and found everything was palletised. The pallets all had double-walled, sealed boxes on them, stacked two wide and two high the length of the container. The first two rows of four pallets contained dried goods, mostly rice, but the remaining twenty pallets each had three people inside," the officer reported.

"Excellent, thanks Tim. Give me a breakdown please," Nick requested.

"All adults sarge, forty-two males and eighteen females. Not sure about nationality yet, but there's a mix of European, Asian and African. We'll know more when we get them to Colnbrook," he summarised, referring to the immigration detention centre near Heathrow airport.

Nick felt a flush of sympathy for the poor souls who had likely parted with large amounts of cash for this trip, been trapped uncomfortably inside a small box for more than a day, and now found themselves on the way to detention to await deportation. The only thing that gave him some comfort was that there were no children involved.

He headed back to join his boss who was waiting for him with the four captives, now handcuffed and kneeling, with officers watching over them. Of the four men, one was older and wearing a quality suit, gold rings and chains, and a beautiful Patek Philippe watch, Nick noted; clearly the man they were looking for. The other three were each in jeans, T-shirts and trainers, aged twenty to thirty, and of little interest.

"Bravo Three, you can get these three in the vehicles ready for transport," he instructed the officer nearest him, redundantly indicating the men he was referring to. It was clear to all of them who they were here for.

"Please stand up, Mr. Johnson," he told the older

man once the others were out of sight. With his hands cuffed behind his back, the man struggled to his feet with a belligerent look on his face.

"What's this about then? You've got nothing on me," he spat, tilting his head up defiantly.

"You're under arrest under sections twenty-five, twenty-five A, twenty-five B and twenty-five B brackets three of the immigration act nineteen seventy-one. I'm sure you know what that's about," Nick advised him.

"Trafficking? Me? You're 'aving a laugh, lad. I'm a legitimate businessman. If there's something other than dried goods on that truck, then I know nothing about it and you can't prove otherwise," Johnson shouted, leaning forward confidently.

"I'm pleased to hear you know what that law relates to — most people wouldn't," Nick said sarcastically, "Do you really think we'd go to all this trouble if we didn't have the evidence, Mr. Johnson?" he asked with a smile, "We have surveillance video, text and WhatsApp messages, emails, bank transfers, phone calls, phone tracking and you standing here waiting for a truck full of illegal immigrants to arrive. Not to mention all these tables of food and drink, to feed what? Sixty people? I think it will suffice."

Bravo One interrupted them to inform the boss that officers from the National Crime Agency had arrived and were less than happy. Human trafficking investigations fell under the serious crimes they were tasked to investigate and they didn't take well to the police acting on the information themselves instead of passing it on.

"Leave them to me, Nick," the boss said as he headed off to intercept them.

**14:50 p.m., Monday, 4th October 2021**

The NCA officers had been mollified by being able to take over the case and the five arrested men. There had been mumbled accusations of treading on toes and meddling in things beyond the police remit, but the boss had quickly smoothed all the ruffled feathers.

Nick wasn't bothered at all by the loss of the case. Although he and his team wouldn't be credited for the arrests and break-up of the trafficking ring, they'd had today's excitement and they wouldn't have the tedious follow-up paperwork and endless court appearances to suffer through. Although necessary, it was an aspect of the job he did not enjoy. He was also confident the NCA would make the charges stick, so it was a win all round.

Now back at Scotland Yard, Nick sat at his desk in the open-plan office his team occupied, his sudoku app open on his phone ready to begin a game. There would be nothing more to do today, so he looked forward to getting away early for some much-needed sleep. The boss was in his glass box at the end of the room staring at his monitor, and a few other officers were chatting quietly while waiting for the three o'clock news to come on the TV, hoping to see news of today's arrests.

The phone on Nick's desk rang, startling him. He picked up and automatically provided his rank and name.

"Good afternoon, Sergeant. I'm calling from the chief superintendent's office. He'd like to see you as soon as possible," a pleasant female voice informed him.

"You mean now?" he asked, taken by surprise and immediately regretting the stupid question. He really needed to get some sleep and give his brain a rest.

"If you're free, sergeant, then now would be ideal. The chief super is available at the moment. Should I tell him you're on your way up?" she asked.

"Yes, please do," Nick answered, standing and reaching for his jacket from the back of his chair. He looked behind him to see his boss with eyebrows raised, silently questioning where he was off to. Nick walked to the door, opened it a crack and told him he'd been summoned upstairs.

"Shit, it's probably that NCA lot after your blood. Want me to come along?" the boss offered. It was information Nick had dug up that had created today's operation, and the NCA probably thought a sergeant an easier target than a chief inspector.

"It's alright sir. I'll shout for help if I need it," he joked with a smile, closed the door and headed for the lift, doing up the collar button on his shirt and straightening his tie as he went.

❖

Exiting the lift four floors up, Nick looked around for a clue as to where he would find the chief super's office. There were no signs and no reception desk, just blank doors stretching along a corridor into the distance. Nick wondered who the senior officers were hiding from.

Although he knew which floor the executive staff were on, he'd never been up here and was now at a loss where to go. Obligingly, a young woman leaned out from a door halfway along the corridor to his left and beckoned him to join her, which he gladly did as she seemed very attractive from this distance.

As he drew near, she smiled and asked "Sergeant Foster?"

"That's me," he answered, matching her smile easily now he could see up close that she really was quite stunning. Her shoulder-length blonde hair was cut in a bob to frame her face, and she had green eyes and a sharp nose. She wore a plain white blouse over a simple grey skirt, but they didn't detract from the overall impression. His detective's eyes were pleased to note the absence of a ring on her third finger.

"I'm Emily, the chief super's personal assistant. Follow me, please. I'll take you straight in," she told him, smiling still, and coming fully out of the door to head down the corridor with Nick now in tow. The view from behind was equally good, he observed.

Emily stopped and knocked on the next door along, then entered without waiting for a reply. "Sergeant Foster, Sir William," she announced, using the chief super's formal title, as she stood to one side holding on to the door. Nick entered behind her and came to an approximation of attention in front of the chief super's wide desk.

"Thank you, Emily. That will be all for now," the

chief super said as he rose from his chair. She left the office, swinging the door closed silently behind her. Nick hoped he would have a chance to speak with her again before the afternoon was over.

The chief superintendent was a man close to retirement and had reached his limit in rank a long time ago. Balding and overweight, he was no longer called upon to present to press conferences or be the public face of the police, but Nick knew by reputation that he had made a serious impression as a junior officer and was not to be trifled with.

"Now Foster. Thanks for coming up so quickly. You perhaps already know what this is about?" the chief super enquired.

"I think I do, sir, and I'd like to go on record as saying that the operation was entirely my suggestion and it was me alone that pushed for urgent action rather than passing it on to NCA," Nick said in his most confident voice.

"What? No, no. Congratulations on that, by the way. Stuck it nicely to those NCA buggers!" Sir William told him, clearly delighted, "no, this is something entirely unconnected. Have you seen the news about this English chap killed in Thailand?" he asked, retaking his seat and pointing to a chair opposite to indicate that Nick should do the same.

Intrigued and much relieved at this swift change of subject, Nick sat down and confessed he hadn't been keeping up with the news. "I've been rather busy sir, what with the latest case and a couple of others we have on the back burner."

"Then let me bring you quickly up to speed," the

chief super said, reaching for some papers from his desk to consult. "A British businessman, Mr. David Townsend, was shot dead in his car in a drive-by shooting on the first. What's that? Three days ago? Right," he asked and answered himself, "The Thai police believe it's either a business dispute or mistaken identity, but his family disagrees. They're clearly well connected because they've been making a fuss with the Foreign Office, who've now suggested we get one of our own on the scene as an observer. And that, if you were wondering, is you," the chief super finished.

Nick was stunned. If he'd had to give a list of the ten likeliest things he'd be called upstairs for, this wouldn't have made the list. "I see, sir. And when would I be expected to travel? I assume the case is ongoing as we speak?"

"It is, but they don't seem to be making any progress, so the sooner you get out there the better. Perhaps you can shake things up a bit," Sir William suggested.

"And exactly where is 'there', sir? Bangkok?" Nick asked, assuming a British businessman would most likely be living in the capital city.

"No. Phuket, actually," he delivered with a smile, "and I happen to know that's where you were born and grew up. So, get next door and see Emily to arrange travel for you, and don't forget to keep me updated." The chief super placed the papers back on the desk indicating the meeting was over, so Nick stood, still stunned, and made for the door.

❖

Does a sergeant knock on a secretary's door? Nick wondered in the few slow steps he took to get there. He does if he is a polite young man, he told himself and knocked on the door.

"Come in!" he heard in reply and entered the much smaller but equally neat office.

"Hello again. The chief super said I should see you about my travel arrangements. Apparently, I'm off to Thailand," he told her, still in shock at the news.

"I know, aren't you the lucky one! I've taken the liberty of checking flights for this evening. That's not too soon, is it?" she asked, a crease appearing on her brow.

"No, tonight is fine, but before you confirm anything, I wonder if it would be possible to make my own flight and hotel bookings and claim it on expenses when I get back?" Nick asked, regaining some of his thinking faculties at last. The lack of sleep, a beautiful girl and astonishing news had knocked him sideways.

"Well, I suppose it would, but it's very unusual. A flight at such short notice will be very expensive, you know," she counselled him, her eyebrows drawing together. Most people wouldn't want to carry that kind of expense for too long.

"Understood, but all the same I'd rather do it myself," he confirmed, noting her surname 'Brown' from the sign on her desk.

"Very well then, but you should also know the Met

will only cover the cheapest flights, not necessarily the most direct route. Oh, and you may as well take these," she said, offering printouts of flight availability and a selection of hotels she'd prepared.

"Thank you," he said, accepting the offered sheets, "And also, ... I wonder if you'd like to join me for dinner when I get back?" he added hopefully.

Without a pause for thought, she said, "I'd like that," looking him square in the eye with a smile, as if she'd already been quite certain he'd ask.

"Until then, ... Ms Brown," he finished, slightly flustered, turning to the door.

"Until then, Mr. Foster," she answered.

❖

As soon as the lift doors had closed, Nick called up a number from his contacts and pressed dial. It was answered immediately in English, but with a delightful lilting accent.

"Good afternoon, Thai Airways, Royal First Class service. Kanjana speaking. How may I help you today Mr. Foster?" came the formulated greeting. Even after a couple of years of not flying, he was unsurprised they still had his number in their system.

"Good afternoon Kanjana. I need a one-way flight to Phuket leaving this evening. What do you have available?" Nick asked.

A few keyboard clicks later she said "I have a seat on the twenty-one thirty-five. That will get you into Phuket at sixteen twenty-five tomorrow," not mentioning the change in Bangkok as she knew he was already well aware of it.

"That's perfect. Book that please and have a car collect me at six-fifteen. My address is still the same," he instructed her.

After a few moments she told him "That's done, sir. Is there anything else I can do for you today?"

"That's all, thank you."

"Have a good trip Mr Foster, and thank you again for flying Thai."

I wouldn't fly any other way, he thought, hanging up and pocketing his phone.

❖

"You jammy git!" was the boss's response when Nick returned downstairs and shared his news. "I wish I was offered an all-expenses-paid holiday in Thailand!" he laughed. He'd once been sent to the Isle of Wight on a training course, but that was as far as his police career had ever taken him.

"It's hardly a holiday, sir. I will be working, after all," Nick objected, half-heartedly.

"Even so lad. I reckon detecting is easier with beaches and sunshine than snow and rain. Enjoy it lad, this is the kind of opportunity that comes along but once," the older man said more seriously.

"I will sir, but now I need to get moving if I'm to make my flight," Nick said, consulting his phone to check the time and realising he'd be cutting it fine.

"Right you are then, and don't forget to send us poor plebs a postcard!" his boss shouted at his retreating back as he left. Without looking round, Nick waved a farewell over his shoulder as he opened the door to the stairwell that led down to the underground car park.

# Chapter 3

Nick woke feeling well-rested just before the pilot announced they were beginning the descent into Bangkok. After a visit to the toilet for a quick wash and change of clothes, he retook his window seat to watch the countryside appear below. The stewardess had removed the blankets and pillows and changed the fully flat bed back to an upright seat in preparation for landing. Coffee and orange juice arrived just as he sat down. Both were very welcome. Looking out at the view, he thought how different it was to England from above. Where the English roads and villages looked timeless and rooted in the surrounding fields and woods, the roads and buildings across Thailand looked like scars cut across and into the landscape.

He hadn't been home since Xmas 2019, he realised

guiltily. This unexpected trip was well-timed, too, he mused, because he was not planning on visiting this Xmas either. Time passes so quickly when you get wrapped up in work, he thought to himself. Although he always found time to have regular video calls with his mother, father and younger sister, he had a lingering feeling of being detached from their daily lives and that they were all moving forward without him. He knew he'd have to come back more often if he didn't want to feel more and more like a stranger. Still, living in London had the benefit of being able to see his English grandparents most weekends, and he adored being able to spend time in their company. Now in their eighties, the still lively couple had an endless supply of stories to pass on.

Once the meal service was cleared away, it was just thirty minutes more before they touched down on the runway at Suvarnabhumi. Now dressed in shorts and T-shirt more suited to the climate, Nick grabbed his small holdall and made his way to the front door to disembark. Although there was an airconditioned jetway to walk into the terminal building, the heat coming through the gap between plane and jetway still surprised him. After years away, it was going to take time to acclimatise himself to the heat and humidity he'd once taken in his stride.

The Thai ground staff greeted him politely by name and ushered him to an electric cart for the ride to immigration. He handed over his Thai passport to the officer, who looked up briefly at him before stamping an entry stamp and returning the passport.

Taking his seat in the cart, he was swiftly transferred to the domestic departure gate for his flight to Phuket.

Mum and Dad are going to be really surprised to see me, he thought, getting comfortable for this last, short leg south to Thailand's largest island.

❖

The Thai airways' black Mercedes S-class was waiting at the terminal exit door for him and he was pleased to see his luggage had got here before him and was already being loaded. The driver opened the rear door for him and he climbed aboard, thankful for the air-conditioning and cool leather of the seat on his back. He was already hot and sticky just from the short walk out to the car.

"Where to, sir?" the driver asked in passable English once he'd taken his seat.

"Head south toward Chalong temple, please. I'll direct you to the house once we get nearer," Nick informed him and stretched out to enjoy the forty-minute or so ride south down the island.

Arriving at the junction with Kwang Road, Nick instructed the driver to turn left and left again into a private, gated estate of just a small number of large houses. The uniformed guard at the gate raised the barrier as soon as he saw it was a Thai airways limo and did not ask them to stop, saluting as the car passed despite being unable to see the passenger through the darkened windows. Telling the driver to go straight ahead and take a right at the end, Nick admired the beautiful houses they went past. Very different to my London apartment, he thought, but probably no more expensive. They were mostly off-white painted two-storey villas, each with ample covered parking, swimming pools and servants' quarters. Landscaped gardens surrounding them ensured privacy from neighbours and the gate guard prevented access to non-residents.

Having turned right, Nick had the driver stop in the curved driveway of a house on a large corner plot to the left, undid his seat belt and stepped out into the last heat of the day. He tipped the driver, receiving a small bow for his generosity, then grabbed his small suitcase and holdall before going up the few steps to the double front door. It wasn't locked, so he stepped inside and dropped the bags before closing it behind him. The doors led into an open-air courtyard, so he was effectively still outside. He heard a single bark, then saw a ball of white fluff rushing toward him. Bending down with arms outstretched, he said "Hello Lucky. How are you doing, boy?" and gave the dog a hug and a scratch.

Either the sound of the door closing or the dog's bark had attracted someone's attention because the door to his left opened and he turned to see his father appear.

"Nick! What a nice surprise! Why didn't you let us know you were coming?" his father asked, coming quickly closer to embrace him in a tight bear hug. Although now aged fifty-five, Tom Foster was still a fit man, having the time and money to eat well and exercise regularly. At six feet tall he was a couple of inches shorter than his son and completely bald, where his son had a fine head of jet black, straight Asian-like hair.

"Well, I didn't know myself until late yesterday afternoon. You would all have been asleep by then, so I thought I'd make it a surprise," Nick explained.

"Your mother will be disappointed she isn't here to greet you. She and Jane have gone to Bangkok. They won't be back for a couple more days," his father told him. Jane was Nick's younger sister by two years and was slowly taking over control and running of their father's construction and property development business, something Nick had been groomed for and expected to do.

"That's alright. I've got some work to do anyway. Let's go inside and I'll explain," Nick told him.

❖

Tom said he'd already had dinner and let the maid go for the day, but he could call her to come up if Nick wanted something. The family's long-term Burmese maid and her husband lived in a small apartment above the garages at the side of the house, so were always there if needed. Both had been with the family since before Nick and Jane were born, so they thought of them as older relatives rather than employees.

"I'm fine, dad. I'll sit with you for a while, but I don't think I'll last long," Nick told him. There had been more than enough food and drink on his two flights to see him through the day.

His father turned off the music he had been listening to and they sat down on a long couch in the living room. Nick filled his father in on the reason for this trip at short notice, and his father listened in silence while Nick told him the little he knew about the case and what was expected of him.

"You know, I met Townsend a couple of times over the years. He was a nice enough bloke from what I could tell. He owned a real estate business specialising in land plots here and in Phang Nga. I looked at a couple of potential hotel sites he was offering some years ago, but none of them came to anything," his father told him. Nick was not at all surprised; his father either knew, knew of, or had met anyone who was anyone in Phuket, either through his own business or Nick's mother's family connections.

Nick's father was never short of an opinion on any subject and he wasn't today either. "Listen, Nick, in all the time I've been here, you know I've always made sure to keep clear of the police and any legal troubles, and I'd advise you to do the same. Just observe as you've been instructed and report back. Keep your head down and mouth shut is my best advice," his father told him, quite firmly.

"Don't worry dad, I know how to handle myself," he assured his father, "And now, I think I'll go to bed before I fall asleep where I sit. Good night."

"G'night Nick. It's good to have you home," his father said as Nick stood to go up to his room that was always kept ready for him.

"It's good to be home, dad," he agreed.

**Phuket, 04:00 a.m., Wednesday, 6th October 2021**

As his body clock hadn't yet adjusted to the local time, Nick was up by 4:00 a.m. looking for coffee. He must have woken the maid, Chaw, because she turned up in the kitchen a few minutes later to see what was going on. Delighted to see him, she insisted he sit down, then took over making him a double espresso, knowing without asking that would be exactly what he wanted.

Nick sat outside in the courtyard waiting for his coffee. It was still dark and would be for another two hours or so, but the night was cool and dry. Having drunk the coffee, he changed into swimming trunks, switched on the underwater pool lights and started swimming slow lengths. The water was much cooler at this time than it would be during the heat of the day and it immediately relaxed him. After losing count of the lengths he had swum somewhere around thirty, he climbed out of the water and went back upstairs to shower and dress.

He came back down at seven in shorts and T-shirt to join his father for a breakfast of poached eggs on an English muffin with freshly squeezed orange juice to wash it down. He smiled to see his father eating the same thing he had every day without fail.

"I guess you'll need a car while you're here. I'll sort something out, but for today you can take either your mum's or Jane's," his father offered.

"Thanks, dad. In that case, I'll take mum's car," he confirmed, and they both laughed. His mother's car was a plain white Mercedes C-class; a nice car but certainly not ostentatious. His sister's car was the complete opposite, a canary yellow Audi TT two-seater that turned heads wherever it went on the island, usually very quickly. Nick noted his father hadn't offered his own car, not because he would be using it himself, rather that he hated anyone else driving his cherished Mercedes G-63.

"Oh, and it's your grandfather's ninety-sixth birthday this week. He's having a party on Saturday and you should be there."

"I remember mum told me the last time we spoke. I wouldn't miss that for anything, dad," Nick assured him.

With breakfast over, Nick went back upstairs to change into more appropriate clothing to meet the Chief of Police for Phuket province. Coming back down, he said cheerio to his father, grabbed the car keys and went down the front steps two at a time, feeling energised and ready for anything.

❖

The sun had climbed high enough to be felt by the time he arrived at police headquarters in Phuket town just before eight. He chose to park in the street outside rather than the car park, thinking he did not need everyone seeing the foreign cop arrive in a Mercedes. Picking up his well-worn leather portfolio case from the passenger seat, he put on his sunglasses, locked the car and walked through the gates.

Police headquarters occupied a four-storey, plain fronted, white building, which put Nick in mind of the brutalist architecture popular in communist Russia. It looked an uninspiring and dreary place to work.

He did not know how much the local police had been briefed about him, but he expected it was not much more than name and rank. He had thought about this moment, but had not decided until now. Should he speak Thai? Or stick to English and keep his ears open? If he did, how pissed off would they be if they found out later he could speak Thai? Screw it, he thought, I was sent here as a British police officer; that's what they expect and that's what they will get.

As it was still quite early, there was nobody going in or out as he entered the building through the front door. Approaching the reception desk where two male officers sat, he offered a smile and a cheerful "Good morning." One of them looked up, the other continued two-fingered typing on a battered-looking keyboard, his protruding tongue demonstrating the level of concentration it required.

"Ken I hep you?" the officer asked, suddenly looking interested when he saw a foreigner in front of his reception at eight in the morning. He knew they were expecting a cop from overseas today, so assumed this must be the guy.

"Detective Sergeant Foster to see the Chief of Police," Nick told him, maintaining the friendly smile.

"OK. You sit first. I speak boss you here," the man said confidently in even more mangled English.

Nick nodded and took a seat on one of four hard plastic chairs to the side of reception. He expected to be kept waiting, so was thankful he was in an air-conditioned space, even if it was an uncomfortable seat. Looking around he thought the building designer must have been told to avoid any possible colour or warmth. Everywhere was hard, white-painted concrete. To his surprise, a female officer appeared within a few minutes. She was tall for a Thai, he estimated her to be at least five foot nine, and somehow managed to make her tight brown police uniform look feminine. As she came closer he saw she was pretty, with a small nose and chin, and her dark eyes and soft lips were very sexy.

She stopped a couple of paces away and half-turned away from him before saying, "Sergeant Foster? Would you like to follow me?" in excellent, unaccented English. She didn't introduce herself, so he assumed she was a secretary who would escort him to the chief of police.

"Certainly," Nick agreed and followed the young woman back along the corridor she had appeared from. She led him up a flight of stairs, along another corridor, then opened a door and stood aside to let him enter first. He had been expecting to meet with the chief of police, so was slightly taken aback to find himself in a long rectangular, windowless room with three tables set longways down the centre and mismatched chairs along both sides. A box file stood on the desk nearest the door. The woman closed the door behind them, gestured for him to take a seat, then sat down opposite him.

"My name is Sub-lieutenant Marisa Pondee, but please call me Marky. I've been appointed to accompany you for the duration of your visit. The chief isn't in yet because there was an officer suicide yesterday afternoon. In the meantime I thought we'd go over the case file, then you can meet him later when he's available," she explained.

"That's fine with me. I understand if he's busy and I know he probably wasn't expecting me so soon," Nick said, recovering quickly to this sudden change from what he had anticipated. He kicked himself mentally for thinking she could be a secretary when her rank was clearly displayed on her shoulders.

"The chief was only notified yesterday that an English policeman would be coming. He pulled me off a different case yesterday afternoon, and I only just got up to speed with this new one myself. I commandeered this room for us to use. It's a training room, so it never gets used anyway," she told him with a wry smile.

Nick assessed the officer as he would anyone he was assigned to work with. She had a typically slim Thai physique and wasn't overweight. He guessed she was a similar age to himself, twenty-eight, give or take a year, although it was hard to tell with Thais. She was olive-skinned rather than dark as many southern Thais were, so he guessed she may be from elsewhere in Thailand. The fact that she had a nose worth mentioning told him she probably wasn't from the northeast. Her black hair was obviously long, but she had it clipped in a bun at the back of her head. She had on no makeup bar a faint trace of lipstick and wore no jewellery. Her uniform wasn't old or worn, and her belt, badges and shoes all looked immaculate. A pretty girl, but she clearly took herself and her job seriously.

"I guess you were chosen to work with me because you speak English so well," Nick ventured, attempting to offer a compliment.

"I'd like to think I was selected for this task because I'm an excellent inquiry officer, Sergeant Foster," she snapped, sitting back abruptly.

"Oh ... I'm sorry, ... I didn't mean ..." Nick stuttered.

She smiled, sat forward again and said "I'm kidding. We Thais do have a sense of humour you know. I'd be the first to concede that that's exactly what the chief was thinking, but I do believe I'm a good inquiry officer all the same."

Nick knew that the Royal Thai Police equivalent of detectives were their inquiry officers, and it was one of the few real policing jobs that female officers were able to do, being barred from many other roles.

"I'm sure you are," he said, relieved he had not put his foot in it so soon. "What was it you were working on until yesterday?" he asked, in an attempt to ingratiate himself by showing interest in her work.

"Incestuous rape of a minor," she grimaced, a fourteen-year-old girl raped by an uncle in the family home while her parents were at work. The uncle is in custody and I was completing the file for submission to the prosecutor when I got called away. It will either have to wait, or I'll finish it after normal work hours."

It was obvious she was unhappy at having to suddenly drop the case and Nick guessed that given the circumstances she would want it with the prosecutor sooner rather than later. Nobody wanted a child sexual abuse case held up.

Thinking quickly he suggested, "I tell you what, why don't you finish that up and I'll start going through this file to get up to speed?"

She looked surprised and amused at the suggestion. "You'd find that a little difficult sergeant. It's all in Thai of course."

Nick quickly switched to perfectly enunciated Thai to tell her "I am Thai, I can read it perfectly well, and please call me Nick."

She sat back in her chair again and stared at him for a few moments while she considered. "Does anyone else know you're Thai, Nick?" she asked, also speaking Thai now.

"Well, I think my family and friends are quite ..." he offered with a smile.

"Okay, okay, so you have a sense of humour too. You know what I mean," she scolded him playfully.

"Other than the guy at the reception I spoke English with on the way in, you're the only other officer I've met. I don't think the Met passed on the information, so it's just you and me."

"Well, let's keep it between us for now. It might be useful others not knowing. I don't know quite how, but it can't hurt."

"Fine by me. It'll be our secret," Nick agreed with a smile, glad they were getting along better now.

"Okay, you make a start on this case file and I'll go

and get my laptop to finish up that rape case report," she said, standing to leave.

As instructed, Nick removed the lid from the box and lifted out the single thin file inside to start work right away. Opening it up, he noted the handwritten list of contents on a sheet stapled to the inside front cover. It wasn't a long list.

| Item | Description | Officer | Date |
|------|-------------|---------|------|
| 1. | case description | ST3 Jantasak | 1/11/64 |
| 2. | witness 1 interview | PT Wattana | 1/11/64 |
| 3. | witness 2 interview | ST3 Jantasak | 1/11/64 |
| 4. | SD card video | ST3 Jantasak | 1/11/64 |
| 5. | spouse interview | ST3 Jantasak | 1/11/64 |
| 6. | victim documents | ST3 Jantasak | 1/11/64 |
| 7. | autopsy report | ST1 Ngaan-dee | 4/11/64 |
| 8. | ballistics report | ST1 Ngaan-dee | 5/11/64 |

He removed the seven documents and laid them out on the desk side by side, took out his phone and shot a photo of each one in turn. The memory card was in a small plastic bag also stapled to the inside front cover. Picking up the first document, he read the brief account of events as summarised by Police Lance Corporal Jantasak.

The victim, Mr. David Townsend, aged sixty-one, a British national, resident of Phuket, had just arrived on a flight from Bangkok at approximately 16:30 p.m. and collected his car from the car park, where he had left it the previous day. While the car was stopped at the traffic lights in Thalang, a motorcycle pulled alongside and sat there until the lights changed. As the queue of vehicles began moving, about 17:04, the pillion passenger raised a pistol and shot three times into Mr. Townsend's vehicle. The motorcycle then left at high speed. There was no registration plate on the motorcycle and the traffic monitoring cameras at the junction did not pick up the incident as Mr. Townsend was the seventh vehicle back from the lights.

A neat and precise summary, thought Nick, replacing it on the desk and picking up the second document just as Marky returned. She dropped another casefile box and a very thick, clearly ancient laptop on the table, connected the charging cable and plugged it into a socket on the wall behind her.

"It's an antique. The battery gave up ages ago, so it only works when plugged in," she explained with a sardonic smile.

"What do you do in the field?" Nick asked.

"Good old-fashioned pen and paper, and my phone to take video or photos. I've started using it to record interviews too, so I can concentrate on the person talking instead of writing," she told him, placing her phone next to the laptop.

"Is it okay if I take notes?"

"Sure, as long as you don't copy anything."

"Of course," Nick confirmed, making a mental note to keep his photos private.

Unzipping his leather portfolio, he removed a sleek, slim, Microsoft Surface tablet with keyboard and set it up to his left, along with his phone, a notepad and pen.

"Very nice," she observed enviously, "do you want to use the WiFi? It's not fast, but it works."

"No need, thanks, it connects to my phone."

Marky shrugged indifference and got stuck in to her own work while Nick resumed reading the second document. Police Constable Wattana had taken this witness statement from the driver of the car behind Townsend and it told exactly the same story as in the case description.

The second witness was in the next car in the queue and hadn't seen anything of the shooting, but did have a dashcam and the video was on the memory card. Nick removed it from the plastic bag and slid it into the slot on the side of his Surface.

"Have you watched this video?" he asked.

"I have. There's not much to see, to be honest."

Nick clicked on the file to play the video, then enlarged it to full screen. The motorcycle beside Townsend's car wasn't visible from this far back and with the other car in between, but as the lights changed Nick saw Townsend suddenly slump to the left, then jump again, obviously when he was hit by a second shot. As Marky had said, there wasn't much to see, so he replaced the memory card in its bag.

"Unlikely we'll be able to identify the shooters from what's in here," he said.

"Not from that, no, and to be honest it's not really them we're after. Most crimes like this are ordered by somebody else who pays for it. The only point in catching the perps would be if they could identify that person, and they probably wouldn't be able to anyway if they were hired through a third party."

"You're right, of course," agreed Nick, realising he would have to change his way of thinking.

Catching those who actually commit the crime is not the same as catching those who were ultimately responsible for it.

The next document stated that Lance Corporal Jantasak had identified the deceased from his passport and obtained his address from his Thai driving licence. Once the scene had been cleared, he and the constable had gone to Townsend's home to see if there was any family. That was where they had discovered he had a Thai wife, who they then interviewed. Nick was surprised they had started asking questions immediately after breaking the news of her husband's death, and queried this with Marky.

"Probably just too lazy to go back again and wanting to get it wrapped up. Not what I would have done, but there you see a typical example of beat officers dealing with something they should have passed upwards right away. Sergeant Ngaan-dee took over after that, but hasn't been back to see the widow, as far as I know," she explained.

In the wife's brief interview she had said she couldn't think of anyone who would want to hurt her husband and didn't know of any disputes or disagreements he had with anyone, whether business or personal. Nick made a note that she was not asked why her husband had been to Bangkok, where he had been in the capital or who he had visited. That was at least something to follow up on.

The next couple of documents were copies of Townsend's passport and driving licence, so Nick skipped them and moved on to the autopsy report.

Skipping past the all-too-detailed photographs, he read the doctor's summary; fatal gunshot to the head, second shot to the neck.

The ballistics report stated the gun used was a nine millimetre and three shots had been fired. Two bullets had been recovered from the deceased and the third had gone through the driver's headrest and was found embedded in the passenger-side B pillar.

"Well, there's not much here. Do you know what Sergeant Ngaan-dee is planning to do next? Shouldn't he be here, if he's in charge of the case?" Nick asked.

"Agreed, there's not much in the file. I went through it myself yesterday afternoon. No, I have no idea what he intends to do and I haven't been able to speak to him yet. Hmm, how can I best sum up Ngaan-dee for you? Useless asshole? Yes, that just about fits," she said with some passion.

"Oh dear."

❖

Nick went through the file again and made a few more notes while Marky finished up her report. After she had collected the print-out from another office, signed it and put it in an envelope, she suggested they take a break for lunch and decide on a plan for the afternoon.

"Sounds good to me," agreed Nick, now hungry once more.

Nick collected up his things in his portfolio, Marky locked the training room door and they headed downstairs together. She dropped off the completed report for approval signature as they went past the lieutenant's office.

"We can take my car," Nick offered, "I'm parked in the street."

"Great, 'cos I don't think you want to ride on the back of my Honda," she laughed.

"Any preference?" he asked, opening the driver's door. He would normally always open a car door for a lady, but he considered Marky an equal colleague and so there was no place for old-fashioned chivalry. He guessed she'd never had a man open a door for her anyway, as it was not part of Thai culture to do so, so she would be unlikely to think of it as a slight.

"I'm easy, whatever you prefer, but I don't usually eat much midday."

"Then I know just the place," he told her, pulling out into the busy lunchtime traffic.

Fifteen minutes later he turned into Phuket Marina and parked behind the row of shop, office and restaurant buildings facing the moorings. Nick led her through to the wooden deck and they strolled along to his favourite deli near the end. Marky admired the moored boats as they went.

"Sawatdee kaa, khun Nick. It's good to see you again," said the waitress, using the polite Thai word for 'mister', as she opened the door for them. She looked twice when she saw Nick's companion was wearing a police uniform.

Nick smiled a hello and led Marky to a table near the rear of the deli, away from the few other customers who were seated nearer the windows overlooking the boats. The waitress brought them menus and came back to take their orders a couple of minutes later.

"This is very nice," Marky observed.

"It's one of my favourite places for a snack or lunch. The food's not too heavy and they bake fresh every day."

Marky folded her arms on the table and leaned toward him. "So, I'm intrigued. What's your story?" she asked. "I noted your Asian eyes and hair when we met, but I pegged you as possibly a Chinese mix, not Thai."

"The short version is: born in Phuket to an English father and Thai-Chinese mother, which explains the Chinese-looking part. Went to uni in the UK, stayed on to do a Masters, then joined the Met. That's the London Metropolitan Police, by the way."

"I know what the Met is, I am a police officer," she smiled.

"What about you? Where did you learn to speak such good English and how did you end up as an inquiry officer?" he asked as the waitress brought their drinks.

"I was just lucky to have a good English teacher in high school and I've watched many more English language movies than I care to confess."

"You didn't study abroad?" he asked, astonished.

"Nope, just a three-month 'work and travel' break in the US, which was a lot of fun. All my uni buddies were going, so we went to work in a hotel in Colorado as a group. Other than that I must credit Warner Brothers and Paramount Pictures for my English."

"Well, I have to say I'm very impressed with the level you've achieved. I know it's not easy."

"Thank you. As for becoming a police officer, it came about by accident. Like most people, I didn't really have a career plan while at uni in Bangkok, but my roommate's mother was a long-serving policewoman and she inspired me. I finished my Bachelors in computer science then took a Masters in pre-law so I could join as an officer cadet instead of going through cadet school."

The part she didn't tell him was she had dreamed of carrying a gun and chasing bad guys into abandoned buildings, arresting them single-handedly after a shoot-out. Her partner would be single and handsome, and they would likely have an affair. Here she was years later, though, sitting in a cafe explaining to a foreign cop why she joined up, never having chased as much as a stray dog.

"That's very similar to me. I took PPE at LSE for four years without any particular goal in mind, then did a one-year Masters in crime and forensic science at UCL once I'd made my mind up to join the force. The Masters allowed me to apply for fast-track entry to detective training without being a beat constable." Nick explained.

"Your Masters sounds interesting, but what's PPE? I've never heard of that."

"Sorry. I'm so used to using acronyms. It's Philosophy, Politics and Economics, very useful for police officers, right?" he joked, "LSE is the London School of Economics and UCL is University College London."

41

Their food arrived and they ate in silence for a few minutes. Nick was struck by how similar their routes into their respective police forces had been, but had no doubt hers had been tougher, being a female in a male biased environment. With their sandwiches finished and plates removed, Nick brought the subject round to the case in hand.

"I'd like to visit the victim's wife if that's possible."

"Sure, there are no restrictions on us making inquiries."

"Then let's head there before going back to the station," he suggested.

Nick paid the bill and they left the deli to walk back along the boardwalk to the car.

"Excuse me just a minute," he said, holding up a single finger before ducking into a gift shop.

Marky followed him in and saw him head to a rack of postcards. Quickly selecting one and asking for a stamp, he paid and zipped them inside his portfolio.

"For the plebs back home," he told her by way of explanation.

"Where is home exactly?" she asked.

"Good question. I guess Phuket will always be home because it's where I was born and where my parents live, but I've been in London for the last ten years and I feel more and more comfortable there. Where are you from?"

"Phuket born and bred." she told him proudly.

❖

Townsend's house was on the edge of a golf course

in Kathu, so Nick took the shortcut past the British International School to get there. The road that surrounded the golf course had high walls and gates for most of its length, hiding the houses facing the course. Townsend's house was the same, having just enough space to pull a car off the road in front of a tall gate. Nick dropped his window and pressed the button on a post to their right. There was no response, but the gate began to slide open a few moments later. He drove inside the small compound and parked next to a newish blue Toyota SUV.

A typically petite Thai lady came out to greet them and introduced herself in English as Mrs. Townsend. Nick and Marky both expressed their condolences and were invited inside.

"Please, call me Tik," she told them, offering seats in the spacious living room. The room had a glass wall overlooking the golf course and Nick admired the view.

"Did your husband play golf?" he asked, not wishing to jump straight into uglier matters.

"At least once a week, yes. It was his only hobby and his second love after me, he liked to say."

It was a beautiful house, tastefully furnished with lots of polished hardwood. Townsend had clearly done very well selling land and property over the years. They complimented the house and chatted about the view for a few minutes while Tik made iced tea. Nick removed his notepad and pen from his portfolio and prepared some questions while they waited.

"I'm very glad you're here," she told Nick,

retaking her seat, "I know David didn't have any enemies or business problems, so his murder is because of something else entirely. The other officer who came didn't seem very interested and I didn't feel it would be investigated properly, that's why I contacted David's family for help. His son is a barrister." Turning to Marky she said in Thai, "I mean no disrespect to the police, but the officer was too keen to simply dismiss the inquiry." Marky nodded her understanding.

That explained why the Home Office had acted so quickly, thought Nick. They wouldn't want anyone high profile creating a public fuss.

"I see. You said 'other officer'. Weren't you visited by two officers on the day of the shooting?" Nick asked, curious about the discrepancy.

"Yes, but then a different officer came on Monday." Marky and Nick looked at one another in puzzlement.

"Do you remember the officer's name?" Marky asked, equally baffled by this news.

The woman hesitated to think for a moment, then said "No, and I'm not sure he even gave his name. I just accepted he was a policeman because he was wearing a uniform. I know he was a sergeant though, from his three stripes."

Marky was busy swiping on her phone while Tik was talking, and now she turned the screen to show her a photo of a police officer. "Was it this man?" she asked.

"Yes, that's him," Tik confirmed.

Marky turned the phone to show Nick the photo

with a name underneath 'Police sergeant Mongkon Ngaan-dee'.

"Mrs. Townsend, — Tik, have David's possessions been returned to you yet?" Nick asked.

"No, I haven't seen anyone since that officer on Monday," she told him, sniffling as she did.

"I've only just read the written reports and I haven't seen the record of his belongings yet. I'd really like to hear it in your own words, so do you mind telling us again what occurred the day or so before David left and what he would have had with him on the day he died? Particularly paperwork and any phone or laptop."

"He'd been busy since the previous weekend finalising a sale, so he was at home most of Monday and Tuesday, on the phone, you know?

"On Wednesday he went to the Land Department in the morning to be there for the transfer and came home by about three in the afternoon. We went to an Italian he liked nearby to celebrate that evening.

"Thursday morning he played golf early, about half-past six. He didn't like to go too late because of the sun. I don't know what happened while he was there or who he talked to, but when he came home he showered, changed and booked a flight to Bangkok right away."

Nick interrupted to ask "How did he seem? Was he angry, upset, anxious, nervous? Did he say why he was going?"

"No, he was his normal self. He didn't tell me anything and I just assumed it was business, although it was very unusual for him to go to Bangkok alone like that because all his property sales are in Phuket and Phang-nga. As far as I know, he only took a single change of clothes, his phone and tablet. He didn't have any files or papers that I saw, but I could be wrong," she told them but was quite obviously beginning to struggle with her emotions now.

"That's fine Tik. Just a couple more things then we'll leave you in peace. Did David speak Thai? And did he keep an office elsewhere, or work from home?"

"Yes, he spoke Thai very well. He could read too, because of his work. His office is through here," she said, standing to lead the way. She showed them through to a room that also had a view of the golf course. A large map of southern Thailand was on one wall and a well-stuffed bookcase against another.

Nick went directly to the desk, then turned to ask "Do you mind if we look around?"

"Not at all. Please go ahead," Tik said, then left them to go back to the living room.

Nick looked through the few items on the desk. Most were the usual fixtures of a man's workplace; framed photos, a mobile phone stand, some stationery items, but there was no computer. A notepad had a few scribbled notes relating to property, but no names or phone numbers. He reached under the desk for the wastepaper bin but saw that was empty too. He turned to Marky and she shook her head, nothing, so they left the room to return to the living room.

"Did David use a computer?"

"He used to, but last year it broke down and he

said he didn't need one anymore as he'd started using a tablet along with his phone."

"Right, well thank you Tik. We won't bother you any longer, but we'll keep in touch and keep you updated, okay?" Nick put away his notepad and turned for the door. Marky followed him after offering her condolences again, in Thai this time.

"Thank you both for coming," she said, dabbing her eyes with a tissue, then "you know, I can't believe he's gone. When the phone rings, I think it's him. It just doesn't feel possible."

"We'll do our best to get to the bottom if it, Tik. It won't take the pain away, but at least it may give you some answers." Marky told her.

Tik saw them to the door and waved them away as they drove out the gate.

"Is it normal to visit a deceased's spouse and not make a record of it for the file?" Nick asked as they headed back to the station.

"A lot of officers will do the minimum amount of work, just shuffle the papers and run the clock down on cases. Ngaan-dee strikes me as one of them. If we hadn't gone to see Mrs. Townsend, nobody would ever know he'd been. And with him being the investigating officer, he wouldn't expect anyone else to make a follow-up visit without his knowledge," she replied just as her phone rang. She spoke in Thai for a few moments, then hung up and told Nick that Colonel Orntong, the chief of police, was in the station and ready to see him.

"Ngaan-dee will be there too apparently, as it's technically his case," she told him without enthusiasm.

"I look forward to meeting him. By the way, I don't really understand how it's his case, but you and I are given the freedom to do what amounts to a parallel investigation. It seems a bit odd if you don't mind me saying."

"It is, I agree, but the only instruction I was given was to chaperone you and investigate as necessary. The chief didn't say anything about working with Ngaan-dee, and I'd much prefer not too."

"I see, well maybe all will be revealed when we get there."

"Don't hold your breath."

❖

Marky suggested parking the Mercedes in the station car park in full view of the staff, knowing very well that a show of wealth was a good way to get instant respect in Thailand. Nick did as instructed, then followed her inside and back upstairs. She went directly to the office at the end of the corridor where a uniformed secretary said they should go straight in.

The chief's large office overlooked the front of the building and had a fine view of the street and car park. He clearly was not a man who liked clutter. His desk held only a large blotter, a stack of wire file trays and a telephone. A filing cabinet had two framed photographs on top, one of the chief in civilian clothes with a woman, presumably his wife, and the other of the same woman with two young men, possibly their sons. A side table supported a television and a mismatched collection of unlabelled box files.

The chief rose from behind his desk as they entered, as did the officer already sitting opposite him. Marky stopped and saluted the chief before introducing Nick in Thai.

"Welcome sergeant. We happy you come to Phuket," the older man said in English and beamed at him, then spoke to Marky again in Thai.

"The chief apologises for his poor English and asks that I interpret for him," she told Nick, trying and failing to hide a small smile, knowing he already knew.

Marky turned to the other officer and introduced him as Sergeant Ngaan-dee. The man stepped to Nick and offered his hand, which Nick accepted. "Pleased to meet you," he said without warmth or sincerity.

The chief waved his arms across his desk to indicate they should all sit, then called his secretary to make coffee. Nick knew this conversation would take some time, with Marky having to translate back and forth, but they'd made their bed now and would have to endure.

Through Marky, the chief asked how Nick expected to proceed, so sentence by sentence Marky gave his reply. He knew he had been sent as an observer, but suggested he approach it as if it was an entirely new case given him to investigate. Alongside the Thai officers, of course. He hoped this would be possible, and brought the chief and Ngaan-dee up to date with what they had already done today; their review of the file and visit to the victim's wife.

"Do you have any objection, sergeant?" the chief asked Ngaan-dee.

"No sir, as I already said, I think this is a simple case of a business dispute. It's unlikely we'll ever apprehend the actual shooter or driver of the motorcycle as they were most certainly just hired for the job. A long and difficult investigation may eventually reveal the person who hired them but will be very challenging and take a lot of time and resources. To be honest, I have many other closable cases that are more worthy of my time."

Nick didn't like this man already and he'd only completed four sentences. His entire body language was off, too, thought Nick. He is far too cocky and confident for a sergeant.

"That's settled then. Sub-lieutenant Pondee, this case is now officially yours and you will work on it with the farang. Ngaan-dee will pass on anything new he has."

Nick didn't find being called 'the farang' offensive, as it only meant 'the foreigner', but it was quite dismissive when everyone else was being referred to by name and rank. He suddenly thought less of the chief too.

"Thank you, sir," Marky said, looking pleased with the outcome.

Nick interrupted to ask the chief, "I just have a couple of questions for the sergeant before we conclude, if that's alright?"

"Go ahead," said the chief after Marky translated.

Nick turned to Ngaan-dee and looked him in the eye, "You visited Mrs. Townsend on Monday, but there's no record of it in the file."

Marky translated almost as Nick spoke, anticipating what he would ask.

"And?" he answered in a bored voice.

"Well, when will the report be available?" Nick persevered.

"She didn't tell me anything new, so there was nothing to record. I'm not going to waste my time pointlessly writing up a report that no one will ever read."

"I see. And what about the victim's belongings? Where are they? And his car?"

"Still with forensics," he said, standing, "if that's all, sir?" he asked, turning to the chief.

The chief nodded without looking at the sergeant and Ngaan-dee left the room without another word. Nick was a little shocked but Marky seemed unperturbed and not at all surprised.

The chief spoke quietly to Marky for a few moments and asked her to explain to the Englishman that Ngaan-dee was not the best example of officers on his force. He hoped that he would have a better experience with any others he worked with.

"Thank you, sir. I can confirm that my brief experience with Sub-lieutenant Pondee so far has been first class," which she had to translate while hiding her embarrassment.

"She's an excellent officer. That's why I chose her," he said, which Marky was too modest to translate in full. The chief excused them and they returned to the training room along the corridor to regroup.

"I hate that kind of officer and the bad reputation they bring on all of us. The chief feels the same, I'm sure." She was still clearly annoyed by Ngaan-dee.

"There are bad apples in every organisation. The rest of us just have to try even harder," Nick told her, knowing more than a couple of people who were swanning along in the Yard, just killing time until retirement.

"There are so many bad apples here, they're rotting the entire barrel. The public has no respect for the police, only fear. This is not the way it should be. We're here to 'Serve and Protect' as the Americans say." This was clearly not a new subject for her. "And for women officers, it's even more difficult. We're held back, even though we work harder and are usually smarter than most of the men. There's a glass ceiling we have to break through, but nobody has managed it yet. The Royal Thai Police force is like an old boy's club and the rules are designed to hold us girls back," she finally finished.

"Okay, have you got that off your chest now?" he inquired with a grin.

"Yes, sorry. It annoys me whenever I think about it." She smiled and her demeanour immediately switched back to the open and friendly manner he'd experienced so far.

"So I see, now where is forensics?"

Nick wanted to go to the forensic department to track down Townsend's belongings. Without a clue from something in the car, he couldn't see how they were going to get any further. Ngaan-dee might have been right on the money when he said it would be a challenging case to close.

Marky made a quick phone call, then they headed back outside. She told him they wouldn't need the car, as the forensic's building was on the same block as headquarters. After a short walk down the street, they turned into a fenced yard and she showed her ID to the gate guard. Entering the warehouse-like building they came to a reception counter the width of the room, preventing outsiders any access to the interior. A man greeted them and Marky told him what they were there for. He left them for a couple of minutes, then returned carrying a cardboard box with 'Mama Noodles 30-pack' on the side. Clearly a tight budget, thought Nick, suppressing a smile and a humorous comment.

Marky slid the box along the counter to the other end, then opened the flaps to look inside. There was a single sheet of paper listing the items, which she handed to Nick to read for himself.

1  Samsung S21 mobile phone

2  Samsung S10 tablet

3  leather wallet, 2,140 Baht in notes, driving licence

4  passport

"That's it?" he asked surprised, expecting more.

"They won't have bothered itemising clothing, so I guess that's all there was other than clothes."

"Can we take these with us or do we have to do this here?"

"I can sign them out if you want to take them back to the station," she offered.

"Let's do that," he said, dropping the sheet back into the box and folding the flaps down.

❖

Back in the training room with both devices now switched on and placed on the desk, Nick wasn't surprised to find them locked.

"I'll call the wife. See if she knows," Marky suggested. She made the call and spoke for a couple of minutes with Tik.

"She knows the code pattern, so I asked her to add me as a friend on the Line app, draw it out on paper and send it as a photo," she explained, and they waited in silence for a minute until her phone pinged.

"I also asked her if anyone else had requested this and she said no," Marky told him with raised eyebrows. "Ngaan-dee clearly wasn't going to pursue this any further."

Marky opened the Line messaging app and showed Nick the unlock pattern drawn over nine dots, which he swiped into the phone. He opened up the call record and started jotting down the numbers used since the previous Wednesday. There were only four and they kept appearing one after another. Marky pointed to the second one and said "That one's the wife's number."

"Great, then we're already down to three to follow up. Can we find out who these numbers belong to or should we just call them?"

"We can find out from the service providers who they belong to if you have a couple of months to spare, otherwise I suggest we simply call them." She typed in the first number on the list and pressed dial, then immediately pressed the red cancel button when she saw a name appear on her screen.

"This number is already in my contacts," she told him, a look of astonishment on her face.

"Who is it?"

"Police Captain Wanchai Gerdpon, the officer who committed suicide yesterday," she told him, stunned and completely confused. Her mind was racing trying to make a connection between the two dead men.

"Try the third number. That was only dialled once," Nick suggested. She dialled it and quickly discovered it was the booking office for AirAsia. She thanked them, hung up, then dialled the final number, which had last been dialled on Thursday evening when Townsend would have been in Bangkok. It rang and rang, so Marky put it on speaker to wait. Eventually, someone answered in Thai, "Hello, can I help you?"

"Yes, who is this please?" Marky asked in Thai.

"Would you mind telling me who's calling first please?" came the polite reply.

"This is Police Sub-lieutenant Pondee, Phuket Police. Who am I speaking to?"

"This is Police Sergeant Poonsak, Din Daeng Police Station, Bangkok. Can you tell me why you're calling this number?"

Marky explained that they were investigating a shooting and had found the number in the victim's phone log.

"Whose number is this?" she asked the officer in

Bangkok.

"It belonged to a newspaper reporter who jumped out of his sixteenth-floor apartment window last Friday morning," came the reply. Nick and Marky looked at one another in stunned silence.

❖

They agreed they didn't know what to make of these two revelations, so agreed to call it a day and meet again the following morning to share any ideas they had overnight.

Marky beeped her horn and waved as she sped past him out of the car park on her blue Honda PCX scooter. Nick waved back and climbed into his mother's car, thinking hard how he could make a three-way connection between these people who had all turned up dead within five days of one another. He drove home on autopilot, arriving in time to join his father for dinner.

"So how was your day with the men in brown?" his father asked, attempting humour.

"In a word, odd," Nick told him.

Nick recounted the meeting with the chief and the sergeant, explaining how the lowly sergeant was openly disrespectful to his boss and quite brazenly admitted he didn't follow proper procedure. He told him that he had been removed from the case — without complaint — and a more competent female officer had taken over.

His father then listened in amazement as Nick told him the news of the two phone calls they had made. Nick had no qualms about telling his father the details of the case; he knew he could trust his discretion implicitly.

After the meal, they both changed to swimwear for a game of one-on-one volleyball. Tom Foster unhooked the net from the post on one side, then waded across the pool and climbed out to attach it to the other.

"You're taller, you can take the deep end," his father told him. Nick smiled to himself and dived in, taking up position in the deeper half of the pool, knowing very well it was a considerable handicap moving in the deeper water. His father had used the excuse of his greater height ever since Nick had overtaken him at age fifteen.

The four by eight metre pool was the perfect size for a match between two players, and they continued until dusk when his father declared it a draw.

"How is six games to five a draw, dad?" Nick asked.

"Only a couple of points difference after more than an hour of play? I'd always call that a draw."

"So how many points difference counts as a win?"

"That always depends on whose favour they're in, of course." his father laughed.

"You're a hard man to beat," Nick told him, also laughing now, as they headed upstairs to shower and change.

Nick joined his father in the living room for an hour before finding he still hadn't adjusted to the local time and said he would have to go to bed early again.

"That's probably a good idea. Your mum and Jane will be back tomorrow and you know they'll want to catch up with you."

"I'll do my best, no promises."

"Fair enough, g'night Nick."

"Night dad."

# Chapter 4

Nick managed to sleep a little later than the previous day, but he was still downstairs at half-past five for coffee. It had rained overnight, leaving the garden and terrace damp and the air humid. Chaw appeared as if by magic and brewed his espresso, then he took it outside to sit and think about the case. He'd brought his portfolio down with him and now opened it to remove his notebook. He started listing down what he knew to be the facts in the case.

There weren't many.

1. Townsend had been to Bangkok.
2. Townsend was murdered when he returned.
3. The reporter in Bangkok committed suicide.
4. The police captain committed suicide (how?).
5. The three of them had spoken more than once in the days prior to their deaths.

Then he moved on to reasonable assumptions.

1. Townsend went to Bangkok to meet the reporter.
2. The reporter had been killed(?).
3. The police captain had been killed(?).

If his assumptions were correct, then there had to be some item or information that they'd been killed to protect. What was that?

Nick wasn't too sure how the police captain fitted in, as he'd died four days after the other two. Had he somehow been involved in or even responsible for their deaths? Did he kill himself out of remorse? Or was he some kind of tidying up of loose ends, only made to look like a suicide?

There was insufficient information at this point, so what he needed was a plan. Finally, he listed what actions they could take.

1. The timeline of calls in Bangkok pretty much confirmed that Townsend met the reporter, so a check of the location log for both phones will confirm it. The priority is to link the two men.
2. Check Townsend's phone and tablet for any information he'd saved.
3. Look further back in Townsend's phone for the first contact with both of them.
4. Find out how the police captain died. Was he possibly murdered too? Or was it a clear suicide?
5. Was the reporter also murdered?
6. If 4 & 5 were murders, then look into the final movements and calls/messages of both of them.

Looking at his list, it was obvious they needed to go to Bangkok. He checked the time on his phone, six-twenty. Would Marky be up yet? He called anyway. She answered on the fourth ring.

"Unlike you, I don't have jetlag you know."

"I'm really sorry to wake you, but we need to go to Bangkok. Can you pack a carry-on bag and I'll pick you up shortly?"

"I can't just leave Phuket without permission. I need to clear it with my lieutenant. We need to get flights approved anyway."

"Can you call him? Don't worry about the cost of the flights; the Met will cover that on my expenses." He didn't really think they would, but she didn't need to know that.

"I guess so. Let me call you back." She hung up and Nick headed upstairs to pack a bag, shower and get dressed. Marky called back as he was packing to say her boss had agreed but mumbled something about crazy farangs. Nick laughed and told her to send her location in Line, promising to call again once he had booked their flight.

He called Thai airways and got seats on the nine-fifteen flight, so quickly showered, dressed and headed back downstairs. Tom was having breakfast when he appeared with his bag.

"Leaving already?" he asked in surprise.

"Need to go to Bangkok. I'll be back tomorrow if not tonight," Nick told him, grabbing his father's orange juice and downing it in one gulp. "See you!"

"Make sure you park your mum's car somewhere safe!" his father shouted after him.

❖

Marky had sent her location through, so Nick clicked on it to get the route up on Google Maps. He saw she lived in The Heights condo next to the Tesco Lotus crossroads, so it was on the way to the airport and wouldn't mean a detour.

The condo entrance road led to both the underground parking and the circular road in front of the main entrance. Marky had said she would be waiting at the main entrance, so that's where he headed and she came out as he pulled up. She was wearing her police uniform, which he guessed she was obliged to do if she was on duty. She opened the rear door and dropped her bag on the back seat, then climbed in with a cheery 'good morning'.

"Well, this is an adventure," she said, smiling, "I haven't been back to Bangkok since I graduated uni more than five years ago."

"I'm sorry I dropped this on you so suddenly," he told her, looking across.

"No problem. In fact, I'd come to exactly the same conclusion; we need to see the reporter's phone and also see what their investigation shows. I was planning to ask permission to travel today, but you beat me to it."

Marky sat back and relaxed as Nick guided the Mercedes through the early morning traffic. Heading through the green light in Thalang, they both looked over at the spot where they knew Townsend had been so coldly shot dead a few days earlier. Neither

THE DEAD OF PHUKET

spoke.

After a few minutes, Nick broke the silence with "That's a nice condo you live in, good location too."

"Yes, I love it there. The project started about the time I joined the police, so I was able to pay the down-payment monthly while it was under construction. The mortgage is a stretch on my salary at the moment, but it'll get easier."

Nick had never thought about money in the same way that most people did. In fact, he never thought about money at all. With his parents' wealth, all the money he needed was there whenever he needed it. He tried to be self-sufficient, living off his salary, but his father knew he could not afford London property prices and had bought a fabulous wharfside apartment when Nick first moved there for university. It had always been planned as an investment that would be sold when Nick graduated, but years later he was still in London and still in the apartment. He did not take his privileged position for granted though, he knew he was lucky and did not abuse the opportunities he had. If anything, he had worked harder at school and university than the other kids had, as if he needed to prove he was worthy. He had passed every exam he had ever taken and was top of his class more often than not. He was sure this was all in his own mind though, because his parents never mentioned it.

"Where do you stay when you're in Phuket?" she asked him, bringing his thoughts back to the moment.

"At my parents' house, they still keep my old

room ready for me. I've never had my own place here because I was eighteen when I left to study in London and still living at home. My younger sister still lives at home too. I haven't seen her or my mum since I got here though. They were in Bangkok when I arrived and they're coming back today."

"Oh, that's a shame. You'll miss them."

"It's okay, we'll catch up tomorrow, then we have a birthday party on Saturday where we'll spend time together."

"Nice. I love family parties, but it's not something we do so often now everyone is grown up and living away from home."

"You're welcome to come to this one if you like," Nick suggested on the spur of the moment.

"I can't intrude on a family birthday party."

"I assure you, it will be more public than private. It's my grandfather's ninety-sixth, so there will be people coming from all over the place. Trust me, you'll get lost in the crowd."

"Really? You don't mind?"

"Not at all. It would be a pleasure."

"Then I will, thank you."

❖

After leaving the car in the safest spot he could find in the airport's multi-storey car park, they walked over the footbridge and took an escalator up to Departures. Nick headed for the Thai Airways Royal Silk Class check-in desk. Marky followed uncertainly.

Nick handed over his Thai ID card and Marky did the same.

"Do you have any check-in baggage?" the clerk asked.

"No, just carry-ons."

"Here are your boarding passes and ID's. Have a pleasant flight and enjoy your stay in Bangkok."

"Thank you."

Nick led the way to domestic departures and straight into the Royal Silk lounge. They dropped their bags on a couple of armchairs, then headed straight for the buffet. Neither had eaten breakfast before leaving.

Seated with a plate of food, coffee and juice each, Marky said "I can't see the RTP stumping up for anything other than economy class for lowly officers like us. The Met must be very generous."

Nick smiled. "I honestly don't know what the Met regulations are on flights and so on, but I do know what I prefer."

"Have you ever investigated a murder?" she asked out of the blue.

"No, I haven't. I've done pretty much everything else you can think of, but it's a separate team that handles murder at the Yard."

"You're based at Scotland Yard?" she asked in surprise and disbelief.

"I am."

"Wow. It must be a thrill working there."

"It is, even now. It still gives me a buzz when I turn up for work. A lot of famous detectives have solved a lot of famous cases there. I hope I can live up to expectations. How about you?"

"What, murders?"

"Yes, ever worked one before?"

"I've never been the lead investigator, but I've worked on two with my lieutenant. The first was straightforward, a husband strangled his wife at the dinner table, called the police and confessed. It would have been hilarious if it hadn't been so tragic. He said he didn't like her cooking and had finally snapped."

Nick almost choked on his croissant, "Seriously?"

"That's what he said, I swear. The other one was a Thai woman, an ex-bargirl, who killed her German husband after she found out he had a new girlfriend and was planning to divorce her. Knowing she would lose her cushy life with the house, car and bar business, she hired two ex-policemen to do the job. All three got caught in the end, which was very satisfying."

Their flight was called, so they picked up their bags and made their way to the gate. They walked past the queue waiting to board and were comfortably seated by the time everyone else was allowed on to the plane.

"I could get used to this," Marky observed. Nick just smiled.

**Bangkok, 11:35 a.m., Thursday, 7th October 2021**

Din Daeng police station was an identical building to the one they were working from in Phuket, so the RTP clearly did not waste money on new designs. Marky had asked her lieutenant to call ahead to let them know they were coming, so she was pleased when the officer she had spoken to on the phone yesterday met them at reception.

"Come on up," he told them, heading for the stairs. They followed him to the second floor and into a room similar to the training room in Phuket. There was a similar box file on the desk and a second box marked 'property'.

"Please have a seat," he offered, gesturing to two chairs on the other side of the table, "coffee?"

"We're fine thanks," Marky replied for both of them.

"So, I'm Sergeant Poonsak and I guess you are Sub-lieutenant Pondee. Who is this with you?" he asked, flicking his eyes toward Nick.

Nick chose to answer himself, in Thai, "Detective Sergeant Nick Foster of the Metropolitan Police, London, here as an observer."

The officer pursed his lips and nodded slowly, without commenting, then removed the lid from the box file. Nick saw it had as slim a file inside as their own case did in Phuket. He wondered at the point of the box files but guessed it would be another one of those Thai mysteries he never figured out. Poonsak opened the file to the cover document and turned it toward them. They both leaned in to read the contents. Again, it was similar to their own file.

Marky turned the page and they read the case description together. The deceased, Suttichai Borirak, aged forty-eight, a reporter with the Bangkok Times, had fallen to the pavement below his sixteenth-floor apartment window at around eight-fifteen on the morning of Friday, October 1. Witnesses had called the police, who had been able to identify him as the resident of apartment 1623. They had found the apartment door locked and had used the manager's master keycard to gain access. The sliding glass door to the balcony was wide open and there was no sign of a disturbance. The conclusion was that the victim had jumped to his death for reasons as yet unknown.

"Was there any evidence that anyone else had been in the room recently?" Marky asked.

"Nothing I noticed when I searched. The only clothes and shoes in the room looked like they belong to the victim. There was a single used coffee cup in the sink waiting to be washed. I didn't see anything out of place or that made me suspicious."

"Did you check the condo's CCTV?"

"No. Again, it wasn't deemed necessary. It presents as a straightforward suicide."

"What about a phone, computer, anything like that?" Nick asked.

"They're here," Poonsak said, reaching for the box marked 'property'. He removed a Huawei phone and an Acer laptop, placing them both on the desk.

"Have you been through them?" This from Marky.

"The computer, no, as there didn't seem to be any point. I tried calling the last incoming number hoping it might be family, but got no answer until you called me back. It was lucky the box was still sitting on my desk at the time, otherwise nobody would have heard it. The devices will stay here until family claim them, if we can find anyone."

"Is it okay if we go through the file and take a look at the phone and computer?"

"Be my guests. I'll leave you to it. Dial one-two-two on that phone to reach me if you need anything," Poonsak pointed to a phone at the other end of the table, stood and made to leave the room.

"One last thing before you go," said Marky, "have you spoken to his employer?"

"Yes, I contacted them to ask if they had a family contact, but they don't. Call me when you're done," he repeated and left abruptly.

They looked at one another, equally taken aback at his casual interest in the case.

"Macho pride. He doesn't want anyone looking over his case, which is understandable, I guess. I probably wouldn't be happy either, but I'd like to think I'd be more gracious," she remarked, shaking her head.

Nick switched on the phone while Marky opened the laptop and held down the power key to start it up. She hoped it had juice because there was no charging cable in the box. While checking in the box she found a set of keys with a keycard and what looked like a car remote and door key, which she showed to Nick. Other than that the box was empty.

Luckily the phone was not locked. Going through the call list, Nick saw Townsend's as being the last number dialled, presumably by Poonsak, as he had said. Prior to that, he had either called or been called by Townsend and had recently called out to one other number. Nick noted down the second number to check out later.

No photos or files were on the phone, but the location history on Google maps showed the reporter had left the Bangkok Times newspaper building at fifteen thirty-two on Thursday and gone to Siam Paragon shopping mall. There were too many possible locations in the mall to know exactly where he'd been inside, but he'd remained there until just after seven o'clock in the evening, when he had gone back to his apartment. His phone showed it had not moved again until brought to the police station. Having checked Townsend's phone himself, Nick knew that he too had been in Siam Paragon around the same time. After checking calendar, notes and tasks apps, Nick concluded there was nothing else to be found in the phone other than the location and the number.

"Location shows they were in the same place at the same time, so I believe Townsend definitely came here to see the reporter. And there's another number we can follow up," he told Marky, switching the phone off.

"Excellent. That's some progress, at least."

Marky had the laptop switched on and used the touchpad to open 'recent files' in the Windows menu. It was empty. As were 'documents' and every other folder she tried.

"That's very strange."

Nick was watching from beside her and agreed.

"Let me try something," she said, opening Windows file explorer. She knew any recent folders used would appear in 'quick access', but the most recent file there was an expense claim from the previous month. She closed all the open windows and clicked on the Google Chrome browser shortcut on the desktop. Opening Drive, she finally found some recently used files.

"Here we go."

The reporter's folders were well organised and simply labelled. Under 'stories' she found several subfolders with a few names she recognised from recent major news stories. Although she did not recall seeing the reporter's name before, he was clearly a high-level writer for one of the country's better-known tabloids. It would take time to go through all these, she thought, so clicked 'My drive' to get to the home screen and started going through 'suggested' documents at the top. These were the reporter's most recently used files.

The first one she opened was untitled and contained only the name 'Tida Yemyim' in Thai and what she assumed was the date '4/8/15'. Checking the document details she saw that the file had been created at nineteen forty-six on Thursday evening.

Nick was still looking over her shoulder and said "That's not long after he got back from meeting Townsend." He noted down the name and date.

Marky checked the remaining files in 'suggested', but they had not been opened any later than Thursday morning.

"It has to be relevant," said Nick, "do you think someone tried to clean out the laptop and missed the online files?"

"No, I don't think anyone wiped his laptop; I think he kept it that way. It makes sense that he used Drive to save all his work. Keeping it in the cloud meant he wasn't at risk of losing data to a hardware failure and could open his work from anywhere."

"Okay. Well, if there's nothing more here, what do you say to visiting his apartment?"

"You read my mind," she said, shaking the keys she was already holding.

❖

Poonsak offered to accompany them to the condo but was easily put off. His offer had been more out of politeness than a real desire to go along. He did arrange for a police vehicle to drop them off, though.

At the condo's front entrance, Marky pressed the keycard against the electronic door lock, it buzzed and she pushed the door open. They took the lift to the sixteenth floor, where they found the keycard also opened apartment number 1623.

Standing just inside the entrance with the door now closed, Nick observed "We'd have at least rubber gloves on if we were in London, and a full bunny suit if this was a murder scene."

"All the bunny suits got used up in the Covid pandemic," she told him in jest, "only forensics use them here, but usually by the time they get called in several heavy-booted officers will already have trampled the scene and poked around anyway."

The condo was three rooms, the combined living and dining space they had entered into, and a bedroom with a bathroom off. They both went directly to the sliding glass doors that opened to the balcony. Nick slid the door open and they went outside to look down over the railing.

"That's a hell of a long way down," Marky observed, "it would take some guts to jump from here."

"I think we can be sure he didn't jump. I know anything's possible, but it's simply too unlikely that he met somebody the evening prior, made a note from that meeting when he got home, slept through the night then suddenly decided to dive off his balcony the next morning."

"Agreed, let's see if we can find any evidence to support the idea," Marky agreed, turning to go back inside.

Nick offered to take the bedroom and bathroom while Marky remained in the living area. The bedroom was neatly kept and the bed was made. Other than an electronic alarm clock and bedside lamp the room was bare. Checking the wardrobe he saw the usual selection of shirts, T-shirts, shorts and trousers. Two drawers contained underwear, socks and a couple of belts. A suitcase lay on its side on top of the wardrobe with a layer of dust showing it had not moved for some time. The bathroom was equally spotless, as if it had not been used since last being cleaned. The expected soap and shampoo were in place in the shower cubicle and a bath towel hung on a wall-mounted rail. There was nothing of interest here, Nick concluded, so went back through to see how Marky was doing.

"Nothing in there. You find anything?" he asked.

"Yes, I have," she said quietly, pointing to the

security bracket on the back of the door. A stainless steel bolt shape protruded from the door. Nick was familiar with these security devices and knew there should be a folding U-shaped part on the door frame which hooked over it. It was a sturdier and more modern version of a door chain that enabled the door to be opened a small amount to talk to visitors without allowing access. The bracket that should be on the door frame was missing, but its mounting was still screwed in place. "I've looked. It's nowhere in this room, but it could have been broken before. We just don't know," she added.

"That's not something that gets broken by accident," declared Nick, "so I think we now have all the more reason to want to see CCTV footage."

Locking the door behind them, they headed down in the lift to find the condo office or security. On the ground floor, a sign pointed the way to the condo management office, so they followed where it indicated. Marky explained to the two staff what they needed and one of them got on the phone to call security. A young man turned up just a minute later and led them back to his office.

The windowless room was low-lit, had a single desk against one wall and a number of lockers against the opposite wall. A keyboard, mouse and two monitors were on the desk. Each monitor showed twelve camera views. The right monitor was rotating through floor after floor of the building, while the left one appeared locked on the ground floor and car park views.

"How long do you keep video?" Marky asked the

young man, who appeared extremely eager to be assisting the police.

"About two weeks. It constantly overwrites as the disks get full, but around two weeks."

"Perfect, we need to see the sixteenth floor last Thursday morning from say, seven o'clock."

The man clicked and typed and a new window appeared with four camera views; one of the lift doors and three of the corridors.

"There are four cameras per floor from the second floor up. More than that on the ground floor and parking, of course," he told them, which explained why the monitor was scrolling through different camera views. There must be more than a hundred cameras in all, thought Nick.

"Can you speed it up?" he asked in Thai, surprising the young man who had been wondering why there was a foreigner with the Thai policewoman. The man did so, clicked double-speed, then four-times speed.

"That's fine," Nick told him. They would not miss anything at this speed, but it would only take fifteen minutes to cover an hour. They stood in silence, there being only one chair, both of them looking intently at the view of the lifts. The doors opened several times as people entered to go down, but nobody got off on the sixteenth floor. They remained like this for fifteen minutes and Nick saw the time marker on the video had passed eight o'clock.

"Back to normal speed please," he said and the operator obliged with a click of his mouse.

They watched and waited another eight minutes,

then the doors opened and two men walked out. Both were wearing the pink windbreaker jackets of a popular food delivery company, crash helmets, and bandanas over their mouths and noses like wild west cowboys. They almost instantly disappeared out of view of the lift camera, but immediately reappeared on both cameras watching the reporter's corridor. One showed them walking away and in the other they walked toward the camera.

The cameras were good quality and showed colour video, so they could see the men were dark-skinned and of similar height and build. One was carrying a transparent plastic carrier bag, which clearly held a foam food container inside, of the kind used for takeaways. They stopped outside apartment 1623 and one man nodded to the other, who stepped to the wall opposite the door. The first man held up the bag in front of the door's spyhole and knocked twice on it. The video did not have sound, but they could see him lean in to say something after a moment, although the door did not open. He said something else, then the door opened little more than a crack and he lowered the bag and smartly stepped aside.

The second man surged forward and shouldered the door, which must have given way immediately because he disappeared from view. The first man followed him inside and the door closed a few seconds later.

"Stop it there," ordered Marky and the young man clicked his mouse to freeze the screen.

"It looks like they used the pretence of being food

delivery drivers in order to get the door open," Marky offered, "but I doubt that's what they really are."

"Agreed, and they would have had no problem accessing the building dressed like that, particularly at a busy time of day with so many people leaving for work. They could even just walk in as someone else went out."

"Okay, continue please," and the man clicked again.

Still slightly shocked at the casual violence, they waited and when the clock on the screen said eight-nineteen, the door opened once more, the men came out, closed the door and walked unhurriedly back to the lift. They had been inside less than three minutes. The security man had gone white, being aware of what this meant, but snapped out of it when Marky told him to make two copies of all the video from the parking, ground floor and sixteenth floor. It didn't take him long to burn two CDs and hand them over. Marky thought CDs a little quaint in 2021 and hoped they still had a player at the station.

"Do you want to check his car?" Marky asked as they left the security office.

"We're here, so we might as well, but I doubt there'll be anything there."

Rather than wait for the lift they took the fire stairs down to the underground parking. It was spread over four levels, each occupying half the area of the building above, with ramps between them. Marky pressed the remote; nothing. She started walking between the two rows of cars on this level and tried the remote again as she went; still nothing. Nick followed her down the ramp, where she tried again, finally hearing a beep and flash of lights in reply from an older model white Honda Civic parked near the next ramp down.

Nick opened the driver's door, checked the side pocket, centre console and under the seat but found nothing of interest. Marky joined from the passenger side and tried the door and glove compartment without success. They both climbed out, opened the rear doors and looked there with the same result. The boot revealed nothing either, so the car was a bust.

"As expected," Nick said.

"Let's get back to Din Daeng and light a fire under Poonsak, then we should be able to make it home today."

"Sounds like fun," he agreed and they headed for the lift to take them back above ground.

❖

Marky did not waste time going to see Poonsak but instead went directly to his boss to tell him what they had discovered and give him one of the CDs. To his disappointment, she had told Nick he would have to wait in the office they had been in earlier. She shouldn't wash dirty laundry in front of a foreign cop, she said, and he thought that was reasonable enough.

Marky was back in twenty minutes and had another officer with her. Nick saw from his insignia that he was a lieutenant and guessed this was

Poonsak's boss.

Nick stood and the man introduced himself and shook his hand. "Thank you for the excellent work. I appreciate your help," the man said in passable English.

"It was Sub-lieutenant Pondee who spotted the broken door that led us to the CCTV, sir," Nick wanted to be sure Marky was properly credited for her work.

"Nevertheless, you've both done a good job here and I'll make sure it's reported back to both your senior officers. If there's anything else you need, please contact me directly," he said, nodded, and left the room.

❖

"Result!" said Nick, when the lieutenant had left.

"Yes, I rather enjoyed that," Marky laughed, "what now? Back to Phuket?"

"Well, it's only half-past three and we're in Bangkok, so we could hang around, do some shopping or sightseeing, have dinner, then head back later. What do you think?"

"Sounds great. I have nothing to get back for, but don't you want to get back to see your mum?"

"Nah, we'll catch up tomorrow. Nobody waiting at home for you?" he asked.

"Nope. No time for men in my job," she told him without a trace of irony.

"I know the feeling," said Nick, taking out his phone to book flights then call a cab. Marky excused herself and left the room with her bag.

Nick had packed everything back into the boxes and collected up his own things by the time she returned, now changed out of her uniform and with her hair freed from the usual bun.

"I didn't fancy walking around Bangkok in a police uniform. This is what I brought for travelling back tomorrow," she explained with arms out to show off the different clothes. She had changed into a simple cream coloured top and a pair of skintight jeans over flat Vans slip-ons. The result showed off curves in all the right places.

"A huge improvement over institutional brown. You look great," he complimented her honestly, "the cab should be here in a minute. We'd better get moving."

They went back downstairs and waited just a short time for the yellow and red cab to arrive. They climbed in and Nick told the driver to take them to EmQuartier mall. Twenty minutes later they pulled up in the taxi rank at the ground floor door. The main front door was on the first floor, accessed from the raised walkway of the Skytrain.

"I think a snack first, don't you?" Nick suggested.

"Good idea, we completely forgot about lunch."

Nick led the way to Au Bon Pain and they selected sandwiches and drinks, then took a seat and waited for them to be made.

"Give me that other number you found and I'll try calling it." she told him.

Nick opened his portfolio, pulled out his notebook and read out the number as she typed it into her phone. She waited with lips pursed as it rang, but eventually it went to voicemail. She left a message to call her back and made a note to herself to try it again later.

Marky realised they had not called the Bangkok Times where the reporter worked, so Googled the number. She dialled and asked for the editor or news editor. After a short delay, she spoke with a man for a minute then hung up.

"It occurred to me we hadn't thought to go to his office, but his editor says they hotdesk, which means nothing personal is ever left at a workstation," she explained, "Luckily for us."

Nick nodded in agreement, mentally kicking himself that he hadn't thought of it.

Having eaten their sandwiches, they went for a leisurely walk around the shops. Marky marvelled at the bags in Longchamp and the dresses by Issey Miyaki on the ground floor. The mezzanine left her speechless, with all the top brand names on show.

"It's a dream to be able to shop in stores like these. I need either a lottery win or a rich husband," she laughed.

"I think the second is a far likelier prospect than the first."

"More likely neither," she countered.

On the first floor Marky wanted to look in Jaspal. "It's still expensive, but not as crazy as the designer labels," she told him. Nick sauntered while she browsed the rails, eventually completing a circuit of the shop to find her admiring a sleek black dress.

"What do you think?" she asked, showing it off by

holding it against her.

"Stunning."

She reached to return the dress to the hanging rail. "Why don't you try it on?" he suggested.

"Because it costs almost a month's salary," she whispered.

"It's free to try," he persisted.

"Well, if you don't mind?" she hesitated, clearly tempted to see how it looked on her.

"We have time, go ahead."

She was gone just a few minutes, then reappeared to model the dress for him. "Well, what do you think?" she asked again with a huge smile, twirling in front of him. The dress was shimmering black material that only really began just above her breasts; above that were only two thin straps to hold it up. It clung to her breasts, waist and hips as if cut to fit, then tapered out into fine pleats to end above her knees.

"You look amazing. It could have been made for you."

"I love it too, but I was only trying, remember?" She walked up and down some more, checked every angle in the mirror, then headed back to the changing room to remove it.

They continued slowly up, floor by floor, mostly just window shopping but occasionally entering a shop if something caught their eye. When they ran out of shops to browse it was nearly seven o'clock, so they took the lift back down and headed for the taxi rank where Nick instructed the driver to take them to State Tower on Silom.

Half an hour later the lift doors opened on the sixty-third floor directly into a restaurant. The concierge came forward to greet them, made a Thai 'wai' greeting with her hands in a prayer-like gesture while dipping her head and said "Welcome back to Sirocco, mister Nick. Your usual table is prepared for you if you'd like to follow me."

She led them to the edge of the open-air rooftop, and now Marky was genuinely speechless as she took in the nighttime view over the Chao-phraya river and skyscrapers of the capital. They were so far below, the lights glittered like jewels spread over the ground. Waiting staff appeared like ninjas to draw their chairs back and spread their napkins, then left them with a winelist and menus.

Marky leaned forward to whisper "This is really something!" She had a wide smile on her face and did not even look at the menu as she took in all the surroundings in the restaurant and below.

"I'm glad you like it. I always come here when I'm in town. You must try the oysters," he advised. Marky checked the menu and was shocked at the prices of the dishes, but did not comment, having realised by now that Nick was a man of some considerable means.

They shared oysters and wine, then split a wagyu steak and Dover sole. With no room for dessert, Nick asked for the bill, telling her they would need to leave to make their twenty-two fifteen flight.

❖

They didn't talk much on the flight back, nor in the car. Each was thinking about the case and what their next move could or should be. Nick dropped Marky off at her condo, where she thanked him for a memorable afternoon and evening, then he dropped all the windows, switched off the air-con and enjoyed the cool breeze for the rest of the journey home.

It was well after midnight by the time he arrived home and everyone was already in bed. As he hadn't thought to call, he couldn't expect anyone to be waiting, he realised. He went upstairs as quietly as he could, showered, and slept a dreamless sleep.

# Chapter 5

Marky was in the office before Nick arrived and tried calling the number again that they'd found in the reporter's phone. Still no answer. Nick turned up at eight-thirty with coffee and croissants.

"Hot latte, no sugar, correct?"

"You could be a detective one day," she teased him and told him there was still no answer on that number. She was glad of the coffee and pastry. Putting together a plan of action would be easier with caffeine and calories.

"Thank you, I'll do my best," he said with a dip of his head, "as far as I can see, we have three possible leads now, and that phone number is one of them. The second is the name and date we found and the third is the officer who committed suicide."

"I can put in a request to trace the name, but

honestly from experience, it could be weeks before we get anything back, and even then it could be a long list. If you want to look at the suicide, I feel I need to speak with my lieutenant first, or maybe even the chief."

"Understood. I can see how this could be awkward. Might I suggest waiting until you know your boss is out of the building, then going directly to the chief? He has the authority to approve it right away and I think he'll be more amenable, and if your boss is out of the way you have an excuse for bypassing him."

"Sneaky, but I like it," she said, "let's leave it until after nine, then I'll see where my boss is at. In the meantime, there must be something we can do with this name and date."

"OK, here are some ideas we can try locally; social security, income tax, hospitals — er, that's all I've got."

"And driving licence and vehicle registration."

"Great, we have a plan for the day."

They chatted while they finished their coffees and croissants, then as the clock ticked past nine, Marky said she was going to check on the lieutenant's whereabouts. She was only gone a few minutes and came back to report that he had left early for court and would be gone all day. Using the desk phone she called the chief's secretary to see if he could spare five minutes. The answer was yes, so they locked the door and headed along the corridor.

On the way, Nick told her he felt uncomfortable continuing the pretence of not understanding Thai and asked if it would be okay with her to let the chief know. She agreed it would be a good idea to at least tell the commanding officer, and let him decide beyond that.

Being shown into the chief's office by the secretary, both Marky and Nick offered a respectful 'wai' to the boss and greeted him in Thai.

"You learn fast!" said the chief, laughing heartily. Nick never failed to be amused by how much Thais loved it when farangs made an effort to adopt their customs.

"Sergeant Foster has something to tell you, sir," Marky began. The chief indicated they should sit and told his secretary to make them all coffee. Neither of them wanted more coffee, especially instant Nescafe, but it would be impolite to refuse the generosity.

Nick continued in Thai, "Sir, I feel I should inform you that I am half-Thai, half-English. I wasn't deliberately keeping it from you, but the opportunity hadn't arisen to brief you." The last part was not quite accurate, but it was pre-emptive.

"So you're a half-child!" exclaimed the chief, using the Thai word for mixed-race children. He seemed to be even more amused at this news than he was at being greeted in Thai. "Well, that's just perfect. I will be honest with you too, sergeant. I didn't like the idea of a foreigner snooping around our business, but now I know you understand how things work here, I'm a lot more comfortable with the idea. Just excellent!" he said, laughing even louder now.

The secretary brought in coffee on a tray with

sachets of sugar and creamers. The chief roughly tore the ends off two of each in one swipe and dumped them into his cup. Although he did not normally, Nick added sugar too, knowing the coffee would be bitter. Marky did the same.

"The main reason we wanted to speak with you, sir, is to ask permission to look at the death of Captain Wanchai Gerdpon as perhaps not being suicide. We've discovered a clear connection from him to Mr. Townsend and have also connected his death with a second murder in Bangkok."

"That's impressive work. Give me the short version."

Marky expertly summarised how they had made the connections and been to Bangkok on the previous day. She also told him about Poonsak's failure to properly investigate the suicide and that she had passed on the CCTV footage to his boss.

The chief did not answer immediately but sat quite still thinking and rubbing his cheeks with his left hand. Finally he spoke, "Well, you two have achieved a lot in two days," he admitted, nodding, "let me call Captain Gerdpon's wife, then we'll go to see her together. Once I've introduced you and explained what's happened, you'll be free to interview her yourselves."

"Thank you sir."

The chief leaned forward and said in a more serious tone "You must understand how awkward this is, Pondee. It was bad enough having an officer's suicide in the news. We need to tread very carefully to avoid starting talk of murder before it's confirmed.

To that end, we'll keep it between the three of us for now."

"Understood sir," they said in unison.

"My secretary will let you know when I've spoken to the wife," he said. Though polite, that was a clear dismissal, so Marky and Nick stood.

They thanked him again as they left his office, both having avoided touching the coffee.

❖

"Did you get to see your mum yet?" Marky enquired when they had returned to their makeshift inquiry room.

"Yes, the four of us had breakfast together this morning. She understands I'm busy with this case, but expects me at the party Saturday evening and at home on Sunday. I told her I wasn't sure about Sunday because we don't know what will come up."

"Well if there's nothing urgent, I could do with a day off myself to catch up with housework. Laundry and cleaning don't take care of themselves."

"Don't they? I wasn't aware," he asked sarcastically with a smile.

"Oh, I forgot, you probably have a team of servants who follow you around."

"Well, it's not a team ..." he said and they both laughed, taking their usual seats at the desk.

Marky tried the number again while they waited, but without success. They compared all the numbers between Townsend and the reporter's phones, including the two other numbers they were aware of;

the captain's calls and the numbers that had been dialled from the reporter's phone.

The captain and Townsend had phoned back and forth a number of times, as had Townsend and the reporter. There were no calls between the captain and the reporter, and he had been the only one to call the unknown number.

"Well, that got us exactly nowhere," Nick concluded.

Marky believed that cases were stories, with a beginning, middle and end. Sometimes the information and evidence came in the wrong order, so it didn't make sense at first. Most cases were like that; you started at the middle or end and had to work your way back to the beginning. Once you had all the pieces, then you had a complete story. At the moment there were still too many pieces of this particular one missing to see where it would lead.

The phone on the desk rang and Marky answered it, saying only 'okay' twice before hanging up.

"That was the chief's secretary. We're to take our own car and follow him. He'll leave us to it once he's done the introductions," she told him. Nick grabbed his portfolio, Marky locked the door and they headed for the car park.

Marky pointed out the chief's car, a silver Toyota Camry with the purple police shield and sword on the front doors, as it pulled out from its allocated space near the front door. Nick fell in behind as the chief's driver headed through town. Passing Suan Luang park the car indicated left toward Panwa cape, eventually turned right, followed a twisty road for a couple of kilometres, then turned into a housing estate.

The terraces were all identical narrow townhouses of three storeys, each with a space in front to park one vehicle. Given the many different colours they were painted and the number that had extensions built to the front or carports added, Nick guessed this was not a recent housing development. The streets in the estate were narrow and made even more difficult to negotiate by the number of cars parked on the road, and the children, dogs and cats running everywhere. The Toyota stopped in front of a house midway down a street and Nick pulled up behind it. He hoped he was not blocking somebody's driveway, but it would be difficult to do otherwise.

The chief's driver quickly got out to open the rear door for him and he climbed out, straightened his uniform and waited for them to join him. Reaching the front door, they removed their shoes and the chief took off his hat. A large, framed photo of the dead officer stood on an easel inside the door and beyond that a white coffin was raised up on a plinth. Nick could hear the low hum of the chiller unit in the base keeping the coffin cool. The whole area was surrounded by flowers, some with silk bands printed with the names of the individuals, organisations and companies that had sent them. Nick noted one was from Phuket police headquarters, while others were on behalf of other stations around the island. A few older people sat quietly on plastic chairs placed against the wall opposite the coffin.

One of the ladies stood up and offered a 'wai' to

the chief with head bowed. "Colonel Orntong, thank you for coming again. Please sit. I'll have tea made for you."

"That's alright, Noi. I won't stay. As I said on the phone, I just wanted to come to introduce my officers."

Nick was pleasantly surprised to hear he was now one of the chief's own officers.

The colonel turned to include Nick and Marky into the conversation, "This is Sub-lieutenant Pondee and Sergeant Foster. They're working on a case that has a connection with Wanchai. They'd like to ask you a few questions, but they won't take up too much of your time."

The last was added for their benefit, thought Nick.

"Certainly, colonel. I'd be happy to help." The lady smiled at them in welcome. "Please come through to the back where it's more private," she offered, gesturing to a sliding door at the back of the room.

The colonel nodded at them, said goodbye to Noi, turned to 'wai' the coffin, then went back outside to put on his shoes and leave. They followed Noi through to a kitchen cum dining room. She closed the sliding door behind them and offered seats at the dining table. The room was cluttered with large plastic storage boxes, piles of clothes and children's toys. Stairs at the side of the room led to the upper floors and even the staircase was being used to store items. They sat down and got out their notebooks while Noi made tea and brought it to the table on a tray with glasses of cold water.

"We're sorry to disturb you at this difficult time

and we'll try to be quick," Marky began.

"Take your time, dear," Noi reassured her. "My husband didn't kill himself and if you can prove that I'd be delighted," Noi said with conviction.

Thrown off guard for a moment, Marky asked "Why are you so certain of that?"

"Because he was a very happy man. He loved his family, he loved his job, we're not rich but we have no money troubles as many do. He just wouldn't do such a thing. It's utterly inconceivable."

Nick doubted little would be gained from talking to the wife, so interrupted to ask if it would be alright for him to have a look around. Noi said he could look all he wanted, but please leave the mourners in peace. He decided to begin upstairs and excused himself to navigate the congested staircase.

On the first floor was a bedroom to the front and a smaller room being used for storage at the back next to a bathroom. From the storeroom, he could see that the neighbouring house at the rear was barely four metres away. The developer had really packed these houses in.

He did not know what he was looking for, but nothing stood out in either of these rooms so he went up the next flight of stairs to the top floor. This floor was one large bedroom with an en-suite bathroom at the back again. Two large wardrobes, a dressing table and a bed comprised all the furniture in the room. In keeping with the rest of the house, there were plastic boxes here too, storing even more stuff. About to go back down he spotted a tall cylindrical bag covered by a towel with a beer brand printed on it. He lifted the towel to discover a set of golf clubs, cleaned and ready for use.

Arriving back downstairs he found Marky and Noi chatting about funeral arrangements, so clearly she had finished with her questions. Marky looked at him and raised her eyebrows to silently ask if he was done.

"Mrs. Gerdpon, did your husband play golf?" he asked.

"Yes, he did. He took it up a couple of years ago and played every week in Kathu."

"Do you know any of his golf partners?"

"Sorry, no I don't. As far as I know, he was in a group of several players and any two or three of them would meet up for a game whenever they were free."

"Any foreigners?"

"Oh yes, probably more foreigners than Thais, I think."

"Thank you for your time Mrs. Gerdpon, you've been very helpful," he thanked her and Marky did the same, standing to leave.

They both stopped to offer a respectful 'wai' to the coffin on their way out and smiled a silent goodbye to the other mourners. Noi saw them out to their car and watched them drive away.

"What did you get?" Nick asked as soon as they were back on the main road.

"He shot himself with his own revolver, in his car, in front of their house. Lots of neighbours heard the gunshot and a motorbike, but no one saw anybody in the street immediately afterwards. The only other thing out of the ordinary was that he took a day off work on Tuesday, the twenty-ninth of last month. His wife said it was unusual and unplanned, he was gone all day until late evening and she didn't know where he'd been. What about you? What was that about golf?"

"He has a nice set of Ping golf clubs in his bedroom. Townsend played golf in Kathu too, remember?"

"Of course. I see what you're getting at. We need to speak to Tik again and maybe go to the golf course," Marky caught on quickly, "we're friends on Line now, so I'll message her to tell her we're coming."

"Okay. Any chance forensics were called to Gerdpon's scene? He was a policeman after all," Nick enquired.

Marky rolled her eyes in reply, "No, so you can forget about gunshot residue. The cremation is tomorrow, so if we want to ask for a test, we'd need to do it today."

"I don't think we'll need it, but let's keep our options open."

"Agreed."

❖

Tik was surprised to see them again so soon.

"Do you have some news already?" she asked eagerly before they had even got fully out of the car.

"Sorry, no, just a couple more questions," Marky answered. Tik looked deflated and disheartened for a moment but quickly recovered herself to smile and invite them inside.

Seated around the same table with glasses of iced tea, Nick asked if she knew any of David's golf partners.

"There are quite a few, some he played with more than others. I've met at least three foreigners at club functions, but I know he played with some Thais too."

"Any policemen?" Marky asked hopefully.

"Not that I know of, but David knew I wasn't interested in his golf, so we didn't really talk about it."

"What about the name Suttichai Borirak?" asked Nick, "ever hear David mention him?"

Tik thought for several seconds, then shook her head and said "Sorry, no."

"Alright, thank you Tik. That's all we wanted to ask."

"I'm sorry I wasn't any help," she said dejectedly.

"Don't worry, we're making progress," Marky told her and smiled encouragement.

❖

The drive from the Townsend house round to the golf club was very short, and they were soon parked in front of the clubhouse, a low, wide, single-storey building with an overhanging shingle roof. As they walked inside, Marky asked if Nick knew that all Phuket's golf courses were built on old, disused tin mines.

"Yes, I know my Phuket history. And did you know that the mining families were mostly only granted mineral licences for the land, and that they conveniently forgot to return it to the government when they were done mining?" he challenged her in return.

"No, I didn't know that, but it explains how just a few people ended up owning half the island. I've often wondered how anyone could afford so much land. I'm disappointed but not surprised to hear it was stolen."

"Sort of, yeah," he agreed, "but that was a long time ago and those families have done a lot for the island since. They gave land and funds for a lot of school and temple building, for example."

"Right, land that wasn't theirs in the first place," she argued.

"You're going to love my grandfather," Nick told her with a laugh.

She did not have the chance to ask him what he meant by that because they'd now arrived at the reception desk. Nick asked to speak with the manager, and the receptionist invited them to take a seat while she called him.

The open-air lobby had rattan sofas and chairs spread around, so they sat down to wait. There were few people in the clubhouse, but several on the course. Looking across the fairways of the first few holes they could see some of the houses built around the edge of the course. Nick pointed to a house in the distance and said "I'm sure that's the Townsends' house."

Marky looked to see where he was pointing, but the manager arrived at just that moment to take her attention.

The club manager was a Thai man, dressed in loafers, grey shorts and a purple polo shirt with the club logo embroidered on the left breast.

"Good morning. I'm the manager. How can I help you, officers?"

They stood and Marky took over, "We're investigating the death of Mr. David Townsend, one of your members."

"Oh yes, we were very sorry to hear about that. It was a dreadful thing to happen to such a nice man."

"Would it be possible to find out who Mr. Townsend's most recent golf partners have been?"

"Certainly, everyone has to book a tee time in advance and we keep good records. If you'll come with me to reception I can look it up for you."

They followed the man the short distance back to the reception desk, where he went behind it and began tapping at a keyboard. Nick prepared his notebook in anticipation, but it was unnecessary as the manager shortly presented Marky with a printout.

"This is a list of dates, times and partners Mr. Townsend has played with for the last three months. Will that be sufficient or should I go back further?" he asked.

"No, no, this is great," Marky said, accepting the offered sheet.

"Please make yourselves comfortable while you look at that and I'll be here if you have any more questions," the man said with what appeared to Nick to be a genuine smile, although he knew you could never be sure. Thais were masters of the smile for all occasions.

Nick turned to return to the seat they'd just occupied, but Marky took his elbow and said, "No need to sit down, look at this," and showed him the printout with her finger under the booking on Thursday, September 30.

'Mr. David Townsend & Captain Wanchai Gerdpon at 06:45 a.m.'

It was near enough lunchtime, so they decided to eat while they took in this new information and tried to work out what it meant.

❖

"May I summarise?" asked Marky once they had ordered. Giving a briefing or just verbalising the information helped her organise the material in her head, and often threw up new avenues to explore. Occasionally it revealed links that hadn't joined up previously.

"Please do."

Nick had driven them up a narrow lane into the hills above Kathu. Although a lot of the island's greenery was now thanks to rubber plantations, a lot of it was still natural, untouched jungle. The lane had finally ended at a Thai restaurant perched on the hillside, overlooking a man-made pond. It was open-air, but the covered veranda and cool breeze ensured it wasn't uncomfortable, even in the heat of the day.

"Captain Gerdpon met Townsend to play golf. Something he told him or gave him sent Townsend off to Bangkok the same day. Townsend met a reporter in Bangkok to pass on the item or information that evening, I imagine for it to be published. The next day the reporter is dead, Townsend is dead, and four days after that the captain is dead. Sound about right?"

"It does. We don't know any more than that, and the only clues we have yet to follow up are the number that never answers and the name and date we found in the reporter's Google Drive."

"Correct, so not a lot to go on then."

"Do you know what car the captain drove?" Nick asked, out of the blue.

"I didn't ask, but I can find out. What are you thinking?"

"Between his phone and the car's navigation, if it has any, we can maybe work out where he went on that day he took off. It might be something, it might be nothing."

"His wife let me check his phone at the house. It was an old model iPhone with nothing useful I could find. But the car's satnav idea is good, I like it," she said, picking up her phone to find out.

"And try that unknown number again, would you?" he suggested as their food arrived. He had ordered iconic 'pad thai', a fried noodle dish with shrimp, peanuts, egg and bean sprouts. As a personal rule to avoid disappointment, Nick never ate Thai food outside Thailand, so this was going to be a treat. Marky had gone with minced pork fried with basil over rice; way too spicy for Nick's stomach to deal with yet. He started in on his food while she made the calls.

When she put down her phone and picked up her cutlery, she told him the unknown number still did not answer but Gerdpon's car was in the police pound. It was planned to be cleaned before being returned to the captain's wife but had not yet been touched. The officer promised to get forensics in to take a look at the navigation system and call her back.

Her phone rang as they finished their food and she answered with a curt 'Pondee'. She listened for a moment, then hung up and smiled at him, "the car's destination will be with us shortly."

"Damn, that was quick," Nick said, both surprised and impressed.

"Forensics were already on site, finishing up with Townsend's car. The officer I just spoke to has checked the GPS and said the captain only used the car's navigation system for one trip on the Tuesday he took off work. Rather than waste time pulling the route off onto a laptop, he would just see where it had been set to go and send us the destination."

Nick guessed the captain did not need navigation in Phuket, so it made sense that the only recent route would be wherever he'd been that day. "That's good work. While we wait for the location, what do you think we should do next?" he asked, thinking it was early Friday afternoon and they could not achieve much more today. With luck, she would agree and they could call it a day.

"We could follow up on the unknown name we have, at least with the Land Transport Department.

I've always found them cooperative in the past," she suggested, to his disappointment.

"Okay, let's do that."

❖

The drive from Kathu to the land department took them half an hour, so it was after two when they arrived. Wearing her police uniform, it didn't take Marky long to get the attention of a senior clerk and explain what they needed. He led them behind the counter to an office with a computer on the desk. Marky handed him the name and he typed it into the system to search.

"Here we go. Miss Tida Yemyim, born April 5, 1994, took a motorcycle test and was issued a licence on December 19, 2013," he announced as if he had completed a magic trick.

"And the address she gave?" pushed Marky.

The man studied the screen some more, called up a copy of her licence and turned the screen for them to read for themselves. Marky leaned in and read out, "26/4, Soi Tesaban 4, Phanom, Suratthani."

Her phone pinged to say a Line message had arrived. She opened it up and said, "It's the location come through." She looked up at Nick with a victorious grin, and said, "Phanom, Suratthani."

Nick smiled back and said, "You know where we're going next, right?"

"Obviously, but not today. It's too late now. How about an early start in the morning?"

"Fine by me. Seven okay?"

"Deal."

❖

On the way back to the station, Marky tried the number again, but there was still no answer. She left yet another message.

Nick dropped her right at the front door of police headquarters, no longer caring if anyone saw the foreign cop in a Mercedes. Heading home, he figured he could be there before four. Arriving at the house and pulling into his mother's parking spot, he was taken aback to see a bright red Jeep Wrangler occupying the last of the four covered parking spots. Nice car, shocking colour, he thought, shaking his head as he walked past it, wondering who could be visiting.

His mother was in the kitchen with Chaw, preparing the dinner. He leaned over her from behind to kiss her on the cheek and say good afternoon.

"Hello, dear. Have you had a good day?" she asked.

"Yes, thank you. What are you cooking? It smells great." One of the things he disliked about living by himself was cooking for one and eating alone. It led to a lot of waste and more often than not he just could not be bothered by the time he got home. Frozen ready meals and takeaways didn't make for a healthy diet. His mother's cooking was a mix of Thai, Chinese and western, often fused together on the same plate.

"You'll have to wait and see. I assume you're joining us today?"

"I am. We're done for today, although I'll be out again tomorrow."

"Oh Nicholas, you know it's grandaddy's birthday! You'd better be there," she scolded him, using his full name as always.

"I will, I will. By the way, I invited my colleague too."

"That's nice, what's his name?"

"Marky, and she's a 'she'," he corrected her.

"Ooh, finally my son is bringing a girl home!" she laughed.

"It's not like that, we're colleagues."

"A mother can dream," she huffed, "now get out of the way while I work. Go and see what your father's up to," she shooed him out of the kitchen.

Nick found his father in his den, which he insisted on referring to as his office although he no longer worked. The walls were covered with photographs of villas, houses, condos and hotels, all projects his father had built over the years. Tom was sitting at a wide desk viewing artist impressions of a new project and had a 3D view of the same project open on a screen.

"This is the new hotel ideas your sister brought back from Bangkok, care to take a look?"

Nick had zero interest in design or construction but chose to humour his father rather than decline. He pulled up a second chair to take a look at the concept drawings. The style was industrial, with lots of rusty looking steel and iron, plenty of unfinished wood and roofs of corrugated sheets. Nick could see how this would fit in well in the setting of an old tin mine, which is where he already knew it was to be located, having video-called with his sister often enough. She talked of little else.

"The theme will continue throughout the hotel, in everything from the reception counter to the breakfast buffet and restaurant," his father explained, "but of course the room furnishings will be contemporary. People want to see eccentric decor, they don't necessarily want to sleep with it."

"Looks great, dad, when do you break ground?" Nick asked, hoping his lack of interest didn't show.

His father was too enthusiastic to notice. "The environmental approval is already in, as we didn't need a finished design for that, just an outline with the number of rooms. That means we can start as soon as we finalise the design, which is why your sister is chasing me to decide," Tom explained.

"Where is she, anyway?"

Tom looked at his watch, "She usually gets home around four-thirty, so any minute now I expect." They both heard the dog start barking in excitement at that moment, so guessed it was her. The office door opened and Nick's sister Jane came in with Lucky in tow.

"Hi Nick, hi dad. So what do you think?" she asked, always business first.

"I think it's great. You've done a good job, so why not call tonight's family dinner a celebration of your first completed design," Tom told her. Nick was sure his father would have misgivings about some elements of the design and would want many changes, but it was considerate of him to give her this moment.

"Thanks dad!" she squealed with delight and ran off to give their mother the news.

"Tell me about your day then. How is the case progressing?" his father said, turning his attention back to Nick.

"We've connected three separate deaths together, two here and another in Bangkok. As to the who and why we don't have a clue. All we have is a mysterious woman in Phanom who we plan to visit tomorrow." Nick explained.

"Phanom? Sounds familiar, but I can't place it."

"Suratthani province, this side near the border with Phang Nga province. Not too far for a day trip, and don't worry, I'll be back in plenty of time for grandad's party," Nick assured him.

"You'd better be or we'll both be hearing about it for a long time."

Nick said he was going to shower and change before dinner and left his father to look over the designs again. Chaw must have gone up after he'd arrived to switch on the air-con because his room was nicely cooled when he got there. The time difference was still taking its toll, so he decided to have a nap before going back down. Dinner was always at six sharp, so he had plenty of time, but he set an alarm on his phone just to be sure he didn't sleep through.

❖

Nick was showered, dressed and back down in

plenty of time for dinner. The doors onto the courtyard, which had been open all day, were now closed and the lights over the dining table were lit. The table could easily seat eight, but the superfluous chairs had been removed and there were now just four seats and four place settings.

Admiring the table, he saw his mother had selected the finest crockery, cutlery and wine glasses she normally reserved for entertaining guests. She was pulling out all the stops to spoil him, he thought, and appreciated it.

"Need any help?" he shouted through to the kitchen.

"You can open the wine if you like. It's on the top shelf," his mother replied.

His father had already selected the wine and put it on the top shelf of the wine fridge in the pantry. Nick took out one of the bottles and read the label 'Amarone Riserva 2012'. His father was making an effort too, it seemed. He opened the bottle and placed it on the table to breathe next to the centrepiece of fresh flowers. He saw his mother had been up to change also and was now dressed almost formally. He regretted his choice of shorts and T-shirt immediately and went back up to put a shirt on.

By the time he came down a few minutes later everybody else was already seated. He took the remaining chair and opened his napkin over his lap.

"Where did you disappear to?" his mother asked.

"I felt underdressed, so went to put a shirt on," he admitted sheepishly.

"Don't be silly, you're at home now," she said, but

107

Nick surreptitiously took stock of his father and sister, and they too were more than casually dressed. It appeared they were making a concerted effort to show him what he was missing living alone in London. It was not until Chaw switched off the overhead light that he realised the candles on the table had been lit also.

Chaw now appeared bearing a large oval platter and placed it in front of his father, who rubbed his hands in anticipation. Even before it was cut, Nick knew this was his favourite dish, beef Wellington. Just how far were they prepared to go he wondered?

The maid reappeared moments later with two plates of sauteed potatoes and grilled veg and placed one in front of Nick and the other his mother. After another quick trip to the kitchen, she returned with two more plates, one for his father and the last one for Jane. Her plate already had a mini Wellington on it, which Nick knew would be her vegetarian version.

His father cut the Wellington in half, then half again, served himself a slice, then allowed Chaw to serve Nick and his mother. Red wine sauce and béarnaise sauce were already waiting on the table. Once he saw his mother and father begin, he picked up his own knife and fork to savour this decadent treat.

"Did you eat anywhere nice in Bangkok yesterday?" his sister inquired.

"Yes, I went to Sirocco. Haven't had good oysters in ages."

"I could have guessed, you're so predictable. Mum and I tried Vertigo at the Banyan Tree. It was terrific."

They ate quietly, enjoying the easy company of family and the delicious food his mother had spent hours preparing. Nick remembered the Jeep he'd seen parked outside when he returned home.

"What's with the fluorescent red Jeep, dad?" he asked sarcastically.

"Ah, I'm glad you asked. Your mother needs her car back. She has things to do tomorrow. I've got that on loan from a dealer friend for a few days to see if I like it. Let me know what you think."

Nick was momentarily speechless and Jane smirked at his expression, as even she had been shocked by the colour.

"Okay, but don't be surprised if I don't catch any bad guys. They'll see me coming from a mile away in that thing," he said, only half-joking.

They ate without further conversation, each enjoying this seldom cooked feast. Tom cut the last piece of Wellington in half and shared it with Nick, who had been tempted to ask for it anyway. With the main course over, they finished the red wine and waited as Chaw cleared away their plates.

Passionfruit panna cotta accompanied by a light Lambrusco completed the meal, then they all went to sit in the living room. The chatter was light and easy, and they spent two hours filling each other in on all the small news and details they had overlooked during video calls.

Eventually, Nick said he must retire if he was to get up early. He thanked his mother for the wonderful meal and kissed her good night, gave his father a hug and fist-bumped his sister.

Despite his earlier nap, he was asleep within a minute of laying his head on the pillow.

# Chapter 6

"Seriously? How do you even get up there?" Marky asked with a huge grin. She was standing with the passenger door of the Jeep open and had just discovered there was no side step to climb up. Grabbing the handle on the A-pillar she pulled herself up and flopped into the passenger seat, pulling her regulation uniform skirt back down to cover her knees, "it clearly wasn't designed with skirts in mind."

"I think this is my dad's idea of a joke," he explained, laughing at her difficulty getting in. As much as he felt conspicuous driving the red car, he had to admit it was a lot of fun. The instant power from its V6 engine meant the weight of the vehicle was irrelevant, and it took off like a sportscar from a standstill.

It was exactly seven as they began what Google Maps said would be a three-hour drive. From experience, Nick knew that it would take a little less, as the Maps app was always pessimistic. Or perhaps he just drove too fast, he thought.

"Did you have breakfast, or do you want me to stop?" he asked.

"I've eaten, but another coffee would be good."

Nick was pleased he finally had a partner, albeit temporary, who understood the importance of coffee to the proper investigation of a case.

They set off north up the bypass and Nick pulled into the first PTT petrol station, knowing the Amazon coffee was drinkable. Marky didn't move but looked across and said quite seriously "I'm not climbing in again."

Nick laughed and got out himself to fetch their coffees. Back on the road, he brought up a matter that had been bothering him since the previous evening. "You know we're probably in danger, right?"

Marky turned to look at him and said levelly, "It had crossed my mind. If somebody has already killed three times to cover something up, they probably wouldn't hesitate to do so again."

"So we need to keep our eyes open at all times. You're safe enough in the police station, but remember how easily those guys broke into the reporter's condo. When you're on your bike, you ..."

Marky interrupted him, "I know how to take care of myself," she said sharply.

"I'm sorry, I didn't mean to suggest otherwise."

"Fine, when we're together we can watch one another's backs, otherwise it's every man for himself."

"Or woman," he said, grinning, to break the tension.

"Or woman," she agreed, mollified.

With that said, Nick checked the rearview mirror to see if they were being followed. There was less traffic now they were north of the airport and he could not see any vehicles that he recognised from earlier. Satisfied, he reminded himself to raise his awareness level.

Not long after they'd crossed the bridge to the mainland, Nick turned east toward Phang Nga town. They hadn't spoken since he had mentioned their safety, so he decided to try a lighter subject.

"I know I haven't seen how a team properly investigates a murder here, but I can tell you everything I've seen so far is very different to the way we do things back home."

"So London is home? You weren't too sure the other day," she mocked him.

"It is at the moment," he confirmed, wishing he had not spoken.

After a few moments of silence she realised he was not going to continue, so said, "Tell me about how things are done then."

"As I already told you, I haven't been actively involved in a murder inquiry, but my training covered it and I see and hear things around the station. As with any crime, the priority is to contain the scene as quickly as possible, then cordon it off to prevent contamination of any evidence. Forensics will go in next to gather everything they can, and they're very thorough, including fingerprints, photos and video. The senior investigating officer, either an inspector or chief inspector, will want to do a walkthrough himself, and he'll have a detective sergeant with him at all times."

"Why's that?" she asked.

"They work as a team and the sergeant gets on-the-job training and experience from working with the more experienced officer. Anyway, anyone who enters the scene has to be signed in, so there's a record of everyone who entered the cordon. Likewise, a record is made of everything recovered from the scene. It's all bagged and taken away, possibly to be examined further, say for DNA or prints. Then a team will be pulled together. It will vary, but there will always be an Action Manager, ..."

Marky interrupted again to ask what the so-called Action Manager's job was.

"Think of him as being in charge of the 'to-do list'. He'll make sure everything is followed up and hand out new actions to be completed. There will also certainly be an intelligence officer; he, or she," he looked across at her as he corrected himself, "is responsible for technology, specifically finding stuff. It could be vehicle registration searches, addresses, the national inquiry database, company registrations, fingerprints, you name it."

"Makes me think the RTP will never get there," she observed, knowing the resources and desire to put such a system in place did not exist.

"There's more," he said, "such as an exhibits and disclosures officer to record all the evidence, a crime scene manager, possibly a search adviser if there will be any organised searches, a financial specialist perhaps, a family liaison officer, the list goes on."

"Okay, I get that there are lots of roles involved, but what about the actual investigating?" she prompted.

"The SIO will maintain a 'murder book'. It sounds ominous, but it's really just a case file where the inquiry team record every step of the investigation, like witness statements, forensic reports and crime scene photos. A timeline will be put together, plotting all the events leading up to and after the murder. That will usually be on a whiteboard, and other boards will have crime scene photos and photos of everyone connected to the case. One of the most useful boards is the 'association chart' that shows how people are connected to one another, either as family, workmates, friends, etc," Nick paused for breath and to think a moment, "you know what? I think the thing that resolves most cases is not the number of people on the team or the resources they have, it's the fact that every possible lead is followed up. Nothing ever gets left out. Murder inquiries are solved by sheer doggedness and perseverance, and that's exactly how you and I are going to solve this one," he finished emphatically.

He looked across at Marky and she smiled and nodded to show she agreed with his resolve.

❖

By nine forty-five they were passing the turning to Phanom temple a few kilometres south of the town. A few minutes later, Nick turned right onto the 401 highway. This road ran straight as an arrow and he followed it for another kilometre before slowing to turn right. His phone was connected to the car's Android Auto, with the dash screen open on Google Maps. It showed the street they were looking for was somewhere off to their right.

Nick turned into the narrower road with buildings on the left and right, most of them shops. A hundred metres further in was the first right turn and he noted this was Soi Tesaban 1, with single-storey houses along its length. Continuing on they passed soi 2, then soi 3 and finally came to Soi Tesaban 4. Nick turned in and drove very slowly, looking for house numbers.

"These are the higher numbers at this end, so 26/4 must be at the other end," Marky told him. He continued slowly down the narrow street. This was clearly a poor area; the houses were unmaintained and had never been painted since they were first built at least a decade ago. There were few cars in evidence, but he spotted a couple of battered pickup trucks, and mostly older model motorcycles, some with sidecars. Adults and children alike stopped to stare as the bright red Jeep crawled slowly past. They finally came to the last house, showing the number 26/6. There didn't appear to be any houses ahead, but it was heavily overgrown on both sides of the road and hard to tell. They continued on. The concrete road was in poor condition and full of potholes, so Nick took it carefully.

They had nearly given up on finding more houses when almost a kilometre in they came across a terraced row of five single-story homes to their left. These looked to be in even worse condition than the ones they had passed earlier and were completely surrounded by fields overgrown with trees and grass. Nick pulled up just before they reached the houses and switched off the engine. He struggled to get the Jeep far enough off the road to allow other vehicles to pass, but doubted this road saw much four-wheeled traffic.

They climbed out and both collected their notebooks and phones before walking towards the houses. There was no one to be seen anywhere, not even a dog in sight. With no numbers visible to help them, they guessed the second one from the end ought to be 26/4, assuming they ran from 26/1 to 26/5. In the small outdoor area under the front roof of the house was a very old Honda Cub motorcycle, which looked as if it was still used as it had a crash helmet hanging over one of its wing mirrors. The front of the house was a wooden door and a single window with curtains drawn inside.

Marky knocked on the door and they waited, surrounded by an eerie silence. After thirty seconds with no answer, she tried again, more loudly this time. This time the door opened a crack and they could see half a young woman's face in the darkness of the interior.

"Miss Tida Yemyim?" enquired Marky in her friendliest tone.

The girl shook her head but did not speak.

"Do you know anyone of that name?" she persisted.

Again, a shake of the head.

"This is 26/4 Soi Tesaban 4, right?"

The girl replied 'ka' in place of yes.

"What's your name?" insisted Marky.

The girl hesitated, then quietly said "Ning", obviously a nickname.

"Your full name please," pushed Marky.

"I told you I don't know anyone of that name," she said, more loudly this time. The girl made to close the door, but Marky already had her foot in the way.

"Your name," she said again, insistent now, taking her phone from her pocket and unlocking it. While the girl hesitated, Marky swiped the screen a couple of times, then Nick saw her press a green circle. A phone immediately began ringing in the room and Marky asked sweetly "aren't you going to get that?"

Defeated, the girl opened the door and stood aside to let them enter.

❖

The room was gloomy, having no light on and the drawn curtains blocking much of the daylight from outside. The only pieces of furniture were a TV and a fake leather two-seater sofa with foam showing through several rips. A ceiling fan was turning slowly overhead, cooling the room a little. Down the side of the house, a corridor led to where Nick guessed there would be a bedroom, bathroom and possibly kitchen. Marky sat down on the sofa while Nick remained standing with the door to his back, now closed.

The girl sat on the sofa as far away from Marky as she could, with her arms folded and the combative look still on her face. "What do you want?" she demanded, "I know nothing 'bout anything."

Although she looked clean and her short hair was washed and brushed, her T-shirt and shorts were old and worn. She looked to be about mid-twenties, which matched with the year of birth they had from the driving licence.

"We're not the first police to visit you recently, are we?" said Marky gently, and from the girl's body language they both knew it was true.

The only answer they got was a defiant raise of the chin and continued stare.

"Ning, three people have died and we think you know something that can help us find their killer. So tell me why the policeman came to see you."

Nothing but steely eyes.

"Fine, don't help us, but what if the same people come looking for you? That seems quite feasible to me, even if I don't know the whole story. We found you very easily, so they probably will too."

This seemed to get through to her because the girl relaxed and dropped her arms onto her lap. "If he hadn't come, they wouldn't be dead, would they?"

"The policeman is one of the three that have died," Marky explained.

Ning looked down and shook her head slowly, then began to speak in little more than a whisper. Nick saw Marky was recording on her phone, so did not bother taking notes. "He wanted to know what happened when I worked in Phuket. It was a long time ago and I just want to forget about it."

"We're sorry to dredge it up again, but we have to catch the person responsible."

"Hmph," the girl said, looking directly at Marky and shaking her head again, "you have no idea who you're dealing with."

"Then help us."

The girl was silent for more than a minute, but they waited, saying nothing. Finally, she seemed to reach a decision and started talking, slowly at first, "I worked at Amnesia nightclub in Patong as a waitress. Just waitressing!" she repeated sharply and looked them both in the eye in turn. Nick understood she didn't want them to think she'd worked as a prostitute, as many 'waitresses' did in Phuket's party town.

She continued "Sometimes after the club closed, around two in the morning, the boss would host private sessions to drink late with his friends, VIPs, police, bigwigs and so on. The doors would be locked, the music would be turned down and some of the staff would have to stay behind to serve them. Of course, there would be girls there too. You know what I mean?"

"We understand," Marky assured her, knowing the girl meant the 'hostesses' that would be available to the guests.

"I never liked working the boss's 'special' nights because the men always thought they could grope every female in sight. The extra money and tips were welcome but it was like a free for all and I hated it. One night there were a few younger men there too, but they sat separately from the boss's group, as if they were tolerated but not part of the in-crowd, you know? His usual guests would be older men." She hesitated as if reluctant to go on.

"You're doing great," Marky reassured her. Nick saw she was almost on the edge of the sofa, hanging on every word. He smiled, knowing that feeling well.

"I'd been serving the table of young men so as to avoid going near the boss's awful friends. I thought they'd be easier to handle, but one of them started grabbing me and I told him to stop it. The next time I passed him, he pulled me down to sit on his lap. His friends were all laughing and encouraging him, but I was scared because he was holding me down. In the end, I slapped his face hard to make him let me go. That made all his friends jeer at him, but he finally gave in and let go of me."

Ning hesitated, clearly finding it difficult to find the words. After another minute of silence where they again waited quietly for her to go on, she said, "I was angry, embarrassed and crying, so I ran upstairs to the staff locker room. He must have followed me because he was right there when I went to close the door. He slapped me hard and I fell to the floor. Before I could get up he was on me and pushed me face down into the tiles. I couldn't move because he was sitting on my back and had a hand on the back of my head. His other hand pulled my skirt up and he started trying to get my panties down. I was struggling to get away and must have been holding my breath. Finally I screamed and he grabbed me around the throat with both hands. He told me to be quiet or he'd hurt me. I was so scared that after that I just lay completely still and quiet."

She stopped again, tears now visible on her cheeks, but apparently determined to finish her story now she had come so far.

"I won't say it. You can imagine what he did. It was over quickly and then he stood up. He kicked me hard in the ribs and said something like 'that's what you get when you slap someone'. I pulled my skirt down to cover myself and stayed where I was, scared to move, then heard the door shut. By the time I managed to sit up one of the other girls came in and saw me there. My underwear was still on the floor and I was crying, so she knew without asking what had happened. She used her mobile to call the police."

"What happened when the police came?"

"Hah, nothing. By the time they arrived everyone had left and there were just a few staff remaining to clean up. The other girl had stayed with me in the locker room after going to tell the boss what had happened. She came back to sit with me and the boss opened the door to look in for a moment but didn't say anything. Two policemen eventually came. One poked around the room while the other asked me questions. There was no sympathy, he just noted my answers in his notepad."

She stopped again, but Marky knew there had to be more. They waited quietly until she was ready to continue.

"Another man turned up after a few more minutes and spoke with the policemen. I couldn't hear what was said. Then they left. That was it. I wanted to put my underwear back on because I felt vulnerable, but couldn't find them. The man told me he was a lawyer and that he would help me. He said something to the girl who'd found me and then drove the two of us to Patong Hospital. The lawyer spoke to a nurse. She checked me over and said nothing was broken, just gave me a painkiller and a morning-after pill. I didn't see a doctor. Then he took me home."

"What was the lawyer's name?" asked Marky.

"I don't know. I didn't know he was the boss's lawyer and I'd never seen him around the club before."

"What was the other girl's name? The one who found you."

Ning shook her head again "one of the hostesses. We didn't mix, so I didn't know their names."

"That's okay, did you go back to work at the the club afterwards?"

"I didn't leave my room for more than a week because I had bruises on my face and neck, but mostly because I felt ashamed and didn't want to face anybody. In the end, I had to go to work because I had bills to pay, but when I got there I was told I'd been fired. I started looking for a new job, then the following week there was a deposit of one hundred thousand Baht into my account. I guessed it was hush money, it couldn't be anything else, so I came home and I've been here ever since."

"When did you start work at the club?"

"I went to Phuket when I was eighteen, so about 2012. There was no work around here when I finished high school. I worked in a few places before Amnesia, but I'd been there about a year when it happened."

"And when did it happen. Do you remember the date?"

"The fourth of August, 2015. I'll never forget that date." As expected, that matched with the date they'd found with her name in the reporter's Google drive.

"I'm sorry for the questions Ning, but I have to ask. Do you know who did it to you?" Marky asked softly.

The girl shook her head, "No, he was just another customer who knew the boss and got to stay inside drinking after hours. I didn't know any of them."

"Can you describe him?"

"He was about twenty. Very dark-skinned. Typical Thai with the usual dark hair and eyes. There's nothing special I can tell you about him, he looked ordinary, like thousands of other people."

"Do you live here alone?"

"My mum died of Covid in January. I've been alone since then."

"I'm sorry to hear that. Do you have a job?"

"I sell fried chicken and sticky rice in the afternoon and evening. I used to do it with my mum, but it's just me now," she said.

"The policeman who came a couple of weeks ago. What did he want? What did he ask you?"

"He told me he was one of the officers who'd come to the club that night. I didn't recognise him after so long. He kept apologising and said he'd felt bad ever since about abandoning me and wanted to make up for it. I felt like spitting in his face. He should have done his job properly back then. He didn't stay long and he didn't explain how he thought he could help. I didn't really care to be honest."

Marky hesitated a few moments, then said "Look, I want to be frank with you. After all this time, with no evidence, no witnesses, and no DNA, it's going to be nearly impossible to prosecute anyone."

"I know that. I told you, I just want to forget."

"Not being able to charge the person who did that to you doesn't mean we can't go after the other policeman, the club owner, the lawyer and anyone else who let you down that night."

"Do what you like as long as you keep me out of it."

Marky turned to look at Nick and they exchanged a look of understanding. She turned back to Ning and said, "I want you to save the number I called you from just now. Answer if I call you, but don't talk to anyone else if you don't recognise the number. We are doing our job and I promise you we won't drop it."

Totally unexpectedly, Ning surprised Marky by embracing her in a hug. She sobbed for a moment, then let her go and whispered "Thank you".

❖

Neither of them said anything as they walked

back to the car, but once the doors were closed Marky said "Wow".

"Quite. Good thinking with the phone number, by the way."

"Thank you. Let's see if we can find some lunch, but more importantly a strong coffee." The girl's story had struck a nerve.

"I'll second that," he said, turning the car round in the narrow street and getting them pointed back in the direction of the main road. "You handled her very well," he complimented her.

"Thanks. Sadly I've had too much experience dealing with rape and abuse of girls. It's all too common."

There were no cafes or restaurants they could see among the few buildings on the 401, so Nick continued on, passing the junction with the road they had used to come north and told Marky they would take the longer way home via Khao Lak. Soon enough they saw a sign announcing a restaurant ahead, and Nick pulled into the Fireback Cafe after another hundred metres.

"Unusual name," he said as they got out of the car.

"It's the name of a pheasant that's the national bird of Thailand. You ought to know that, being Thai," she admonished him.

"Then I've learned something today, thank you."

Fireback Cafe was a steel-framed building with a corrugated metal sheet roof and wooden floor. It was built at the top of a steep slope dropping into the valley below and had a wide view over the tree-covered hills. The tables and chairs inside were also welded steel topped with wooden boards. Everything that could be painted had been painted black.

The restaurant was deserted other than the waiting staff, so they had a free choice of seats. Marky led the way to a table at the edge that enjoyed the view of the hills. A young man followed them, smiled once they were seated then dropped menus on the table. They looked the menu over in silence, then Marky asked if Nick had decided what he was having. He said he had and she called the waiter back to take their orders.

"So, what does Ning's story tell us?" she asked after the waiter was out of earshot.

"Well, it seems to me to be a stretch that three people have been killed to cover up a rape that happened, what, six years ago, and that there's no record or evidence for?"

"Agreed, but it's obviously the thing that kicked off the murders, and even if we've now got the why, we still don't know the who. Somebody is clearly concerned enough to want to stop the story from becoming public."

"The only clue we have from here is the lawyer, so we need to find out who he is," declared Nick.

"That's not all we have. We can try to find out who the other officer was with Gerdpon that night, and the club owner is worth looking at, if only because he has wealth and connections. He's just the kind of person that can cover up shit like this," Marky said, clearly disgusted at the thought.

"You're right, and he wouldn't want that kind of

news getting out about his club and after-hours drinking sessions. But again, I don't see it's worth murdering someone over."

"Life is cheap. People have been killed for less," she said, but stopped talking as the waiter brought their food and drinks, set down a selection of condiments, then left them to it.

"So who do you want to start with?" asked Nick.

"See if we can find out who the second officer is, then the club owner and then the lawyer."

Nick nodded in agreement, then they ate their lunch in silence, enjoying the unspoiled view below.

❖

There was no more talk of the case as they continued the drive home. The road took them through Khao Sok, undulating and winding as it made its way through the valleys, but climbing occasionally as it left one valley to enter the next. Nick was glad they'd come back by this route as the scenery was fabulous. The area was mostly still pristine thanks to being part of a national park.

As they turned south toward Khao Lak, Marky asked about the evening ahead. "You haven't told me anything. I don't know where it is, what I should wear, how I'm getting there, what time it is, nothing."

"Right, of course. Well, it will be a buffet rather than sit down meal, simply because there will be too many people. It will be very formal and a lot of Phuket's elite will be there."

"I'm not sure I have anything to wear that I'd describe as formal."

"Don't worry about it. Wear what you feel comfortable in; you'll look good in anything," he reassured her with a smile.

"I thought this was a family birthday. It sounds more like a major event. Just who is your grandfather, anyway?"

Nick had expected this question sooner or later, and although not reluctant to share his family background, it was not something he told many people.

"My mother's maiden name is Ying-jareun-paisan. Her father is Chun-hiang Ying-jareun-paisan," he told her, looking over to gauge her reaction.

"What!? You have got to be kidding me! They're like Phuket royalty."

"I thought you might be surprised."

"Surprised!? Well, I'll tell you right now - I'm not coming. You can forget it. I'll look a complete fool amongst that lot. It'll be like a meeting of Phuket's gentry."

"Don't be like that," he implored her, "I wouldn't have invited you if I didn't think you'd enjoy it. You'll be fine. Besides, my mother is expecting to meet you."

Marky sat quietly for the next few kilometres, then finally said "Okay, but you better promise to stick by and keep me right. I don't want to look an idiot."

"You could never look an idiot."

Now she was over the initial shock and her decision had been made, she wanted to know more about what to expect.

"Right, well, I've explained about the food. There'll also be a bar and waiters circulating, so plenty of alcohol. Grandfather won't appear until everyone has arrived — we should be there by seven — and then he'll make his entrance and take a seat. He's old, so he'll stay seated throughout the evening and all the sycophants and wannabes will take it in turn to congratulate him and brown-nose."

The last part made her laugh as she imagined it, "and where is the party being held?"

"At his house in town."

"Whoa, you mean the old mansion next to the district office, right?" Everyone knew this house, the largest and best-kept Sino-Portuguese house on the island, that had been passed down from generation to generation of the Ying-jareun-paisan family.

"That's the one," he admitted, barely suppressing a smile, "my parents will be there much earlier and my sister is bringing one of her girlfriends, so I'll pick you up at six-thirty if that's alright?"

"That's fine, assuming I can find something to wear," she repeated, mentally cataloguing her wardrobe to see what could possibly be suitable. Now that she had made her mind up to go, excitement was kicking in as she thought about the house and the people she would see there.

"And will we be arriving in this red monstrosity?"

"No," he laughed, "mum and dad will take his car, so I'll be able to use hers."

"Thank heaven for small mercies. I'll be able to get out with my dignity intact," she joked, now fully back on board.

Marky's mind drifted to what she knew of Ying-jareun-paisan history. Most Phuket people grew up knowing about the famous four families that had grown rich from tin-mining on Phuket, and as far afield as Phang Nga and Krabi. Nick's family were pre-eminent amongst them. Tin mining had begun in the mid-1800s, peaked toward the beginning of the twentieth century, then slowly declined until the last mine closed in the 1970s when it was no longer commercially viable.

"Tell me about your family," she prompted.

"You mean my parents and sister, or the Ying-jareun-paisan clan?" he asked, suspecting it was the latter that intrigued her.

"Your family's history in Phuket. I don't know much beyond the little I learned at school."

"I'll do my best, but my mother is the expert on family history," he warned her, "My grandfather's great-grandfather came to Phuket from Penang sometime around 1870. What does that make him? My great-great-great-grandfather? Something like that.

"Anyway, he wasn't a wealthy man, but he had a bit of money saved and he arrived when tin prices were depressed and crushing government taxes had begun. He took a gamble with what little money he had, and could borrow, to buy mines from people desperate to get out of the business. I guess a lot of people thought it was all over, but he believed

131

otherwise.

"Eventually, the Chinese started rioting in Ranong and it spread all the way down to Phuket. While that was going on he bought up even more mines with more borrowed money. By the time the authorities had calmed everyone down, he'd managed to put together a substantial portfolio of mines and other property. The taxes were rescinded, the price of tin went up and he soon became a very rich man."

"It sounds so easy," she remarked, "opportunities like that don't come along nowadays."

"Opportunities are always there if you're smart enough to see them, just look at Bezos and Musk," he corrected her.

"So go on, this is interesting," she encouraged him, now fully engrossed in the story.

"He made money, he had sons, they continued the business and expanded it. They bought land. You know the Chinese collect land like other people collect stamps," he quipped, "by the time my grandfather was old enough to take part in the business the second world war had begun and the demand for tin was huge.

"When the dust settled from that, the price began to drop again and the family looked to diversify. Remember, this is way before tourism came to Phuket, so hotels weren't even thought of back then." He stopped to think for a minute, then continued, "the land that had been acquired was turned to rubber and palm oil plantations, some was rented out to tenant farmers. The mines that had been decommissioned became development land for housing estates, some was returned to the government to build a reservoir.

"By the sixties, with car ownership properly taking off, the family opened car dealerships and petrol stations. As tourism grew from the early 80s, they built their first hotel north of Patong. Dad's company built the second and that's how he and mum met. Those are really all you see of the family business now in Phuket, but there's still a lot of undeveloped land both on the island and the surrounding mainland."

"So you're even richer than I already thought you were," she said, poking fun at him.

"Not really. I won't deny my parents are wealthy, but there are literally dozens of cousins out there, many of whom work day-to-day in the family businesses. None of it belongs to just one person."

"Your mother has brothers and sisters then?"

"Oh boy, does she! Grandfather had four wives and I think thirteen children in all. He married his first wife when they were young, but took a 'minor' wife just a few years later. She lived in a house right at the top of the island and he would visit her and their children when he was touring his properties. With the first wife he had three sons and with the other one, he had a son and daughter. After the first wife died, he remarried to a younger woman and had another three children, two more sons and two daughters. The last one of those is my mother. He took yet another 'minor' wife after all those were born and, get this, she came to live in the main house with them! They must have been very different times."

"I'm not shocked. I think a lot of that used to go on, and still does today to some extent," Marky told him.

"And from those thirteen children, he ended up with somewhere in the order of forty grandchildren, including me. The older ones of those already have children of their own and that's why there'll be so many people attending tonight. I said it would be a crowd!" he laughed.

"So come on, you've had a walk through my family history. Tell me about yours."

"There's not much to tell and it's certainly not as fascinating as yours. My father is originally from Phuket, his parents had a small hardware store in Samkong. He went to university in Bangkok, where he met my mother. She was from Bangkok, so they married there and lived in Bangkok for a couple of years. Eventually they moved down here and I was born. That's about it."

"And what do they do?"

"Dad works for the Forestry Department and mum teaches maths at Nanakit school. I have a younger sister, who married last year and is now pregnant, which is good because it's taken the spotlight off me," she joked.

The conversation had filled the time all the way back to Phuket. Having come over the bridge, Nick slowed the car as they approached the police checkpoint to enter the island. Marky handed over her police ID and they were waved through without delay. He dropped her at her condo, then headed home to relax before showering and changing to come back to pick her up.

❖

Marky hurried inside as soon as they pulled up, knowing she had just a couple of hours to get ready. The security guard beckoned to her from the window of his little office at the side of the entrance hall, calling her name "Officer Pondee." She didn't have any time to waste but went over to see what he wanted.

"A package arrived while you were out miss. It wouldn't fit in your postbox, so I have it here. Just a moment." He disappeared out of view from the small window but returned seconds later with a cardboard box about fifty by forty centimetres and a few centimetres high.

"Thank you," she said, accepting the box and checking the label. It gave no clue as to what it may be, but she knew she hadn't ordered anything this size. She did a lot of her shopping online with Lazada and Shopee, but usually only smaller items. Intrigued, she began pulling it open in the lift on the way up to her apartment on the fifth floor.

It was not yet fully open, but through the gap she had made in the side she could see, and now feel, that it was the dress she had tried on in Jaspal in Bangkok. This could only be the work of Nick Foster, she thought, partly angry at his arrogance and partly thrilled that she had the perfect item to wear this evening. He must have been thinking the same thing, she mused, now smiling. It wasn't going to take very long to get ready after all.

❖

The man's phone rang and he answered after checking the caller ID, "You have news?" he demanded.

"They drove off the island. We lost them the other side of the bridge."

"Idiot," he hissed in reply.

"I'm sorry boss. We were using motorbikes because it's easier to follow them around Phuket, but we couldn't keep up once they got onto the mainland. The farang drives very fast."

"Where are they now?"

"We waited at the bridge and picked them up when they came back. He dropped her at the condo then went back to his parents' house. Jun is outside the condo and I'm in Kwang Road."

"Let me know when they leave," he instructed, "and Tia, don't lose them again. You've messed up enough times already this week."

"No boss, sorry boss," he replied, but the line was already dead.

❖

When Marky walked out of her condo building to join him in the car, she took his breath away. The dress had looked good on her in the shop, but the full effect with hair done, makeup applied, stiletto-heeled shoes on and carrying a dainty clutch bag was more than he had expected. The fact that she was wearing it meant she was accepting of his gift, as he had been in some doubt as to whether he ought to buy it at all. He hardly knew her, after all, so he was was both relieved and pleased.

He jumped out to open the passenger door as she made her way over. An exception could be made when they weren't working.

"Thank you sir. That's very kind of you," she smiled, and carefully entered the car as elegantly as she could. Nick closed her door and got back in the driver's seat.

"Thank you for this, but you really shouldn't have," she told him.

"Please think nothing of it. You look a million dollars, so it was worth every Baht."

"You're very generous. I must admit, I was quite angry when I first saw it, but I agree with you, it looks good on me," and she laughed with genuine pleasure, "thanks again."

He smiled in answer and pulled back out into traffic, stealing the occasional look at the beautiful woman beside him. She's going to put the cat amongst the pigeons tonight, he thought.

It took no time at all to reach their destination. A large marquee, open on all sides, had been set up to cover half the road and the entrance pathway to the house. It was red carpeted and brightly lit, and white-uniformed concierges waited to open car doors. Three police cars were parked in the street and several officers were standing around unobtrusively, controlling traffic and preventing rubber-neckers from slowing as they passed in the other lane. Nick pulled under the marquee, stopped the car and said "There's valet parking, so we can get out here." He handed his remote to the waiting concierge, then paused while Marky joined him. He offered his arm, which she took without question or hesitation, and walked her slowly toward the large double wrought iron gates that were the entrance to the grounds.

A man stood at a lectern just inside the gates and greeted them with a 'wai' and "Good evening Mr. Nick and Miss Pondee" as he ticked them off his list. Very efficient, she thought. Nick walked her a few more paces inside, then stopped to one side of the path to let her take in the house and gardens, a place he knew very well from his childhood.

Behind them now was a wall of ornate concrete pillars with fencing of wrought iron bars between them, stretching in both directions from the entrance gate. Borders of shrubbery and flowering plants ran the length of it, interspersed with tall palms, both inside and outside the property. Tonight, there were lights strung from pillar to pillar and from the trees. Between the borders and the house was a swathe of green grass so flat and well kept it could grace the golf course she'd seen yesterday.

The house was two storeys with a portico standing out proudly in the centre of the wide facade. Wide stone stairs swept up from the path to the level of the portico, where she could see people already waiting inside. Wings went off to each side of the main part of the house, and it seemed to go on forever. It was an immense building. With light coming from all the ground floor windows it was like a palace from the foreign movies she had devoured as a child.

The upper floor was in total darkness, but the garden lights provided enough illumination to make out verandas with stone balustrades in front of some of the rooms. The roof was tiled with the small orange clay tiles that traditionally topped off houses of this period.

"My grandfather's grandfather started building the house in the 1890s but never saw it completed. My great-grandfather finished it and his family moved in at the end of 1903. Grandfather was born here and has lived here all his life," Nick told her.

"It's amazing," was all she could think to say.

"Let's go inside. I'll introduce you to my parents," he suggested and began a slow walk toward the front door under the portico. A waiter appeared as they entered to offer sparkling wine from a silver tray. They took a glass each and Nick leaned in to whisper, "Take it slow, it could be a long evening."

The room was square and the height of the two storeys. A magnificent chandelier hung in the centre of the ceiling and reached down to illuminate the polished stone floor of yellow and brown hues. The floor was deeply patinated from years of use and she was stunned to think it was over a century old. Open arches led off to each side into adjoining rooms and two doors stood closed in the rear wall with a tall side table between them. A plain plank of wood with Chinese lettering in gold hung on the wall above the table.

As Nick had reached to take his glass from the tray

his suit jacket had fallen open and Marky had spied the label 'Tom Ford'. Nice, but not too extravagant for a member of the Phuket aristocracy, she thought. Now in the light, she could better see what he was wearing; the charcoal suit over a plain white shirt with the collar unbuttoned, and a pair of black loafers whose brand she hadn't yet determined. Overall his outfit was understated but very stylish.

Nick saw his mother at the back of the adjoining room fussing with staff over the tall flower displays around a large red and gold chair. "There's my mum. Prepare yourself," he grinned as he led her through.

"Nicholas, there you are!" his mother exclaimed when she saw him approaching, "and who is this fabulous young lady you have with you?" she inquired as if she had no idea who he was bringing.

Nick was delighted that Marky beat him to it and introduced herself with a 'wai' and "Good evening, Mrs. Foster. I'm Marisa, but please call me Marky."

His mother dipped her head in acknowledgement of the 'wai' and said "It's a pleasure to meet you Marisa. Please make yourself at home and enjoy your evening. You must excuse me for now as I have a lot to do. We'll talk again later." And with that, she swept away.

"I should have told you she doesn't approve of nicknames or abbreviations. You will forever be Marisa to my mother." He looked around the room, then told her "Sorry, I can't see my dad. We'll find him later."

Marky had noticed that Mrs. Foster was wearing a ruffled black off-the-shoulder dress, not dissimilar to

140

her own, but being an amateur expert on brands she knew it was Versace, not Jaspal. She suddenly felt altogether better about accepting the gift. She had also quickly taken in the matching Versace shoes, easily identified by the large gold safety pin on the side. As if that wasn't enough to stop you in your tracks, she had set it all off against a diamond choker at her throat. In all her life, Marky had never encountered anyone dressed quite as finely as Mrs. Wanpen Foster.

"Let's find a seat before there are none to be had," Nick suggested, "it's too long an evening to be standing all the way through." He clearly had prior experience.

Once they'd found seats on a sofa of red and gold brocade, Marky leaned in to whisper, "Thank goodness you bought me this dress or I'd have looked a proper yokel. There's nothing in my wardrobe that would have been suitable here."

"Don't mention it."

Marky sipped her drink and took in her surroundings. This room was a large formal space. All the furniture was against the walls and was either plain, dark wood or red and gold painted wood. The floor was tiled with dark red and cream clay tiles in a checkerboard pattern. They too were highly polished and looked as ancient as the house. Tall windows overlooked the front garden and two more chandeliers, less imposing than the one in the entrance, hung from the ceiling. Nick's mother was still supervising the finishing touches to the oversized chair on a dais, primping and adjusting the flower displays that surrounded it. She guessed this was where Nick's grandfather would sit once he'd made his entrance.

More and more people were arriving as the time neared seven. The room was filling up, with groups forming as friends and acquaintances began to congregate together into their cliques. Marky had not recognised anyone yet, but Nick had pointed out many faces for her and provided a running commentary.

An overweight man in a pale grey safari suit was a gold shop owner but was widely known to make more income through his underground moneylending. He moved through the crowd greeting everyone as if it was his own house and party they were attending. An elderly woman outfitted totally in black was the widow of another Thai-Chinese family patriarch. He'd died many years ago, but she still wore black every day. Nick whispered there had been rumours of a possible romance with his grandfather when they were young, but he did not know the truth of it and guessed nobody ever would. There were hotel owners, slumlords, importers, the owner of Phuket's largest shopping mall who had flown in from Bangkok for the evening, rubber plantation owners, property developers, even a massage parlour owner. Mayors and underlings from many municipal areas were in attendance, each looking underdressed among the wealthy elite. Government officers arrived in dress uniforms adorned with medals, notably without their spouses.

The thing that was apparent to her as Nick

provided background on each new arrival, was that all the business people had a pale Thai-Chinese appearance, while all the darker-skinned, full-blood Thais were politicians, police and local government officials. The wealth was in the hands of the descendants of the Chinese, but the authority lay with the Thais. She knew very well though, that one couldn't operate without the other. The two power groups had coexisted and cooperated to manage the island and benefit together for decades.

A gaggle of senior police officers arrived together in full uniform. Marky recognised Colonel Orntong amongst them but didn't know the others, so assumed they must be from other stations around the island. Their insignia showed them to be a lieutenant colonel, two majors and a captain. She wondered if she should greet the colonel, but was unsure of the protocol. A decision was unnecessary as a loud gong sounded three times at that moment. Nick stood and she quickly followed his lead.

The double doors at the back of the room opened smoothly away from them as if controlled by invisible hands. There must be people behind the doors she guessed; this was pure theatre. As they opened wide they revealed a man in a gleaming white suit with wispy white hair to match. He wore polished black leather shoes and the only colour about him was the corner of a red handkerchief poking out from his breast pocket. It was impossible to see into the room behind him as there was a carved wooden screen blocking the view. The crowd had gone silent at the sound of the gong but broke into applause and shouts as he began a slow walk into the room. He took small careful steps, typical of an elderly person no longer sure on their feet, then Nick's mother appeared at his side to take his arm. Although it looked as if she was simply accompanying him, Marky was sure she had a firm grip and was in fact helping him maintain his balance. Neither of them smiled nor acknowledged the cheering crowd as they made their way to the waiting chair. A small hesitation as he negotiated the single step, then he turned carefully and sat down. He did not fidget or move to make himself comfortable but sat erect for a moment looking around the room, taking in the applause. Finally, he raised one hand, nodded his head slowly, once, and the noise died down immediately.

"Thank you all," he said in a surprisingly strong voice that belied his frailty, "every year I imagine this will be the last birthday party I must pay for, yet here we are again." This was greeted with laughter and Marky saw a flicker of a smile on the old man's lips.

Nick leaned over to whisper "He's not kidding about not wanting to pay for parties. He's a typical stingy old Chinaman in that respect."

"A special thank you to my wonderful daughter Ka-hung for arranging everything," he bowed his head in Nick's mother's direction, who smiled and looked at the floor. Marky assumed this was her Chinese name. She made a mental note to ask if Nick had one too. "I am pleased to see many family members here, as always, but my will remains unchanged from last year," he continued to more laughter. "Especially some who have not been with us for some time," he said, directing his steely gaze toward Nick, but then softening into a smile. "Please, everyone enjoy yourselves, eat and drink your fill, and I will try to speak to as many of you as I am able before I fall asleep," he finished and the crowd applauded once more.

People gradually returned to their own interrupted conversations and the babble and chatter filled the room once more. Nick told her they would have to do the rounds of the room but suggested they get something to eat first. He led her back through the arch into the entrance hall, then through the opposite arch into an identical room. This one was decorated in a similar fashion to its twin but had buffet tables laden with food around two walls. Uniformed staff waited to assist with plates and to serve if asked.

"What are these rooms normally used for?" Marky asked, unable to imagine that rooms of this size and grandeur would have an everyday purpose.

"Just for functions, so not very often. I'm sure they were used more often in the past. When we visit we don't normally come in the front door. We park round the back and come in through another door. The ground floor living quarters are all at the rear of the house," he explained, "believe it or not, grandfather lives very simply, with just a cook and cleaner to look after him."

"Hey, farang!" she heard shouted from behind them and they both turned to see a man of similar age to themselves approaching with arms spread wide.

"Hey, coolie!" Nick countered when he saw who it was. The two embraced for a moment, then stepped apart to take in one another's appearance. "You're still skinny and ugly," he said. Marky thought this unfair, so guessed he was being ironic. The man was quite handsome, with fair skin and beautiful eyes. Like Nick, he was wearing a tailored suit over a white shirt. The ensemble was casual and elegant at the same time.

"And you still think you're tall, dark and handsome!" the other man laughed. "Who is this delightful looking lady you've no doubt bribed to accompany you this evening?" he asked with a huge grin while taking in Marky's tightly fitted dress.

"Marky, I'm sorry, but I must introduce my cousin Tang-ju. You can forget you met him once he leaves," he joked.

"It is a real pleasure to meet you, Marky," the man said, "but please call me Beum," he said, taking her hand between his own.

"We were about to eat. Will you join us?" asked Nick.

"I can't, I'm afraid, my mother is alone, so I need to get back to her. Just wanted to say hi and get to meet this lovely woman," he said, still holding on to Marky's hand, "perhaps later" he said directly to her, and with that, he was gone.

"You two seem very close," she observed.

"His mother is my aunt, my mother's half-sister. We went to the same schools, and although he was a year below me, we shared a driver and so spent a lot of time in the car with one another."

"You were chauffeured to and from school?" she asked, feigning shock.

Nick knew she was joking, so replied, "isn't everyone?"

Turning back to the vast buffet spread, Marky noted that every item she could see was finger food. Everything was dainty and bite-sized, and there was nothing that could not be eaten while standing chatting. They took gilt-edged plates and cotton napkins offered by a waitress, then helped themselves to a number of items each. The food was a mix of Chinese dishes, Thai dishes, even some Japanese, and Marky took a sample of each.

Returning to the sofa, they were pleased to find that no one had taken their places. Once they'd sat down to eat, yet another waiter appeared offering wine, which Nick declined so Marky did the same. She ate more carefully than she ever had before, using either chopsticks or a serviette to pick up the food, thereby avoiding greasy fingers. Bites were taken hovering over the plate to prevent crumbs falling on her dress, and she was relieved when she had finished to see she was still clean and presentable.

Once they were done with their food, Nick signalled for a waiter to take away their plates, then he turned to her and asked "Ready to do battle?" He stood and offered his hand to help her up, which she took and joined him, then took his arm as he made his way into the congested crowd.

Nick quickly picked out his father in the packed

room and made his way in his direction. His father was in conversation with an older Thai couple, so he didn't interrupt, but stood beside him patiently until he'd finished. His father squeezed his arm to indicate he'd seen him and should wait. Soon enough, he was able to excuse himself and turned to Nick and Marky.

"Good evening, Miss Pondee. It's a pleasure to meet you," he said, bowing his head to acknowledge her 'wai'.

"Likewise, Mr. Foster. I feel honoured to be invited this evening."

"Nick has told me something of your exploits together this week," he said, "it sounds like an intriguing case."

"It is certainly different from those I usually work, that's for sure," she told him, noncommittally.

"Who's here that I ought to speak to dad?" Nick asked.

"Your grandfather of course, all the aunts and uncles you can find, and if there's time left after that try to charm the Chalong Municipality officers. Our next project is in their area," his father added quietly.

"Okay, see you later," he told him and led Marky toward a woman sitting alone on a sofa. She was holding a near-empty champagne flute and appeared to be unsuccessfully attempting to catch the attention of a waiter for a top-up.

"Good evening, auntie. May we sit with you a moment?" he asked, but sat before she could answer and indicated Marky should do likewise.

"Hello Nicholas," she replied without looking at

them, continuing her scan of the room for a waiter.

"How are you, auntie? I saw Beum earlier, he looked well," Nick persevered.

"Fine, fine. Nicholas, be a dear and get auntie another drink, would you?" she said, pushing her glass into his hand. He rose to do as instructed, raising his eyebrows to Marky as he went. Marky sat in silence, unsure what to say. The woman ignored her.

"Here you are auntie, I brought two," Nick said, passing two full flutes over, "We'll leave you to enjoy yourself." The old woman nodded and took a gulp, but did not speak.

"Well, that was awkward," Nick said with a crooked smile once they were out of earshot, "that's Beum's mother, who you can see has a bit of a drinking problem. I'm surprised he's left her alone like that."

Looking around and seeing no family he recognised, he said, "let's get in the queue to see the old land thief." he joked and led her in the direction of the throne-like chair. Nick's mother was standing guard to his grandfather's left, making sure no one monopolised too much of his time.

Seeing them approach she leaned down to whisper with the person kneeling beside her father, who promptly rose, gave a brief 'wai' and moved away. She politely blocked the path of the next person in line to allow Nick and Marky to jump the queue. Nick kneeled to his grandfather's left and Marky carefully lowered herself down beside him. They both sat Thai-style on the floor with their legs folded to their sides, Marky with her hands palms down on her thighs.

Nick leaned forward with hands in a 'wai' at his forehead, then laid his hands and head on his grandfather's lap. The old man placed both his hands on Nick's head and leaned forward to say something that Marky could not catch over the general hubbub. Nick sat back on his heels, with his hands now grasped by the old man. Although his face showed no emotion, his eyes gave away that he was delighted to see Nick.

"Ah-gong, I'd like you to meet a good friend," Nick said, using the Chinese word for grandfather, and turning to Marky, "this is Miss Marisa Pondee. She's a police officer."

"Welcome to our home, Miss Pondee," the old man said, "I hope you have eaten and had something to drink?" he asked politely.

"We have sir, thank you."

"Nicholas, it is always good to see you, however, many people are waiting to pester me, so please excuse me for now. Why don't you come by for a visit one day soon? And bring this lovely young lady with you," he said, looking directly at Marky with a twinkle in his eye.

"We will, I promise," and with that he stood and she followed, both giving a 'wai' before carefully stepping backwards off the dais.

As they walked away she said, "I'm going to keep you to that!", thrilled at the thought of another visit.

❖

Directly ahead of them was the group of police officers they had seen arriving together. It was too late to avoid them, so Nick went straight up to the colonel, gave a 'wai' and said, "Good evening sir," in English. Marky, beside him, also offered a 'wai' to the colonel and other officers with a 'sawatdee kaa' hello in Thai. Now seeing them standing next to one another, Marky noted how much taller Nick was than the Thai officers. He looked confidently down at them and made no effort to stoop as a younger Thai person would do in this situation. The policemen were no doubt wearing their best uniforms but looked like farmers dressed up in their Sunday suits next to Nick.

"Sergeant Foster! And Sub-lieutenant Pondee! What a surprise," he exclaimed, "what are you two doing here?" he asked, clearly quite taken aback to see one of his junior officers and the Englishman at such an important event.

"It's my grandfather's birthday sir," he told him and watched as the colonel's eyes grew steadily larger in shock, "I invited Sub-lieutenant Pondee to join me. Don't worry, we're not about to arrest anyone!" he joked in an attempt to lessen the shock.

Marky saw the other officers looking her over, so pasted a pleasant smile on her face and looked each of them in the eye in turn. They quickly returned to the conversation between their boss and the farang.

"Well sergeant, you really are full of surprises.

First, you reveal you are, in fact, Thai. Now we discover you're related to the Ying-jareun-paisan family. What other surprises do you have in store for me?" he asked jovially.

"There are no more sir, I assure you. If you'll excuse us, there are people we must see."

"Of course. I'll see you both on Monday for an update on your case," the colonel said to them as an order, not a question. Marky looked back as they walked away. As expected, all the officers were watching her and turned away quickly when she caught them. Oh, life's simple pleasures, she thought, smiling to herself.

❖

"Did you know your auntie has a drinking problem?" she asked quietly as he surveyed the room again.

"No, I didn't. I knew from my mother that she and my uncle had divorced a few years ago. Beum's father was a gambler, but worse than that, auntie found out he had a mistress. I guess it was all too much for her."

"That's a shame, but quite typical of Thai men," she observed.

"We'd better see if we can find you a farang or Chinaman or Indian or something then!" he laughed. She poked him in the side playfully for his insolence. Marky had dated several men while at university in Bangkok, but only ever slept with one of them. That had ended when she'd returned to Phuket, and she'd been alone ever since.

"Ah, there's another aunt and uncle over there. Let's say hello," he said and set off across the room again.

They continued to mingle for the next two hours, only sipping at their drinks, but noticed that others were enjoying the free refreshments without restraint. Nick introduced various family members, including his sister. Where Nick's mother was elegant and stylish, his sister's look was simple yet fashionable.

For this special evening Jane was wearing a mid-length Dior cotton printed dress. It had a flared cut, cap sleeves and shirt collar, with a matching belt to cinch the waist. She wore black Gucci ankle boots with a chunky rubber sole, giving a rebellious edge to her appearance. Her look was clean and free of makeup and jewellery, but Marky guessed her outfit easily cost more than her sub-lieutenant's annual salary.

They weren't able to chat for long as Jane also had to do the rounds and meet as many people as possible. Having been standing long enough to make her feet sore, Marky was thankful when Nick suggested they have a seat and a cold drink. They found space on a sofa and Nick had a waiter bring them glasses of chilled sparkling water.

❖

The crowd had barely thinned out by ten o'clock, but a small number of people had discreetly slipped away. A gong sounded loudly three times again and the room fell immediately silent. Nick's grandfather was helped to his feet by his daughter, who had remained standing at his side the entire evening. Once he was erect, she released his arm and stood back.

"Thank you all again for coming this evening. It has been a great pleasure for me to catch up with so many old friends. Unfortunately, I must now say goodnight before I fall asleep in this chair." There was a polite murmur of laughter at this. "Please stay as long as you wish, there is no need to leave on my account. Good night."

Nick's mother took his arm right away and helped him step down from the dais. With slower steps than when he'd entered the room, he went back through the same doors, which again opened as he approached.

❖

"Well, my duty is done," said Nick, "we can leave or stay, it's up to you." The evening had been less of a hardship than he'd expected, and he would readily admit he'd quite enjoyed most of it.

"Let's stay a little longer, and perhaps have another real drink before we go?" she asked, swishing her glass of water. Marky was in no hurry to leave at all.

"Certainly," he agreed and caught a passing waiter's attention with a raised hand. Two flutes of sparkling wine soon arrived and they clinked glasses. "To a successful conclusion to our case."

"Hear, hear," she agreed.

"Want to mingle some more?" he asked a few minutes later, noticing a definite reduction in the number of people still remaining now his grandfather had retired.

"Sure," she replied and they stood to take in the room once more.

As they made their way into the now quieter crowd, Nick looked to see if there was any family he had missed earlier. He could not see anyone they had overlooked, but Beum caught his attention with a wave to beckon him over. Beum was speaking to a man of his own age and two older men.

"Nick, I'd like you to meet an old school friend of mine. This is Wayu," he said, indicating the young man to his left. The man gave Nick a 'wai', knowing he was older, but also aware that he was a Ying-jareun-paisan. It never hurt to show humility to wealth and power. "This is his father Mr. Apisit Wattana, the public prosecutor for Phuket, and Mr. Jirayu Huangsap, one of our island's leading lawyers," he completed the introductions. The prosecutor was tall for a Thai and wore a well-pressed black suit. The lawyer was a short, mousey looking man with thick-lensed, round glasses and a comb-over. His suit looked like he lived in it on a daily basis, and his paunch threatened to burst his lower shirt buttons open.

Nick and Marky both greeted the two older men with a 'wai', and they both returned Nick's 'wai'. Although they wouldn't normally return a 'wai' to someone a generation younger, they too made an exception in Nick's case.

155

"What do you do, Wayu?" asked Nick, feeling all out of small talk this late in the evening.

"I followed my father into law. Uncle Ji took me on as a trainee in his firm when I graduated," he said, indicating that Jirayu Huangsap was the person he was referring to, although Nick knew 'uncle' was a respectful reference, not literal.

The elder Wattana had struck up a conversation with Marky, and now Nick heard him say "I've seen many case files submitted to my office with your name on. May I say that your summaries are excellently written and always concise."

"Thank you, sir. You're very kind to say so."

"You wouldn't believe how many awful submissions my office receives from some officers. They are barely literate," he laughed.

"I'm sure I would, sir, I work with many of those officers," she assured him, joining in his joke.

"How about going on to a club from here?" asked Beum of the younger members of the group, but looking directly at Marky, "we could go over to Patong," he suggested.

Marky was first to reply with "I'm sorry, I can't. I have a lot to do tomorrow."

"Aw, come on! It's Sunday," he protested, clearly disappointed she had refused.

"I'll join you. I haven't had a night out for ages," said Nick. They both turned to look at Wayu, who had not yet answered. He looked down and shook his head, "Sorry, I can't go either," he told them, taking a sideways glance at his father.

A grown-up, still living at home and still treated

like a child, guessed Nick.

❖

After saying goodnight to Nick's parents and other family members they met on the way out, Marky was impressed to see their car waiting for them under the marquee, doors open ready. His family really knew how to put on a show, she thought.

She hadn't realised how tired she was until sitting in the car and was very glad she hadn't agreed to go on to a club with them.

"Thank you for an amazing time this evening, and especially for not leaving me alone. It was good of you to stick with me all night."

"I told you you'd enjoy it," he said, smiling and turning to look at her, "you sure you won't join us?"

"Really I'd like to, but I can't."

"Beum looked quite despondent when you said no," he offered as they pulled up at her condo entrance.

"He'll recover. Besides, he's already got my number," she told him with a huge grin. She leaned across, surprised him with a friendly kiss on the cheek, said goodnight, then was out of the car and closing the door before he could think of an answer.

❖

Nick drove back to his grandfather's house where he found Beum waiting under the marquee with a driver. He jumped in the back with Beum and let the driver take them to Patong. It wouldn't do for him to be caught drinking and driving, so he never took the chance. Besides, they knew parking would be impossible. Twenty-five minutes later the driver stopped at the drop-off area at the beach end of Bangla Road. They jumped out and the driver went off to find somewhere to wait until they called him back to pick them up.

Beum threw an arm around his shoulder and said "Cousin, it's been too long!" already in high spirits from the champagne.

It really had, thought Nick. They used to go out together often when he was in his final year of high school, and Beum was only seventeen. They had been out together only once since, on one of his trips home, but he could not remember when. His only nights out for a long time had been with his team in London to celebrate the conclusion of a case.

This end of the street was just a few smaller side-of-the-road bars, but they were busy with foreign tourists. Currency exchange booths, pharmacies and convenience stores were still open, even this late at night. With bright neon lights the length of the street and music thumping from every corner, the atmosphere encouraged you to join the party. After six in the evening, Bangla became a pedestrian area, so the entire width of the street was filled with people, some carrying drinks, others taking selfies. The crowd was predominantly male, but there were plenty of couples and groups of girls too.

They walked slowly down the street, enjoying the vibe and dodging the touts encouraging them into go-go bars. Bangla had a number of clubs along its length and a couple of side-streets filled with yet more bars and go-gos. Amnesia club was nearer the other end of the road from where they had arrived, so it took them several minutes to reach it. The club occupied a three-storey building, with its main entrance on the middle floor accessed by a wide staircase from the street. The ground floor was open-air individual bars, but mercifully they were all supplied with music from above and not playing competing tracks like some of the other bar areas along Bangla.

Beum led the way up the stairs. They'd both left their suit jackets in the car, so looked more casual now. The night wasn't too hot, but Nick knew it would get sticky inside if it was busy. The two doormen, one either side of the wide doorway, recognised Beum and waved them through. A hostess picked them up as soon as they were inside; Beum said something Nick couldn't hear over the electronic beat, then she nodded and led them to a second stair that curved up to the top floor.

The third floor was VIP seating areas around the edge of the room. The centre of the room was open to give a view of the dance floor below. The hostess showed them to an empty booth and called over a waitress as they sat down.

"Whisky?" asked Beum.

"No spirits for me, just a beer," Nick informed him and received a look of surprise in return.

"We have to open a bottle to sit here."

"So open one, it's on me."

Beum grinned gleefully and ordered a bottle of Johnnie Walker Black and a Chang beer for Nick. They clinked glass against bottle when the drinks arrived, then sat back to take in their surroundings. The balcony-like area they were on was perched directly above the dance floor, so they could see that down below was almost full to capacity. The club could hold something like two thousand people, Nick knew from the website he had looked at earlier, and it appeared to be getting close to that tonight. From their seats, they had a direct view into the DJ's nest and could see him busily working the decks, bopping his head to the beat. Nick smiled when he saw Beum was already nodding along to the 'pulse', the four-beat bar that typified electronic dance music.

His eyes finally came to rest on an area opposite them, raised slightly higher than the other VIP booths. Several people sat on the black leather couches, mostly Thais with hostess girls, with ice buckets and bottles of spirits on the tables. One man stood out amongst them because he was alone and had a space on either side of him that nobody sat in. While everyone else was drinking to get drunk, he had a plastic bottle of water in his hand.

Nick asked a passing waitress if she knew who the people were in that area, and was informed it was the boss and his friends. So this is the owner, thought Nick, taking stock of the man. He looked about sixty, was slim and still had all his black hair. It was easy to tell he had Chinese blood, as he was quite pale compared to his companions. What struck Nick most was the man's stillness. In the buzzing club, he seemed to move in slow motion, completely unhurried. It took Nick a moment to realise that this was because he felt secure and was supremely confident. He was in his own environment where nothing and nobody could touch him.

A hard man to bring down, if it did eventually turn out to be him behind the killings.

❖

Beum must have said something else to the hostess because she soon returned with two beautiful girls in tow. They were stunning and dressed to kill in skintight dresses that barely covered their thighs. Both were light-skinned, had long hair and the similar facial features that marked them as being from the northwest of Thailand. Nick sighed inwardly.

The girls bent at the knees to 'wai' then sat down, one to each side of Nick and Beum. "Sawatdee kaa," the girl said into his ear, so as to be heard over the music. It was impossible to talk without getting close in, "my name is Noi, how about you?"

"Call me Dancer," he told her, "which is what I'd like to do right now." He stood and offered his hand for her to join him, which she did willingly. Beum and his partner did likewise and they went downstairs hand-in-hand to join the melee.

The dance floor was a crush, but they found some space and joined in the mayhem. Nick raised his hands over his head, closed his eyes and let the music take him. He would have stayed there longer, but after a few tracks the others had had enough and they all went back upstairs. Expensive drinks had appeared for the girls while they'd been away.

Within minutes of sitting down again, Beum's companion had her legs over his and he had begun exploring her curves with his free hand. After ten minutes of empty small talk with his own companion, Nick had had enough and suggested to Beum they leave. Beum groaned and made a face. Nick took out his wallet, gave the girl five hundred baht and handed Beum a wad of thousand Baht bills.

"I'll send the car back for you," Nick told him.

"No need. I'll stay in Patong tonight," he replied, taking the cash and smiling at the girl.

Nick left alone, having got what he came for.

# Chapter 7

Sunday had been a relaxing day for Nick. After sleeping late, he'd taken a swim to refresh himself, then had brunch while his father had an early lunch. His mother and sister had gone shopping and had lunch together in the mall, so he didn't see them until much later. With the meal finished, he'd showered and changed into lightweight clothes, then came back downstairs with his Surface to write a brief report for the chief superintendent back home. It had occurred to him that he hadn't been told how long he could spend on this case, so asked in the email if there was a time limit on him remaining in Phuket.

Today he'd woken at his regular time of six-thirty, so guessed his body clock had caught up at last. He was stuck with the monstrous red Jeep again, but it was slowly growing on him he realised as he parked it in Phuket police headquarters' car park.

The two officers on reception looked up as he came in the front door but did not speak and went straight back to whatever held their interest in their computer screens. Their curiosity in having a foreign policeman on the premises had quickly waned, but Nick was used to the locals' indifference by now and headed directly for the stairs.

He was stopped in his tracks when he opened the door and almost went back out thinking he had the wrong room, but then he heard Marky say "Good morning" and slowly continued in, taking in the complete change since he had last been here on Friday.

The desks had reduced to two and been rearranged in a T format, with two seats facing one another across the length of one desk and a stranger sitting at the other with a laptop open. She was another female police officer, who quickly stood up, gave a polite 'wai' and said "sawatdee kaa, khun Nick". Nick nodded a reply but was too dumbstruck to speak.

Marky stood too, with a wide grin. "Let me show you what I've been up to," she said, stepping to the back wall of the room. The wall now had a large whiteboard hanging on it displaying photographs of everyone involved in the case so far. At the top was a photo of Tida Yemyim, the girl they had found in Phanom. Underneath was written her name, nickname, age and date of birth. Below her were photos of the three men who had already died, again with their personal details written below each. To the right of all this were three more spaces, as yet without full details. She had used male head silhouettes in place of photos and written 'club owner', 'lawyer' and 'policeman' beneath them. This, clearly, was her association board. The last one - policeman - had Nick curious already. Marky didn't speak, but let Nick take it all in in silence. When she saw him nod again, she turned to the second board on the side wall.

The second whiteboard was her timeline, with dates across the top, names down the left, and events written in at points where the two intersected. It began with the attack on Ning way back in 2015, then jumped to the past week with the other three deaths. A vertical line had been drawn down the board and the title 'Actions' had been written at the top of this other section. At the moment it was blank.

"Well, say something!" she said, impatient for some kind of response from him.

"Very impressive. So this is how you spent your day off work yesterday?"

"It is, oh, and this is constable Mayuree Jai-ngaam," she said, remembering and stepping aside so that Nick could see the constable, who was still standing, looking nervous. She had her hands clasped in front of her and head down, not meeting his eye, as if the farang might take a bite out of her.

Hearing her name, the constable repeated her greeting and Nick recovered himself to reply this time, "It's a pleasure to meet you, constable Jai-Ngaam."

"We call her Yu, it's less of a mouthful," Marky

told him. "I stole her from the main office. She'll be working with us now, based here."

"That's great," said Nick.

Before he could ask what exactly she would be doing, Marky continued, "she'll be our information officer, actions officer and whatever else we need, because we can only have one. Yu has excellent IT skills, and her English is pretty good."

"Don't worry about that, I'm sure we can let her in on our secret," Nick said in Thai, causing Yu's mouth to fall open in surprise.

"Finally, I've put everything we have so far in our murder book," she said, indicating a new hardcover case file on the desk. Marky smiled, pleased that he was on board with her project and the three of them sat down to begin work.

Nick put down the coffee carrier and bag of croissants he had been holding this whole time, turned to Yu and said, "You'd better tell me how you like your coffee."

❖

Marky had her notepad open in front of her and even upside down Nick could see she had a list written up. All the same, she looked up and asked him, "Where would you like to start?" which he thought was either gracious or sneaky. It remained to be seen.

"Well, as it happens, I didn't spend all of yesterday relaxing either. You know I love lists, so that's what I did in the afternoon," he told her, removing his own notepad from his portfolio. He laid it on the table between them and said, "Let's compare, shall we?"

Marky smiled, knowing he'd seen her list.

"First, the few facts we have. One, Ning was attacked in 2015 and two policemen attended the scene. The nightclub owner and/or his lawyer had the rape brushed under the carpet, and there it stayed until a couple of weeks ago." Yu had closed the screen of her laptop down and was listening intently as Nick went through his list. "Two, Captain Gerdpon, who was one of the policemen who attended that night, tracked her down after a six-year gap and visited her. He passed on the information about the attack to a golf partner, who in turn travelled to Bangkok to pass it on to a reporter."

He stood up now and moved to the photo board to point at the reporter, "Three, the reporter was killed," he pointed to Townsend, "Townsend was killed," his finger moved again, "and finally Captain Gerdpon was killed. Although there's no evidence for his death being a killing rather than suicide, it's the only way his death makes any sense now that we know more of the story."

His hand fell back to his side and he cocked his head to the side to give Marky a questioning look.

"Exactly what I have, so how about assumptions and actions? Where do we go next?" she asked.

"I've got a couple of ideas. What do you have?" he prompted, giving her the chance to contribute.

"Assumption number one is that the club owner, name as yet unknown, has the best motive for keeping the story covered up. However, as we

167

discussed the other day, it seems a bit over the top to kill three people to do that. This makes me think we're missing something bigger than the rape, as awful as that is already. He had to have known who was in his club that night though, so he must know who was responsible."

"Agreed, but we can only hope the reason is revealed as we progress. We have nothing to go on. As for knowing who did it, he's unlikely to tell us and there's no rape case to prosecute anyway."

"True, unfortunately", she agreed, "and assumption two is that someone knew what Gerdpon was up to and passed it on to whoever ordered or carried out the killings. We can rule out his wife and, I'm sure, Ning, which leaves the question who?"

"Do you have any ideas for who?" he asked, having none of his own and thinking back to 'policeman' on the association board.

"Yes, I think it's a policeman and more specifically the other officer that was with Gerdpon on the night of the rape callout."

"Wow, that's a leap," Nick said, while Yu sat stunned at the idea, "how did you reach that conclusion?"

"By elimination. There is simply no other answer. Nobody other than another policeman could possibly know what Gerdpon was up to, and he may even have spoken to him about it, unwittingly sealing his own fate in the process."

Nick was nodding his head in agreement now.

"Got anything better?" Marky asked sardonically and said no more for a moment. Nick did not reply as he had nothing. "So, to actions then. One, Yu can try to find out who that officer was, and two, you and I can follow up on the club owner and his lawyer."

"Okay, we have a plan."

"Yu, put those actions on the board please," Marky ordered, looking at Nick, not the constable. He smiled at her and she smiled back.

❖

"Ten o'clock on a Monday morning strikes me as an unlikely time to find a nightclub owner at his place of work," Nick declared as he started the car.

"If he's not there, we can have a nose about, talk to anyone that is, get his name and perhaps find out where he lives," she countered.

"I ought to tell you I was there on Saturday night with Beum," he said next, looking across for her reaction.

"Oh, and what did you find out?" she asked, unperturbed, or at least not showing it.

"Nothing. We just went as customers, had a drink and a dance. I didn't speak to anyone or ask anything, so don't fret."

"I wasn't fretting, but I can't see you two dancing the night away together in a nightclub," she joked.

"We danced with girls, not one another," he assured her, then remembered she had seemed keen on Beum on Saturday and regretted it. Stealing a look he saw she was unfazed.

They drove in silence after that, through the crossroads at Kathu and over the hill into Patong. As the road wound down the hill into the bay, it opened up before them and they could see the buildings of Patong Beach in the foreground and the sea beyond, stretching from the hills on the left to those on the right. The tree-covered hills climbed all around on three sides, cradling Patong as if keeping it hidden and separate from other parts of the island. Nick followed the road past the temple at the bottom of the hill, then turned left into Rat-u-thit Road, which ran parallel to the beach road. This road took them through the centre of town, past hotels and restaurants, then past Bangla Road on their right and to Jungceylon and Central shopping malls.

Nick turned left into Jungceylon and said, "This is the most convenient place to park." Even though Bangla was open to traffic until six o'clock in the afternoon, he knew it would be impossible to park on the street there. They left the car in the underground car park, then took an escalator back up to ground level. Crossing the road at the only traffic-light controlled pedestrian crossing Nick had ever seen in Thailand outside Bangkok, they then turned immediately left into Bangla Road.

The first thing that struck him as they entered Bangla was how seedy it looked during the day. Without lights, music and a crowd, it was just another gloomy, dirty street in need of a good clean. At this time of day all the bars, go-go's and clubs were closed, and the only businesses open were the convenience stores and a few shops selling tourist tack. A few people in beachwear were making their way in the direction of the ocean, otherwise there were few people about.

As they'd arrived from the end of Bangla nearer to Amnesia, it only took a couple of minutes before they reached the stairway entrance. There was no point in climbing the stairs, though, as they could see the doors at the top were closed and all the lights were off inside. Unsurprised, Marky set off into the bar area beneath the club. There were a few people about, cleaning up and restocking for the night ahead.

Marky approached one of them and asked if there was another entrance to the club. The woman pointed further inside behind the bars and Marky turned to Nick to point with pursed lips, Thai style, the direction they were going. She led him inside until they reached a service entrance. A truck had been pulled up to unload crates of beer and soft drinks, and the workers were passing back and forth with handcarts.

Seeing no one else of interest they went inside to look around, Marky's uniform giving them sufficient excuse to be somewhere they shouldn't. Spotting what looked like some offices ahead, she pointed them out to Nick then headed in that direction. There were two doors, neither of which had a sign of any kind. The windows had vertical blinds, which were closed.

Marky knocked on the door and waited. It opened a moment later, and the girl opening it was taken by surprise when she saw a police officer. She'd probably been expecting a delivery driver, thought Nick.

The girl recovered to ask, "Can I help you?"

"We're looking for the owner. Is he or she around?" Marky informed her, stepping toward the girl to ensure she backed into the room. The girl stepped back involuntarily and Marky followed her into the office with Nick bringing up the rear. It was a large office with two desks, a computer on each, a couple of filing cabinets and a table with kettle and coffee-making paraphernalia. A closed door led to the office next door. The sign on it said 'private'.

The girl had not responded yet, so Marky asked again, "Is your boss here?" She added a pleasant smile this time and the girl relaxed a little. Her eyes shifted to the office next door for a moment, so Nick guessed that was the boss's office. Marky must have thought the same because she gave up with the girl and headed straight for the door.

"You can't go in there!" hissed the girl.

Marky stopped, turned and asked, "Why not? Is there something I shouldn't see?"

"No, no. It's just, ... he mustn't be disturbed," the girl finally managed.

With an exasperated exhale of breath, Marky turned, knocked on the door and entered without waiting for an answer. Nick saw the girl cover her mouth with a hand.

"Good morning, I'm Sub-lieutenant Pondee, Phuket police. I have some questions for you," Nick heard and followed Marky through the door. A man was sitting behind an ornate wooden desk topped with glass. The desktop was perfectly bare besides a mobile phone lying on a red leather blotter. It was the same man Nick had seen on Saturday night, so his assumption had been correct. Today he was wearing a white Lacoste polo shirt with a chunky gold necklace hanging over it. Attached to the necklace were several gold-framed glass cases with stone Buddhist amulets inside. Clearly he was superstitious.

The man had not even looked up as two people burst unbidden into his office, but calmly continued cleaning his nails with a letter opener. After a pause of nor more than a few seconds he placed the small knife on the blotter, leaned forward and looked at them with a smile.

"How can I help you, officer?" he asked, folding his arms on the desk and giving Marky his full attention. He didn't offer a seat, so they continued to stand.

"Let's start with your name, please."

"Anutin Mee-sombat, but my friends call me Geng," he supplied, slowly and clearly, as if they might mishear.

"Mr. Mee-sombat, please tell me what happened here at your club on August 4 2015," she said.

He feigned surprise and said "That's many years ago. I can't be expected to remember that."

"Let me jog your memory. It was the night that a private guest of yours attacked and raped one of your employees."

Nick had to admit the man was cool. He did not flinch or show any indication that he knew what she was talking about. Marky waited.

"I don't recall any such thing taking place here.

173

I'm sure I wouldn't forget something as serious as that."

"May I see your employee records for that time?"

"Certainly. Gung! Print out an employee list for August 2015," he shouted through to the girl in the outer office. "Please have a seat while we get that for you," he offered, indicating the two chairs in front of his desk. They took a chair each, then Anutin turned his attention to Nick. He switched smoothly to English to ask, "And what is your interest here?"

"I'm a detective sergeant from the UK, here as an observer," Nick replied in English.

"That's quite unusual. What interest do the British police have in this?"

"The case may be connected to the murder of a British national."

"I see," the man replied as his girl appeared with the printout. "Here you are," he said, offering it across the desk to Marky. She looked it over, quickly identifying the name Tida Yemyim.

"Do you have records for Miss Tida Yemyim?" she asked, and Anutin nodded to his girl. She left the room again, they heard a printer whirr into life, then she returned with another sheet of paper. Again she handed it to her boss and he in turn passed it to Marky.

The sheet showed Tida's personal details, her position as waitress, salary, tax and social insurance deductions, but gave no other information.

"Can you tell me why she was fired?" Marky asked.

"I've only ever sacked employees for theft, drink

174

or drugs, so if she was fired it would be for one of those reasons," he answered smoothly.

"Do you have a record of that?" Marky persisted. He looked at the girl, who shook her head 'no', which they all saw.

"I'm sorry I can't be of more help," he said, with the false smile back in place.

"One more thing before we go, what is your lawyer's name?" Nick could have sworn he'd seen the tiniest reaction this time.

"I use a number of legal offices, depending on what the matter relates to," he said, evading an answer.

"The man I have in mind would be your usual go-to person."

He thought for a few moments, unblinking. Finally, he came to a decision and said "You need to speak with Mr. Jirayu Huangsap. Gung will give you his contact details. Now, if you don't mind?", he gestured to the door.

They exchanged a look then thanked him and left his office. Gung closed the connecting door then found the promised information for them.

"That went pretty much as expected," observed Nick on the way back through the bars to the street.

"Yep, coffee time?"

"Sure, there's a Starbucks on the way back to the car," he agreed.

❖

Anutin reached for his phone and dialled a

number he had on speed dial as soon as he'd heard the outer office door close.

"What the fuck?! I thought you'd handled this?" he shouted, then calmed himself, not wanting the girl to hear.

"What's happened?"

"The police confronted me in my own office. They marched straight in this morning unannounced."

"It's all under control, don't worry about it," came the calm reply.

"It'd better be, cos it's you that's going under a bus, not me," he barked and hung up.

❖

"So, Mr. Jirayu Huangsap, your cousin's friend's employer that we met on Saturday," she said pointedly, "is Mee-sombat's lawyer."

They were in Starbucks now with a hot coffee apiece. Marky had chosen a table in a corner to avoid their conversation being overheard. If it wasn't for Nick, she would never have drunk their expensive cappuccino and was always surprised how so many people were willing to part with so much money for a cup of flavoured hot milk. The coffee shop was packed with foreigners and Thais alike at this time of day.

"It's a small world and an even smaller island," Nick offered with a shrug.

"Quite." She pulled out her phone and searched for the lawyer, expecting him to have a website or Facebook business page. "His office is in town, near the court. Shall we pay him a visit?"

"Of course we should, but let's think a minute," Nick said, getting his notepad out, "Mee-sombat will most likely have called him by now, so he'll be expecting us, or even avoiding us until he's prepared himself. Maybe we shouldn't go straight there, put him off-kilter a bit."

"Alright, but we don't have anything else," she pointed out.

"See if Yu has come up with anything on the policeman yet," he suggested. Marky dialled and spoke for a moment, but then shook her head.

"We're already in Patong, so why don't we drop by the station ourselves?"

"That's not a bad idea. We'll do that," she said finishing the last of her coffee and standing up.

"Oh, did you get a photo of Mr. Big for your association chart?" he asked, having seen her fiddle with her phone at a higher than normal position in the man's office.

"Of course I did," she confirmed happily.

❖

Patong police station was only a short distance along the road which Jungceylon backed onto, so they were there within a few minutes. It was yet another plain, white, concrete box, this time of only two floors. Nick parked the Jeep in one of the few parking spaces, then followed Marky inside. She went to the reception desk and asked to see the station commander. The duty sergeant noted her insignia of

IAN FEREDAY

rank, saluted and offered them a seat inside the air-conditioned office.

A female constable turned up after a couple of minutes and asked them to follow her upstairs. Nick thought how similar all government buildings were inside, with their cheap tiled floors, and plain painted concrete walls lit by naked fluorescent tubes. The constable pointed them in the direction of a tatty plastic sofa and offered coffee, which they declined. After another couple of minutes of waiting, the constable returned to take them in to see the station commander.

Marky went through the door first as a uniformed lieutenant colonel stood to greet them. Nick recognised him as one of the officers they'd met with Colonel Orntong at his grandfather's party.

"Sub-lieutenant Pondee and Sergeant Foster, this is a surprise!" he said, acknowledging Marky's salute and waving to two chairs facing his desk, "please sit down."

"My apologies for not calling before coming sir, but we were in Patong following a lead, so decided to come in on the off-chance that you can help us," she explained.

"It's no trouble. How can I help?" he asked, appearing genuinely willing, thought Nick, either because he knew Nick's connections or he liked the look of Marky in an evening dress.

"We've been trying to access online staffing records for Patong station from 2015, but have so far been unsuccessful. Are there possibly any paper records held on-site, sir?"

"Oh, I'm not sure, but if anyone knows it'll be my secretary. I've only been here two years myself, but she's been around since even before the move to this new building. Just a moment," he said, picking up his desk phone and dialling. The same constable came back in and he told her what they needed. Turning his attention back to them he said, "Constable Pacharee will find the information, assuming there's anything to be found. Now, if you'll excuse me...?"

"Yes sir, thank you sir," Marky said and they stood to leave. They saw the constable go off to another room, which Marky assumed was a file store, so they returned to the uncomfortable sofa to wait. After fifteen minutes, and just as they were thinking it was a fruitless search, she finally reappeared holding a ring binder.

"Here we are," she said victoriously, "station staffing records for 2014 and 2015. What date is it you're interested in?"

"August '15," Marky told her and the woman thumbed through the file looking for the relevant page. She stopped, opened the rings with an audible click and took out two A4 sheets.

"I'll make copies for you," she told them and walked back the way she'd just come. She returned with their copies in a buff envelope and handed them to Marky, who thanked her as she struggled to climb out of the sunken sofa.

❖

Marky resisted the temptation to open the

envelope until they were back in the car. She slid the pages out onto her lap and saw they were filled with names, beginning from the most senior ranks down to constables. Starting from the top, she saw a different lieutenant colonel had been station commander back then. There were a couple of majors, four captains, several lieutenants and sub-lieutenants, then the lower ranks were more numerous with sergeants, corporals and constables.

She did not recognise any names as she went slowly down the list, but stopped when she came to Wanchai Gerdpon. Back in 2015 he had been a sub-lieutenant the same as she was now. Continuing down the list she was disappointed not to know any of them as being current colleagues at Phuket headquarters.

"I guess we'll have to cross-check this with a list of staff in Phuket," she said, thinking aloud. Suddenly, she grabbed Nick's forearm, startling him.

"What is it?" he asked, momentarily shocked.

She turned to look at him and said very slowly, "Patong police station, August 2015, Constable Mongkon Ngaan-dee."

"Well, well. Isn't that a coincidence?" he laughed.

"That's no coincidence," she said, sitting back, thinking. "We need to brief the colonel," she said after a minute more.

❖

Arriving back at the station, they discovered Yu eating a lunch of fried rice at her desk. Embarrassed at being found eating in the office, she began to collect up her food to leave.

"Don't be silly, Yu. Sit down and finish eating," Marky ordered, putting their own bag of food down on the desk.

The girl sat back down, still not meeting their gaze, but continued eating all the same. Nothing puts Thais off their food, thought Nick.

"We need to get our boards and file up to date before I ask to see the colonel," Marky told them both, "We need to be well prepared to present this."

"What's happened?" asked Yu between mouthfuls. Marky brought her up to speed and explained that they needed to interview Ngaan-dee, which would require the colonel's approval.

Nick was opening his foam box of noodles fried with soy sauce, but offered, "If you print the photos and update the board, I'll make sure the file is complete." He did not know where anything was outside this room, so couldn't very well do the printing.

"Okay," agreed Marky, attacking her own takeaway.

"What would you like me to do now you've found the policeman yourself?" Yu enquired, hoping to be able to contribute something else after failing to track him down online.

"Call the colonel's secretary and see if he's available later this afternoon. We should be ready by then. And make sure she knows he's to come here for the briefing, not in his office. Better still, offer to escort him because he probably won't even know where this room is."

"Yes, ma'am." She saw they were both now eating too, so went back unabashedly to her own lunch.

❖

The colonel's secretary had said he would be with them at four o'clock and wouldn't require an escort. There was no knock of course, but the door opened punctually at the appointed time and they all stood, Marky and Yu both saluting as he entered. He hesitated to take in the whiteboards, then closed the door behind him. Marky stood aside and offered her chair, moving round to the other side next to Nick and the boards. The colonel sat, folded his arms and said, "This all looks very interesting. Please go ahead."

"Thank you, sir," she said, moving to the association board, now with photographs for everyone involved, including the lawyer which she'd found on the web, "as you know from our previous briefing, we were able to link the killing of Mr. Townsend to the murder of a reporter in Bangkok and also to the death of Captain Gerdpon, which we no longer believe to be suicide." She paused in case he wanted to speak, but he said nothing so she continued, "We have since interviewed a young woman who was attacked and raped in a Patong club in 2015. Captain Gerdpon was one of the attending officers. He was a sub-lieutenant at the time and attended the scene with a constable. The club owner's lawyer somehow convinced them to drop it without arrest or charge, which they did.

"Coming back to the present, Captain Gerdpon visited the girl to tell her he felt remorseful and would try to make up for his past error of judgement. He played golf with Mr. Townsend and passed on the information about the attack to him. Mr. Townsend travelled to Bangkok to give the story to a reporter. Both died before the article was even investigated, let alone written or published," Marky paused for breath.

"That's very impressive work. The fact that you've called me here tells me there's more?" the colonel asked with eyebrows raised.

"Yes sir. We interviewed the club owner, who confirmed that the girl who was attacked worked in his club, although he denied any knowledge of it. We haven't yet spoken to his lawyer who assisted in arranging the cover-up. You'll see that's the second action on our list," she pointed to the action list which had 'constable interview' as item one. "However, we did discover the likely name of the constable that attended with Captain Gerdpon that night. He is still a serving officer and we would like to request that he be interviewed with regard to the events on the night of the attack, but more importantly, the recent events that led to three deaths."

"Are you going to keep me in suspense, officer Pondee?" the colonel asked, now riveted to Marky's narrative.

"I believe the constable is now Sergeant Mongkon Ngaan-dee, sir, and I formally request approval to interview him as soon as possible."

Nick was impressed with her presentation, thinking he would be pleased with himself if he'd done it as well as that. He watched the colonel closely for his reaction, but the older man sat thinking silently for a full two minutes or more before he spoke again.

"So you can't be sure it was him?" the colonel eventually asked.

"No, sir, but I'm as certain as I can be. Presented with the facts we have, I think he'll believe that we do know it was him."

"Very well, but Sub-lieutenant Pondee, I cannot allow an officer of your rank to interview a fellow officer when serious charges may follow."

"But sir ...," she began, but he raised a hand to interrupt her.

He talked right over her, "That is why I am making you acting captain for however long it takes to resolve this in its entirety." They were all stunned, but he had not finished yet, "I will have Sergeant Ngaan-dee brought in for interview first thing in the morning. Tell no one of this," he said, looking at each of them in turn, "we don't want to spook him or allow him time to prepare a story. I will also be present. Let's say nine o'clock in this office." He stood to leave, then turned back to Marky to say, "and leave those boards exactly as they are, hopefully they'll scare the shit out of him."

They took a collective breath once he'd left the room, then Nick offered his hand for a congratulatory high-five, which Marky responded to.

She was beaming and still high on adrenaline.

"We're not done yet," he told her, "we need to prepare our questions and tactics for the morning."

"You can get started on that. I'm going out to get new epaulettes," she told him and left the room still laughing.

# Chapter 8

Yu was first to arrive at seven to make sure the room was ready for the interview. She'd reconfigured the desks to run lengthways again and brought in more chairs. Marky and Nick arrived together half an hour later, with a bag of croissants and three coffees. They sat and chatted about anything other than the case while they drank and ate, then Yu cleaned the table of cups and crumbs once more. Nick complimented Marky on her new insignia and told her she'd earned it.

"It's only 'acting' captain because it's expedient. He'll probably knock me straight back down when it's all said and done."

"Then we need to get a result that makes that difficult for him," counselled Nick, with Yu nodding in agreement, but Marky still looking sceptical.

"I must admit I'm quite nervous," Marky said, fiddling with her notepad and pens, "I've never interviewed a fellow officer before."

"You'll be fine. You gave a great performance yesterday."

"That was just a presentation of facts. Today we're going to be faced with a hostile interviewee. That's a completely different thing. And remember, if we can't get anything out of Ngaan-dee, we have little else to go on that will move us forward."

"You've got this," Nick said to reassure her, "and if you can get done by midday I'll take you to visit granddad for lunch. He's even scarier."

This made her laugh and relax a little, which was obviously what he intended she realised and appreciated him for it.

❖

Marky was checking the time on her phone every minute before the door finally opened at five past nine. The chief entered first, followed by Ngaan-dee with a cowed look on his face. The swagger and insolence had been quickly erased, thought Nick, considering the man anew. He was thankful to note the sergeant had been relieved of his pistol and expected the same was true of his mobile phone.

The chief pointed to a solitary chair on one side of the desk and the sergeant sat. He glanced at the boards, saw his own photograph and the connections that had been made to other people. His eyes widened as he scanned the information and details, then he collected himself and looked down at his lap. Two officers had escorted Ngaan-dee to the interview and one of them now closed the door without a word as they left. As agreed, Marky and the colonel sat opposite Ngaan-dee, while Nick sat behind them where he had a clear view of the man's face. Yu sat at the end of the desk and began recording on her phone.

"Sergeant Mongkon Ngaan-dee," Marky began, "do you know why you're here this morning?"

No response. He did not make eye contact and sat staring blankly at the tabletop as if stunned to find himself in this situation.

"We have evidence that three people have been killed in the past two weeks, one of them a fellow police officer, and we believe you either cooperated or assisted the perpetrators. That makes you an accessory to three counts of murder."

This got his attention and he looked at Marky directly before answering, "I know nothing about any murders and you have nothing to connect me to them. Your board is a bullshit fantasy," he spat, waving a hand dismissively in the direction of his photo. His normal bluster and confidence was returning now.

"We know you were the constable with Captain Gerdpon, sub-lieutenant as he was then, on the night a girl was attacked at a club in Patong. Neither of you filed a report. Your mobile phone is being checked as we speak. I'm sure we'll find an interesting record of calls between you and either Mr. Mee-sombat or his lawyer Mr. Huangsap. That will prove a clear connection," she told him and Nick saw the panic in his face. He did not need to ask who those two people were.

"I haven't killed anybody and I don't know who did."

The colonel leaned forward and almost whispered "Then explain to us why you would call either of the two gentlemen Captain Pondee just mentioned." He was obviously assuming there would be a record; Nick hoped he was right.

Ngaan-dee shook his head, looking down at the tabletop still, "You'll get me killed too. I can tell you what I know, but I want a transfer far away from here. I haven't done anything wrong."

"I can promise you'll never have to work in Phuket again after today," the colonel told him, to Nick's surprise.

The sergeant sat up straight now and addressed the colonel, refusing to acknowledge Marky further. "Wanchai told me he was going to visit that girl," he indicated Tida's photo on the board with an inclination of his head. They knew who he was referring to, so no one looked round, "I called Ji to let him know."

"Jirayu Huangsap?"

"Yes."

"Why would you do that?" this from Marky.

Ngaan-dee hesitated, squirming in his seat, breathing loudly through his nose as he rolled his lips together, thinking. Reaching a decision he told them, "Because he pays me a few thousand Baht a month to keep him informed of anything interesting." Nobody was surprised by his answer, but it silenced them for a few moments. When none of them spoke, he continued, "Look, it's no different to what everyone else does," he said, hands out, palms up, "we all need to make a little extra where we can, you know that, sir."

"Tell me exactly what happened," the colonel ordered.

"When Wanchai came back from seeing her he told me he wanted to make it up to the girl. He said we'd failed her, so I asked him what he planned to do. He told me we couldn't take on people like that ourselves, so he was going to get a friend to pass it on to a big-shot reporter in Bangkok. That would get the story national coverage so it couldn't be ignored and he hoped an investigation would be opened. I tried to talk him out of it because it could only go badly for both of us, but he was utterly determined and said to hell with the consequences."

"So you told Huangsap this?"

"Yes."

"Did you know what he would do about it?"

"No, I had no idea anyone would get killed. I've been passing on bits and pieces of information since back then. It's always been harmless."

"When did you start 'working' for him?"

"Back then, the night the girl was attacked. He offered to pay us both to 'forget' we'd been called out. Wanchai refused because he was always straight. I took the money and he called me a few days later to suggest an ongoing arrangement."

"If Wanchai didn't take a bribe, why didn't he

make a report? Why did he walk away and forget it?"

"They threatened him. He was smart and understood self-preservation. Wanchai was aware even then that they were dangerous people and he didn't know who else they knew, maybe higher-ups in the police. He didn't take their money, but he dropped it all the same."

"It never occurred to you what the fallout might be from giving them that kind of information?" Marky asked.

"I never knew what they did with anything I passed on."

"Then you're stupid," barked the colonel, clearly disgusted with what he'd heard so far, "Wanchai was a far better man than you, and you got him killed."

Ngaan-dee bowed his head, "I know he was," he said softly.

"Do you know what happened to the girl that was attacked?" Marky asked and he looked up, suddenly aware that she had been in danger too.

"No, I don't."

"She had been attacked and raped where she worked, and a week later her employer fired her. Since then she's lived in constant fear and jumps at her own shadow. All of you destroyed that girl's life. You're all equally responsible."

"I'm sorry, but we had no choice. Whether we took the money or not the threat was there. I did the sensible thing and took it. They were always suspicious of Wanchai because he didn't." He was pleading now.

"Did you know about the reporter?"

"No, not until I saw him on your board just now."

"What about Townsend?"

"I got a call from Ji to get myself assigned to his case. It was easy enough because he called right after the shooting and it hadn't yet been delegated."

"Didn't that strike you as a hell of a coincidence?" asked the colonel, shocked how calmly Ngaan-dee relayed this detail.

"No. I had no idea who Townsend was. I didn't know he knew Wanchai, so I didn't make any connection. Ji told me to make sure the shooting wasn't looked at too closely and that's what I did. It was all under control until the farang turned up," he said, glaring at Nick with contempt.

"You said you only passed on information. Now you're telling us you interfered with an investigation."

"Well, ... it was just this once," he said, looking uncomfortable.

"What about when Gerdpon died? Didn't that make you think?" Marky again.

"I was shocked and scared then. It had to be them, I knew that. I was quite sure it wasn't suicide, but I don't know anything more about it."

"You keep referring to 'they' and 'them'. Who do you mean exactly?"

"Huangsap and the owner of that club. I don't know his name, but Ji said he was a dangerous man to cross."

"Did you provide information about Wanchai's address, whereabouts, habits?" the colonel asked, wanting to be completely clear.

"No, no. I never told anyone anything about Wanchai. He was a friend. You have to believe me!"

To everyone's shock, the colonel suddenly rose from his chair and leaned across the table to slap Ngaan-dee open-handed hard across the face. They were all stunned. Ngaan-dee's cheek shone red instantly from the blow.

"You're a disgrace to the police force. You're disrespectful, corrupt and lazy. I won't waste any more time on you," he said, sitting back down, then shouted "Sergeant!" The door opened and the two officers who'd been waiting outside came back in. "Take this man to the cells and make sure his uniform is removed. I'll come down to charge him myself shortly."

"What?! No! You can't do that! You promised me a transfer if I helped you!" pleaded Ngaan-dee as the officers took his arms to lift him out of the chair.

"I promised you'd never work in Phuket again and I'm keeping my word. Take him away!"

❖

The colonel left the office immediately after Ngaan-dee had been removed, still simmering with anger. Nick suggested coffee and offered to fetch it. By the time he returned, Yu and Marky had the desks and chairs back in their former positions. They sat drinking quietly, each with their own thoughts on what they had just seen and heard.

"Now what?" asked Marky despondently, "we now know the 'why' and the 'who', but we have no evidence nor anything we can follow up."

Nick shook his head. "It still doesn't sit right with me. I can't accept they'd kill three people to cover up an old rape, especially one that was never reported."

"Go on, what are you thinking?" Marky prompted.

"Well, even if it was in the newspaper, so what? There would have to be a new investigation and it would quickly conclude there was nothing to go on. Sure, some muck would stick, but it would be forgotten soon enough. People have short memories."

"Then we're missing something."

"We are, but what?" Nick agreed, thinking hard.

"We need a break. How about that promised lunch with grandad?" Marky proposed.

"Good idea. We need to get out of this office for a while. Let's go," he said, reaching for his phone. He made a quick call then told her, "That was his cook. I was just letting her know we'll be joining him."

"You have your grandfather's cook's number saved in your phone?" she asked, dumbfounded and faintly amused.

"I have everyone's number in my phone, especially those who can cook well," he joked as they went down the stairs together.

❖

This time Nick turned into a small lane before arriving at the street which his grandfather's house fronted onto. It followed a high wall for a fair distance, which Marky assumed was the back of the property. The wall was plain other than gold-painted capstones at intervals, clearly intended for privacy rather than to be seen and admired like the one in front. The car stopped at a black painted wooden gate as high as the wall, which slid smoothly aside to let them enter.

The back of the house was as impressive as the front and differed only in that it had a gravel-covered parking area instead of a lawn and flower borders. The back door was also less imposing than its counterpart, and this is where Nick led her once they'd parked the Jeep next to a deep black Mercedes G63.

The door led into a wide, tiled hallway with several doors off to left and right. She could hear laughter and voices ahead, and they got louder as Nick led her farther inside. He turned right through one of the doors into a room with a large round bay window that flooded it with light. A round table stood in the window and sitting around it she recognised Nick's parents and grandfather. Nick's mother was seated between her father and husband. They stopped speaking as the newcomers entered the room.

Nick said hello to his parents and kissed his grandfather's cheek, while Marky gave a 'wai' to all three, eldest first. Nick pulled out a chair for her next to his grandfather and slid it under her as she sat, then took a place next to her.

"It's a pleasure to see you again Marisa. You seem to be spending more time with my son than me," Wanpen said pleasantly, but Marky was unsure if there was a genuine jibe in there or not. If there was, she was sure it was directed at Nick rather than her, so let it slide.

Nick must have thought the same because he said, "Mum, you know I'm here to work. This isn't a holiday."

"Your mother misses you Nick and it's more frustrating than ever knowing you're here but never seeing you," his father told him.

"I know dad, and I do my best, but this case just keeps getting bigger and bigger."

"Tell us about it," chimed in grandfather, and Nick gave Marky an enquiring look to see if she approved. She gave a slight nod that it was okay with her.

Nick started to explain that he had been sent as an observer after the death of an English businessman, but was interrupted by his mother noisily sliding her chair back and abruptly standing up. She dropped her napkin on the table and said, "I'm sorry dad, I don't want to hear about murder over lunch." With that, she walked out of the room.

Nick looked at his father who shrugged with his eyes as if to say 'what did you expect?' He turned to his grandfather and apologised, "I'm sorry ah-gong. It might be better if I come another day."

"Do that Nick. Your mother will cool down soon enough."

Marky stood and the two of them went back down the corridor to the back door. Passing the kitchen he saw his mother helping the cook arrange the food on trays. He put his head in the door and she looked up without speaking, then went back to what she was doing.

"I'm sorry you had to see that," Nick said as they waited for the gate to slide open, "We'll go to a restaurant instead."

Marky did not respond; there was nothing she could think of to say.

He drove into the centre of town and turned into a hotel. "There's a nice restaurant here," he told her as he parked.

The restaurant was adjacent to the lobby and was a huge, high-ceilinged room with a view overlooking a garden. A waitress showed them to a high-sided booth and they took a bench each either side of the long central table.

They looked over the menu in silence, and once they had ordered he looked at Marky and began to explain, "Mum has been angry with me ever since I decided to join the police."

"I thought that might be why. Wasn't sure if it was that or because you'd chosen to stay in the UK."

"Probably a bit of both, but mainly choosing the police. I clearly remember her saying they'd given me the education and opportunity to be anything I wanted, and I'd chosen to be a policeman. She said it in a very derogatory way, I can tell you."

"How different we are. My parents were so proud the day I first put on my uniform," she told him.

"They have every reason to be."

"How did you end up studying and staying in the UK anyway?"

"That's easy. When we were kids we always went

198

to England once or twice a year to visit dad's parents. Granny doesn't like long-haul flights, so they didn't come over here very often. Now they're older they don't come at all. With dad being English and my grandparents being there, it was natural that I'd go to study in England rather than the states or anywhere else."

"Makes sense."

"When I first went to uni in London, either mum or both mum and dad would visit me often, and I always came home for Xmas. We saw one another two or three times each year for a couple of weeks at a time, so we remained close." He stopped to think a moment, then went on, "I already told you I chose crime and forensic science as a masters so that I could join the police, right?"

"Yes, I remember."

"Well, my parents were suspicious right away when I told them my choice of master's subject. Mum pushed and pushed and eventually I told her what I planned to do after graduating. The display you saw today is how she's been ever since."

"I'm sorry, that must be hard."

"It is, but it's also unfair. I have to live my life for me, not how somebody else expects it to be or how they laid it out," he said with some passion.

"Your dad seems okay with it," she observed.

"Yeah, dad is great, and it's made easier by the fact that Jane has filled in where I was supposed to."

"So they expected you to take over the business?"

"That's right. Can you see me discussing building designs or quantity of concrete?" he laughed, "I need puzzles to solve. That's what I joined the police for, the challenge of working out 'whodunnit'."

"I get it, I have the same motivation. If I was moved to any other department I'd quit," she told him.

"I know, I've seen how you are."

"Do you see any way to resolve this?" she asked.

"Not really. On the rare occasions that I come home, mum makes an extra special effort with everything from meals to family days and trips together. She tries very hard to please me but at the same time makes subtle digs."

"Can you see yourself ever moving back here permanently?"

"Easily. As I already said, both here and the UK are home to me, ... or not," he added.

"What do you mean 'not'?"

"It's hard to explain, but I don't feel I really fit in either here or there. Here I'm a farang and over there I'm the Chinaman," he laughed sadly, "neither place can be called welcoming."

She considered for a moment, then said, "It's a shame, but what you've said is true. I've seen people's reactions when we've been together and it's not always pleasant. I hate to say it, but we Thais can be quite bigoted, if not outright racist."

The waiter arrived with their lunch and they stopped talking to eat. Marky watched him closely, thinking that even those blessed with apparently perfect lives still suffered problems and carried burdens just like regular people.

As they finished off the last scraps of food, Marky

asked, "Any ideas on what we do next?"

"Not really. I'm a bit distracted, sorry," he answered glumly.

"Want to call it a day? I can fill the remainder of the afternoon in the office and we can pick it up again tomorrow."

"That would be good if you don't mind? In fact, how about we take a break tomorrow too? I'll spend the day at home and try to appease my mother."

"Sure, that's fine. I've got plenty of paperwork to catch up on and the bad guys aren't going anywhere, after all," she said. The attempt at levity raised a small smile.

# Chapter 9

"We missed our coffees and croissants yesterday morning," Marky told him when he turned up with the usual carry-out tray of cups and a bag of pastries.

"You're both Thai, so I'm sure you didn't want for food," he joked back, then sat down opposite her in his regular spot, "so what have I missed?"

Yu was still a little shy around Nick, but that did not stop her from being first to reach for the croissants. She smiled a thank you to him as she sat back down with her pastry and iced latte.

"Not a lot," Marky told him, "I called Ning to ask her who paid the money into her account. Remember the hundred thousand?"

"Oh yes, what did she say?"

"All she could remember was that she hadn't recognised the sender's name or account number, but she'd known it wasn't the account that usually paid her monthly salary."

"Are we going to assume it was sent by the lawyer, Huangsap?" asked Nick.

"That's what I concluded, so I'm glad you agree. Unfortunately, we can't confirm it because she stopped using that account when she left Patong. There'll be no records after this length of time."

"Doesn't matter, it would have been useful information but it wouldn't prove anything."

"Correct. The slightly more exciting news is that Ngaan-dee asked to see the chief yesterday afternoon. He wants to provide information in exchange for a plea deal."

"What more do you think he has?" asked Nick, surprised at this turn of events.

"He's offering a list of cases he either falsified, fudged or otherwise messed with. The chief told him we didn't need it and left him to stew. In reality, he came by here and told us to dig out every case Ngaan-dee had been involved in since August 2015. Yu has been working on it ever since. He said he'd go back to Ngaan-dee only if we couldn't put anything together ourselves."

"That's a smart move. And what have you found so far?" Nick asked, curious now.

"Quite a lot actually. Although he only ever made it to sergeant, which means he never led a major inquiry, he assisted on many and also dealt with a lot of minor cases himself. Being on any case, either alone or just assisting, meant he had the opportunity to interfere. He could ignore or lose evidence, falsify reports, make sure paperwork went missing, skip interviewing witnesses, and so on. There are plenty of ways he could screw up an investigation."

"What will you do when you have the list of cases?" he asked, not yet seeing how this would help.

"Yu will check through them to find any that were defended by Huangsap. She'll also split them into three more groups; those that the prosecutor chose not to progress further, those that were prosecuted and found unproven, and those that resulted in a guilty verdict."

"That will make interesting reading," he said, impressed once more with her thinking. He turned to his right to see Yu listening to their conversation. Embarrassed at being caught eavesdropping, she blushed and dropped her gaze back to her laptop. He smiled at her cute manner. Turning back to Marky he asked, "So Yu is busy, but what is there for us to do?"

"I think it's time to pay the lawyer a visit," she suggested with a crafty look, "see what we can stir up."

❖

Once they were on their way, Marky said, "There's one other unrelated development I need to tell you about."

"What's that?" he had to ask after she did not go on.

"Your cousin called yesterday to ask me out," she told him, looking sideways to gauge his reaction.

"Beum? Well, well. I hope you said yes!" he

beamed.

"Why do you say that?" she asked without confirming either way.

"Because he's a lot of fun. You'll enjoy it."

"You don't mind?"

"Mind? Why would I mind? It's your choice, nothing to do with me. Why would you think otherwise?" he asked, astonished.

"I wouldn't want you to think I was just going out with him because he's from a wealthy family."

Nick laughed. "Well, I can tell you, if you were thinking that - and I'm quite sure you're not - that he has no money to speak of. My aunt gets a monthly allowance from the 'gong-see' and that's what they live on. Beum hasn't done an honest day's work since he graduated."

The 'gong-see', Marky knew, was a central fund that all Chinese family members who could afford it contributed to. It helped those members that were in need and ensured the family remained strong.

"I see. You've rather put me off. Not because he's not rich, don't get me wrong! Rather that I don't want to get involved with a layabout. I assumed he had a job as he was very well-dressed when we met."

"Their allowance is generous and he's a spoiled only child. Anyway, as I said, he's great fun, so you should go out with him. Who knows, maybe some of your hard-working character will rub off on him," he quipped.

"Well, as I've already agreed, I suppose I'll have to. By the way, you must have noticed that Yu has a huge crush on you?" she asked, amused at the thought.

"Honestly, I hadn't noticed."

"She thinks you look like the half-child TV stars everyone raves about in the TV soaps and movies. Yesterday she interrogated me half the day."

"I hope you kept my secrets," he smiled across as they came to a stop outside the lawyer's office building.

❖

Huangsap's office was in a four-storey 'shophouse' in a less prosperous part of Phuket town, but within easy reach of the police station and court, so provided easy access to the two places he would visit most often. The ground floor frontage was cheap, brown, aluminium framed sliding doors fitted with dark glass. A sign above proclaimed 'Huangsap International Law Office'. Nick smiled while taking in the sign, knowing Thais loved claiming their businesses were international, mistakenly thinking it meant they served international clientele.

Marky slid the door open and they went inside. A number of mismatched steel desks were spread around the room. On one stood an old fashioned typewriter which looked like it still got some occasional use. Another had a computer, but the thing they all had in common was the tall piles of files occupying every possible horizontal space, and spreading to include chairs and the floor. From behind this maze of paperwork, a young man stood up to greet them but hesitated when he recognised them.

"Good morning. Wayu, isn't it?" Nick inquired pleasantly, remembering the young man from the party as being a friend of Beum. He also remembered he was the public prosecutor's son and had told Nick he worked for 'Uncle Ji'.

"Hello again. What brings you here?" he asked, clearly nervous. Nick had thought him something of a weak character when they had first met and he was presenting the same demeanour again today. He looked positively spooked to see them in his office. Police uniforms did that to some people.

"We're here to see Mr. Huangsap," Marky told him, "Is he around?"

Visibly relaxing, Wayu replied, "No, he's meeting dad... sorry, I mean the prosecutor, this morning."

"When are you expecting him back?"

"I can't say, he doesn't spend a lot of time in the office. Mostly he works from home or visits clients. People don't usually come here." That explained the clutter, thought Nick.

"And where does he live?" Marky continued.

"Er, I er ... I'm not sure I should give out that information," he said, flustered now, but worried about refusing a police request.

"We'll get it anyway, so you might as well save us some time," she told him reasonably.

He paused, then they saw his expression change as he made a decision. "I'll write it down for you," he offered and sat back down to do just that, struggling to find space on his desk to write a note.

"Looks like you have a lot of work on," she ventured, looking around the room at all the files.

"Yes, Uncle Ji is a very popular lawyer." He looked up to watch her as if afraid she might grab a file and start looking through it.

"What sort of cases does he take on?"

"Oh, all sorts, but mostly criminal," he said with some pride. Most lawyers dealt with the run-of-the-mill work of contracts, leases, business registrations, land purchases, family disputes and the like. He handed over the address on a yellow sticky note and Marky smiled a thank you.

"And what do you do here?" she asked, causing his initial nervousness to return, despite her affable manner.

"I look after the office and do all the paperwork. Uncle Ji drops by some mornings and afternoons, but mostly he just calls," he told them cautiously.

"That's a lot of work. You must know every case that goes through here then?" she asked sweetly, turning up the charm to full.

"Oh, I do," he replied quickly. She had him hooked now.

"It must be hard keeping track of all these files," she observed nonchalantly.

"Not at all. I have them all in the computer, and although it looks a disorganised mess, they're actually sorted using a system I developed myself," he said proudly.

"Well done you!" she said and made him blush. "And thank you for this," she told him, waving the sticky note.

Back in the car, she showed Nick the address on the note. "Look at this. His office may not be classy, but his home is in a very exclusive estate. He's doing very well for himself."

"Where to next?" he asked.

"Why don't we go to his house? We know he's not there, but it will definitely get his attention when he finds out we've been trying hard to find him."

"Certainly ma'am," he jested.

"I was wondering when you'd show some respect for my rank, sergeant," she joked back.

❖

"So?" he demanded, answering the phone with no greeting or nicety.

"They're at your office."

Silence.

"Boss?" came the nervous query.

"Yes, yes. I'm thinking," Jirayu snapped, "keep me updated," he finished abruptly and hung up.

❖

The lawyer's mini-mansion was as grand as the address suggested. It was a nice estate of large detached properties and they all looked well kept. He wasn't home, as expected, but a maid called his wife to the door to speak with them. She didn't appear surprised that police officers were looking for her husband, simply assumed it was in connection with one of his cases. Marky found it odd though, that the wife would be used to police coming to the house. Surely all such contact would be at the police station, the court or the lawyer's office? Unless of course there was a reason he didn't want to be seen in public with some police officers and vice versa.

They left the wife with a message and phone number for her husband to contact them as soon as possible. She must have called him right away because Marky's phone rang before they had driven more than a few kilometres.

"Good morning, officer Pondee. I understand you've been looking for me." He sounded cheerful and unconcerned, but Marky knew lawyers could act better than many movie stars.

"Thank you for calling, Mr. Huangsap. There's a matter we need to discuss with you. Can you come in to the station?"

"Well, I'm in a meeting with the prosecutor at the moment, then I'm due in court after lunch. Would tomorrow morning around ten be convenient?" he offered genially.

"That will be fine, I'll see you then. Thanks again for calling," she said, hanging up and looking across at Nick. "Smarmy sod, I don't like him at all. He took the trouble to point out he's with the prosecutor just now and will be in court this afternoon, as if he's somebody special and the legal world would grind to a halt but for him."

"Do you just dislike him? Or is it all lawyers?"

"Hmm," she thought a moment, "it could be all of them. Let's get coffee before we go back."

❖

Sitting in the Amazon coffee shop in a PTT petrol

station, Nick finally found the time to read the email he had received overnight from the chief superintendent. He thanked Nick for the update and said they would review it on a weekly basis as to whether he was still needed on the case. As it had taken days to get a reply, Nick guessed the chief was not yet overly concerned at the length of his stay. He decided his next report could wait until mid-week.

"So what did you do with your day-and-a-half off? Did it placate your mother at all?" Marky asked, dying to know the ins and outs of this unusual family dynamic.

"I spent the afternoon at home on Tuesday with mum and dad, then took them all out for dinner in the evening once Jane came home. There were no more tantrums, so I assume mum enjoyed herself. Nobody mentioned what had happened at lunchtime."

"Where did you eat?" she asked, curious to know the details of a restaurant she was unlikely ever to see.

"Do you know Yamu cape?" he asked over the top of his cup.

"Yes, but I've never been there."

"You should. It has a lovely view across the water to the marinas and Coconut island. It's well worth a drive," he explained. "Anyway, there's a small estate of villas right at the end of the cape and past them a hotel sits on the edge of the headland. It has a terrific Italian restaurant and a nice cocktail bar."

"I can maybe afford the drive, but perhaps not the meal," she said grinning.

"Yes, it was a bit pricey," he laughed. "Then on Wednesday we took a boat trip. Remember the marina where we had lunch at a deli that first day?"

She nodded.

"Well, there's a company that does day charters from there. Jane was working, so it was just me, mum and dad. It took us north into Phang Nga bay, then around the top of Yao Noi island. We moored there to snorkel and swim while the crew prepared lunch. Did you know there are hornbills on the islands?"

"No, I didn't. Did you see any?"

"Yes, they were flying back and forth, calling to one another all the time we were eating."

"It sounds amazing."

"Yes, we had a nice day together, so mum has quietened down for now. We'll see how long it lasts. They've already started talking about coming to London for Xmas because I'm not coming here."

"That would be nice for you."

"It would. I don't think dad has spent Xmas with his parents in long enough, so it would be good."

Marky was thirsty for every detail she could get of his life and the way he lived, not through jealousy or envy, but simply because she knew she would never experience these things for herself. While he told her firsthand about fabulous restaurants, boat trips and hornbills she could put herself there in the moment and enjoy it all vicariously.

❖

Back in the office, Yu was smiling, clearly pleased

213

with her morning's efforts. Three sheets of paper were on the desk they shared, one of which was blank. Each was weighted in place with an item of stationery to prevent the ceiling fan from blowing them away.

"What have you found?" Marky asked Yu, taking in the sheets as she sat down. Nick took his seat opposite and leaned forward to read the sheets upside down.

"The sheet under the stapler lists all the cases submitted to the prosecutor that weren't taken any further after review," Yu told them, unnecessarily pointing at it. "There are more than one hundred and fifty over the last five years. That's as far back as the computer records go."

"That sounds like a lot of cases to be tossed out," said Nick, looking at Yu.

"I thought the same, so I did a comparison. We'll come to that in a minute," she said, looking at him with the slightest colouring of her cheeks. "The middle sheet under the hole punch is the cases that went on to be prosecuted, but resulted in 'not guilty' verdicts. There are thirty-two over the same period."

Marky pulled the last sheet out from under a pair of scissors. "Why is this one blank?" she asked, suspecting she already knew the answer.

Yu smiled widely and told them "That's the cases that resulted in a successful prosecution and conviction. Zero." She sat back to let them take that in.

"You mean nobody has ever been convicted in a case that Ngaan-dee worked on? Surely that's impossible!" Nick almost shouted in surprise, looking from one to the other of them and back again.

"I've double-checked. It's quite correct," Yu assured him, more confident now and pleased her work had been able to shock him.

"Can I just clarify a couple of things?" Nick asked, rocked by this revelation. "He only assisted on some of these?" pointing at the sheets, "and in minor cases he was the lead?"

"Yes, these lists are every case he was involved in that led to a submission to the prosecutor. There were another two hundred and sixteen minor cases that didn't get that far as he found they 'did not merit' further action."

After a minute passed in which no one spoke, Nick turned to Yu, "You mentioned a comparison?" he reminded her.

"Yes, I did the same exercise for four other officers, you included ma'am." she said, looking to Marky, "the average amongst them is seventy-four per cent are sent to the prosecutor, ninety-one per cent of those are prosecuted and the majority result in a guilty verdict. Yours were the highest ma'am," she added as an afterthought but got no reaction from Marky.

"Ngaan-dee's percentage?" asked Nick, fearing the worst.

"Over five years, a total of four-hundred and one cases, of which only thirty-two were prosecuted, while one-hundred and fifty-three were not pursued. So only thirty-eight per cent of his cases were sent to the prosecutor and only twenty-one per cent of those were eventually prosecuted. And they all failed."

"Correct me if I've got this wrong, Yu. The average percentage sent by other officers for prosecution was seventy-four, and for Ngaan-dee it was only half that?" Nick asked, becoming numb to the shocks.

She blushed again when he called her by name but said, "Yes, sir."

"And the other officers' cases led to ninety-one per cent being prosecuted and his only twenty-one?"

"Again, correct sir."

Nick and Marky looked at one another blankly across the desk, both trying to think beyond this data to what it meant.

"Yu, do another search, please. Find out who defended the cases that were prosecuted but found not guilty," Marky instructed her.

"I already have ma'am. They were all defended and won by Mr. Jirayu Huangsap."

Nick shook his head in disbelief and Marky's mouth fell open. It occurred to her that it would be necessary to go over every single case he'd been involved in. Clearly many had gone unprosecuted when they shouldn't have and people had got off when they shouldn't have. Their small team could not handle a case review of this magnitude; again, she would have to take it to the colonel.

"What sort of cases has Ngaan-dee been involved in?" she asked.

"Everything you can think of ma'am, from vehicle collisions to murders. I'll prepare a list of all of them if you wish?"

"Do that," said Marky, still thinking furiously.

Nick leaned forward to say quietly, "You know he couldn't get away with this alone. Senior officers must be involved too."

"That's exactly what I'm thinking and why I want the case list, but let's not shout 'conspiracy' just yet," she counselled.

Yu stood up to get the printed list from the printer she had set up in the office, then handed it to Marky.

"Before you look at that, what do you say we get some lunch?" Nick offered, wanting a chance to consider all the new facts.

Marky looked at her watch, twelve-twenty, and nodded agreement.

"Yu, we're going out for lunch, would you like to join us?" he asked, turning to the constable.

She beamed with delight and said, "I'd love to."

Marky smiled at this as she folded the freshly printed sheets and put them in her pocket.

❖

Yu was a lot shorter and skinnier than Marky, but she struggled to climb into the back of the Jeep all the same. It was proving to be a problem for girls in skirts. Nick drove them to the marina and his favourite deli for lunch. The constable was wide-eyed walking along the boardwalk next to the yachts and cruisers, clearly never having been there before. She was awed when the waitress once again greeted Nick by name and showed them to a table. Marky smiled to herself - she was so over the surprises by now.

Once the waitress had taken their order and removed the menus, Marky took out the sheets, unfolded them and placed them on the table. It was a table of case files, with the case number on the left, then the charge followed by the name of the investigating officer. She saw there were names of colleagues she recognised right away, but as she reached the older dates they were all unknown to her. The list of charges was as varied as Yu had said.

"I don't know where we're even going to start with this," she said to no one in particular.

Nick had had the time to think it over, so now offered, "What we now know Ngaan-dee did has a bearing on our case and we can use that. Beyond that though, all these other cases," he pointed at the sheet, "I think should be passed on to someone else. It's a whole new large-scale inquiry."

"I think you're right. I'll take it to the colonel and he can decide what to do with it," she agreed, and continued, "Yu, when we get back, can you break these down to the ones defended by Huangsap?"

"They're asterisked ma'am, like this one," she told her, pointing out an asterisk next to a date.

Marky looked at the list anew, concentrating on those with an asterisk to see what the charges had been. They were a mix of cases, which on quick inspection told her nothing. "Good work, but make me a new list anyway. I'd like to know who the defendants were in the asterisked cases."

Their food arrived and Yu waited until the others had begun eating to avoid making a fool of herself in these strange surroundings. The case was temporarily forgotten while they ate and chatted.

❖

The exit from the marina took them directly onto the main highway running north-south the length of the island. At the first major junction, Nick kept left to continue straight on into town through Sapam, while most traffic was turning right on to the bypass to continue south.

On the outskirts of Phuket town they stopped at a red light in front of the new bus station, the fourth car in the queue in the left lane. Motorcycles continued passing the stopped cars to jump to the front and be first away when the lights changed. As the space in front of the first vehicles at the lights filled up, more bikes waited between the cars and in the narrow lane to their left. Nick had not forgotten to pay attention to his surroundings and immediately noted the trail bike that pulled up next to Marky's door. From what he could see, both the driver and passenger were wearing T-shirts, but what made them stand out were their full-face helmets with tinted visors. Both visors were down.

Nick was about to comment and point them out to Marky when he saw the pillion passenger pull a pistol from a bag slung across his chest. Reacting rather than thinking, he stamped on the throttle and spun the steering wheel hard left. The Jeep did not shoot forward but instead took off at almost forty-five degrees left, slamming into the bike and knocking it over. As the bike disappeared from view, the Jeep bucked as it went over something, then Nick braked hard. Somehow, he had avoided hitting anyone or anything else.

Yu screamed in the back seat, but Marky had seen where he was about to point and understood what he had just done. She quickly opened her door and climbed out over the wreckage of the motorbike. Nick jumped out and ran round to join her. The lights had changed now, and their Jeep was causing a jam as the traffic behind them tried to merge into the right lane.

The bike rider was trapped under his bike, which in turn was now under the Jeep. His passenger was writhing on the ground a couple of metres farther back. Marky collected up the gun which had been dropped and handed it inside to Yu, then got on her phone to call for an ambulance and police assistance.

❖

Extricating the driver had proven difficult as he had a badly broken leg and had been trapped by the not insignificant weight of the Jeep. After jacking the left side of the Jeep up front and rear, the ambulance crew had taken him away with a police officer on board. His passenger had fared better and was only battered and bruised. A police vehicle took him directly to the police station.

Once photos had been taken of the accident scene and they had all given brief statements, they were allowed to continue on to the station under their own steam. The Jeep had a couple of dents and scratches but was otherwise fine. Nick couldn't imagine a vehicle more suited to ramming would-be killers.

His adrenaline was still fizzing when they got back to the station car park. As he switched off the engine Marky turned to him, laid a hand on his arm and said, "You saved our lives just now, Nick. Thank you for being alert. I must admit my mind was elsewhere."

"Any time." he said softly, more confidently than he felt.

❖

Marky told Yu she could go home as she was likely too shaken to concentrate on her work, but the girl insisted on staying to prepare the list of defendants Marky had requested. Yu started that task while Marky and Nick looked at one another silently across the desk.

Finally, Nick spoke, "Well, they've shown how far they're willing to go. Luckily for us it failed — this time."

"Safe to assume they have more on the payroll, so we need to be more careful than ever."

"I agree, so do you mind if I pick you up and take you home each day? It would put my mind at rest."

"I told you I can take care of myself," she insisted.

"I'm sure you can, but you're more vulnerable on your bike and two pairs of eyes are better than one. Besides, it's not like it's out of my way."

"Alright, alright. Don't go on."

The printer whirred and Yu passed over another list, this time of dates, case numbers and defendants.

"These were all defended and won by Huangsap," she told them.

Marky scanned the new list, most recent cases first, but none of the names meant anything to her. "I'm going to need you to get addresses and any other information for as many of these as you can."

"Sure, but that's not in the database. I'll have to pull the case file for each one."

"Okay, you get on to that." She turned to Nick, "You and I can go and have a chat with our would-be assassin."

Yu headed for the file storage room along the corridor, while Marky and Nick headed downstairs to the holding cells.

❖

The cells were at the rear of the police station, where detainees could be brought in directly and discreetly from vehicles, rather than through the front door. A bored-looking officer was sitting behind reception, sweating heavily as he was badly overweight and this area was cooled only by wall fans. He stood when he saw them approaching and saluted Marky smartly. Nick looked around and took in the large communal 'cage' to one side, with floor to ceiling bars. It was currently occupied by four young men, all of whom were asleep on the concrete bench along the back wall.

The officer saw them looking and provided an explanation, "Brought in around four this morning, all out of their minds on alcohol or drugs, or possibly both."

Opposite the communal cell were three smaller cells. These had steel doors with small windows and hatches. One door stood ajar, waiting for its next temporary guest. The other two had names written on the small whiteboards next to each door. One of them said 'Ngaan-dee', the other 'unknown'.

"We're here to speak to the shooter," Marky told the officer.

"Certainly ma'am. Shall I have him brought to an interview room for you?"

"No need, just open the door and we'll have a chat right here in the cell."

The officer selected a key from the row of hooks behind him on the wall and stepped to the first of the three small cells. "He hasn't been talking ma'am. Won't even give his name."

Marky nodded understanding; it was what she'd expected and why she didn't ask for him to be moved.

The door opened and they could see the man lying on the concrete bench, hands comfortably behind his head as if he didn't have a care in the world. He lifted his head slightly to see the reason the door had been opened. There was a momentary look of surprise on his face when he saw Marky and Nick.

"Name?" she asked. No response. The man went back to staring at the ceiling.

"You can be charged whether you give us a name or not. You'll appear in court as 'unknown' and the judge will still send you to prison for attempted murder."

"Lawyer," the man said, unconcerned,

223

maintaining his gaze upwards.

"We'd be happy to oblige. Who is your lawyer? I'll call him myself," she offered with cheerful sarcasm.

"Huangsap."

Marky nodded to the officer and he closed and locked the door. As they turned to walk away, they heard someone call from the other cell, "Pondee!" She paused, thinking, did she need anything from Ngaan-dee? Deciding it could not hurt to listen she turned back to stand in front of the second door but did not speak.

Ngaan-dee's face was at the small window in the door and his eyes were bulging in panic. "Pondee, you've got to listen. Tell the chief I've got lots of information. Please! I can help bring them down."

"Who can you help bring down?"

Ngaan-dee's eyes flicked quickly toward the other cell and back again. He clearly knew who the man in the next cell worked for and had heard the name a minute before. "Not here. I need assurances," he whispered.

She said no more, simply walked away with Nick in tow.

Once they were climbing the stairs and out of earshot, Nick said, "I doubt he knows anything useful."

"Me too. He gave out information, not received it. And I hope we can find out from the old cases exactly what he passed on and when. Let's see what Yu has managed to dig up."

❖

Yu was already back in her seat typing rapidly. She did not look up from the screen when they entered, so Marky left her to it.

There was a note on the desk from the arresting officer regarding the shooter and his driver. She picked it up and read the few lines out loud for Nick.

"Driver has a broken leg. He's not talking and his phone was smashed in the crash. Shooter had no phone. Neither had a wallet or ID on them. The gun has been sent to forensics. It's a nine millimetre."

"The same as was used on Townsend," Nick observed.

She nodded and dropped the sheet back on the desk, then sat down with a loud exhale of breath, blowing out her cheeks, clearly frustrated.

The clicking of the keyboard ended and the room was silent for a moment before the printer began spitting out several sheets. Yu gathered them up, then came to stand next to Marky, placing them in front of her.

She pointed to the first item. "The defendants Huangsap defended and won, ma'am, again listed from most recent. This is the date and case number, the charge, and then the defendant's details. Some have more information than others, and a few of the older files have already been sent to storage so I couldn't get anything."

"That was quick work," Marky complimented her. She read the first item that was from only the previous month. The defendant was Star World Limited Company, represented by its managing director, Mr. Anatorn Pattapong. He operated a taxi cab business and one of his drivers had been in an accident resulting in the death of a motorcyclist. Huangsap had argued that the rider was unlicensed, was speeding, was not wearing a helmet, and had tried to overtake the taxi on the inside when it was already indicating to turn left. No witnesses were called and no CCTV was available. The judge had found the taxi driver free of any blame and the case was dismissed.

The next case was completely different. The owner of a construction company had been caught employing undocumented Burmese workers. Huangsap showed that they were contract employees, hired through a third party company. That company was responsible for their work permits and visas, not his client, he had argued. Again, the case was found unproven.

The list continued in the same vein, mostly businesses or business owners avoiding responsibility thanks to Huangsap.

"Yu, pass me the phone please," Marky instructed and Yu slid it over as far as the cable would allow. Marky dialled and spoke to someone for a few moments, then hung up.

Turning to Yu, she said, "You will brief the colonel on everything you've found. He's expecting you, so get all your paperwork together and get up there."

Yu was horrified at the thought. "But ma'am, this is your case, shouldn't it be you?"

"This is entirely separate. You found it, now you can present it. Don't worry, he doesn't bite," she smiled to reassure the young constable.

Yu got busy reprinting extra copies of everything she had previously prepared and was out of the office a few minutes later.

Nick said, "That was very generous of you."

"We girls have to stick together," she grinned. The adrenaline from the earlier excitement had worn off now, so she suggested they get another coffee.

❖

The Red Spoon coffee shop was a short walk around the corner from headquarters, so was very popular with officers from the main station, tourist police station and the forensic department, which were all located nearby. It was a pale blue painted wooden building decorated with potted cactuses inside and out. They took a seat amongst the few other uniformed customers, and their drinks arrived a couple of minutes later.

"Do you think we'll gain anything from getting a search warrant for the lawyer's office?" she asked out of the blue.

"Possibly, but I doubt it. Those files are going to contain paperwork relevant to each case, but they're not going to have details of how he works them. Any notes or things like that will surely be with him, or even just in his head."

"You're right, not to mention, it would be a mountain of material to go through even if Wayu does have it well organised," she agreed as her phone rang. She showed him the screen and he saw the caller ID was Colonel Orntong. Marky swiped to answer, then listened without speaking. Finally, after a full minute of listening she said "sir." and hung up.

Nick waited, expectantly.

"He wants us back in the office for a meeting at four-thirty. Yu has gone to get the remaining files from storage. She'll be joining us."

❖

Arriving at the colonel's office a couple of minutes early, his secretary told them they should go back along the corridor to the large meeting room. They turned and went back the way they had come and Marky knocked on the door and opened it.

Entering they saw the colonel seated at the head of the long conference table, chatting with two other officers they didn't know to either side of him. Yu was sitting nervously at the nearer end of the table as if she couldn't get far enough away. Marky gave her a reassuring smile. There were several boxes neatly aligned on the table in front of Yu; these must be all the case files she had been going through.

The two strangers stood as Marky and Nick entered and they could tell right away from their shoulder insignia that they were a lieutenant colonel and a major. Marky saluted and the men retook their seats. It immediately struck Nick that they looked like Laurel and Hardy; he smiled to himself but stifled the urge to laugh. The lieutenant colonel had brilliantined hair, parted on one side and slicked across his head. He was short and dumpy where the major was skinny, from his face down.

Marky took a chair one place away from the major and Nick sat down next to her. They all turned to face the colonel.

"Gentlemen, if you would?" directed the colonel.

The older of the two men turned to face Marky and Nick across the table and said, "Lieutenant Colonel Boonsanong Chaiyakan, deputy commander Chalong police station."

They looked to the younger man to their left, who said, "Major Jarupan Sirikant, senior inquiry officer, Ta Chatchai police station."

Everyone turned their attention back to the colonel, who continued, "Pondee, Foster," he began, looking at them in turn, "your shooting inquiry has turned into a proper can of worms. I've called in Chaiyakan and Sirikant to open an inquiry into all cases that have been investigated by Phuket Police Station over the last five years."

Neither Marky nor Nick was surprised to hear this. The colonel continued, "these two officers have both worked under me at different times in different places. They have my trust and I know them both to be men of great integrity. For now, this is not to go beyond these four walls. It will take some considerable time to go through all the cases, so they'll begin with those that your young constable here has already discovered to be questionable," he nodded in Yu's direction, "this meeting room will be used as the inquiry room and constable Yu will now be based here."

Marky would be sorry to lose her, but she was delighted the young officer would have the opportunity to be involved in something as important as this large-scale inquiry. She had no doubt Yu would get a promotion out of this if she did a good job. The colonel was known to reward those that performed well.

"Colonel?" Nick asked and the colonel nodded his permission to proceed. "I hope I don't sound naive when I ask what you hope to achieve?"

"Not at all, sergeant. I'll be happy to explain, in fact, it will be a pleasure," the older man said, looking intently at Nick, "I'm sure you're aware that the RTP doesn't enjoy the best reputation with the public, quite the opposite if truth be told. You're also smart enough to know that not all of us are corrupt. I for one am not, and I know firsthand that these two officers I've called in are not. I believe acting Captain Pondee is also an upstanding, honest officer, and that's why I delegated her to you, rather than Ngaan-dee, whose case it was. I had no evidence against him, but I always had him marked as lazy, if not corrupt. My hope for this inquiry is to weed out all the bad apples in this station, prosecute them when possible, dismiss them from the force where we can, and at least transfer them elsewhere if we can't do either of those. I want to show the public that we really are cleaning house and that Phuket Police Headquarters should be seen as a place people can come to for help when it's needed." He stopped to smile, "like you, I hope I don't sound too naive, but we have to start somewhere."

Nick did not know what to say to that, so nodded and said, "sir."

"Now, I will leave you to brief the lieutenant colonel and major and get them up to speed with what you've found. By the way, this is nothing new to either of them. We've cleaned up together before this, but not to the extent that's going to be needed here. They'll know how to proceed. Gentlemen, ladies," he ended by way of closing the meeting. Everyone stood as the colonel rose and left the room, taking their seats again once the door was closed.

The lieutenant colonel explained that Colonel Orntong had called them to come to headquarters urgently and had only given them an outline when they arrived, so Marky started from the beginning and detailed everything they'd found so far. She had Yu explain what she'd discovered searching through the old cases, then told them the assumption they'd made that senior officers must be involved too. It was simply impossible that Ngaan-dee had manipulated every case himself; the investigating officers had to be complicit. She finished by pointing out that they'd only looked at Ngaan-dee's old cases because it related to their own case, but if what they believed was also true of other officers, then a wider search would be required.

After an hour of explanation and answering queries from the two newcomers, the lieutenant colonel finally excused them at almost six-thirty. Back in their own room to collect their belongings, Marky said, "Do you mind stopping on the way so I can get something for dinner? It's too late to cook anything now."

"I've missed dinner at home too, so how about joining me? We can use the time to prepare for our interview with Huangsap tomorrow too."

"I've never eaten so often with a man I wasn't dating," she laughed, locking the door behind them.

232

# Chapter 10

"We have your shooter in custody," Marky began.

"What do you mean, *my* shooter?" he asked impassively.

"Well, he's asking for you."

"Oh, I see. You mean he's a client." The relief was evident on his face and he visibly relaxed.

Huangsap had arrived late. Marky and Nick were going over the questions they would put to him, with one eye on the clock. Neither was surprised when it went past ten o'clock without reception calling up. Eventually, the phone rang at ten-fifteen and Marky suggested they leave him sitting there for at least as long as he'd kept them waiting.

At half-past they had gone down to the main entrance to find him sitting in one of the uncomfortable plastic chairs, silently fuming, "I've been here fifteen minutes already."

"I'm sorry about that, but we were expecting you at ten. When you didn't turn up we went on to other, more important business," Marky said agreeably, but this failed to mollify him, full of self-importance as he was.

Score one for us thought Nick. He's rattled already.

❖

They chose to interview him in one of the bland, windowless rooms on the ground floor, rather than allow him into their inquiry room where he would be privy to their boards. The small room had a wall fan, but no air-con, so was quickly getting warmer with three of them in it, not to mention smelling of bodies and anxiety from its previous occupants. There were no furnishings other than the Formica-topped table and four of the same plastic chairs Nick had encountered at reception. The few minutes he had spent in one had been bad enough, a drawn-out interview would be purgatory. Huangsap sat opposite them, clearly familiar with these surroundings from representing clients, and Marky's phone was on the table between them, already recording.

"Is that what he is?" asked Marky, "he gave us the impression you two have more of a relationship than that." Neither the driver, now in a cell of his own with a leg in plaster, nor the gunman had said a word, but Huangsap could not possibly know that. He would know better than most that honour amongst thieves didn't truly exist, and when individuals found themselves faced with time in jail it was usually every man for himself. She'd made a point to speak with the custody officer earlier in the morning to make sure Huangsap didn't have access to the two men before his own interview.

Huangsap gazed back at her, obviously feeling he had already answered that question. When Marky didn't go on, he finally said, "I'll see whoever it is once we're finished here," as if whatever they had to ask him couldn't possibly take long.

Nick and Marky had agreed they would alternate the questions and between them had come up with a list of things to put to him, some of which were little more than fishing. It was Nick's turn now.

"Please tell us about your work with Mr. Anutin Mee-sombat."

"He's a client, so that's privileged information," he told them, confirming the first thing they needed; he works for the club owner.

"Then tell us what happened on the night of August 4 2015," Marky demanded without pausing.

His eyes narrowed slightly to give away the fact that he knew what she was referring to, but all he said was, "That's a very long time ago. I'd need to consult my diary to find out."

"No need, perhaps I can jog your memory," said Nick, "it was the night an employee was attacked and raped in Mr. Mee-sombat's club."

"I believe I'd remember something as grievous as that," he said, folding his arms. His body language didn't match his nonchalance, they both thought.

Back to Marky with no letup, "We have two witnesses who put you there that night, and one of them is a police officer."

"They must be mistaken. I don't know anything about a rape."

"There's also the small matter of the hundred thousand Baht you sent to the account of the girl that was attacked." This was the first of their 'fishing' facts. They were quite sure it must have been him that sent the money but had nothing to prove it.

"Yes, I seem to recall something like that," he admitted easily, so their hunch was right, "Mr. Mee-sombat had some trouble in the club and called me. I believe the police resolved it easily enough. Something about an employee causing a problem with a guest."

Marky was outraged and snapped, "We all know what really happened, so trying to twist the facts and blame the poor girl isn't going to fly," she shouted, then calmed herself before continuing, "you arrived very quickly after being called by Mr. Mee-sombat and coerced the police officers into dropping the incident. You even took the girl to the hospital to be checked over. Those are the facts."

"Let's indulge your fantasy and suppose for a moment that what you say is correct. Neither the girl nor the police officers have made any kind of report or complaint. So what are we here for? Can you get to the point of this interview, please? I have a lot to do today." He leaned back in his chair and folded his arms again, poker-faced, waiting expectantly.

It was Nick's turn now. He leaned in and said

quietly, "We are here because ever since that night you have been paying a police officer to provide you with information on cases.

"Hold it right there! That's a very serious charge, so you might want to think carefully before you say any more," he said, raising his voice, then added slowly, "I ... haven't ... paid ... any ... police ... officers," punctuating each word with a pointed finger tap on the table.

"Then explain the payment to the girl and why you were there on the night as the witnesses have told us."

He sat back again, the outburst over and the cautious look back on his face. He's not as smooth as the club owner but he's better prepared, thought Marky.

"I'd like a drink of water, please." he said.

Clever move, thought Marky, breaking up our rhythm and giving himself time to think. Nick opened the door and called to the custody officer to bring in some water. They waited in silence for a couple of minutes until he arrived and placed three bottles of unchilled water on the table.

Huangsap drank deeply, then continued, "Look, I'll say again, I haven't paid any police officers for anything. However, I will confirm Mr. Mee-sombat called me in to help with a problem back in August 2015. He's not the kind of man you refuse, even at three in the morning, so I went there as quickly as I could. I would advise you to be very careful of him too — he's a dangerous man."

Marky drew in a sharp breath. "We don't

appreciate threats," she told him coolly.

"On the contrary, officer, it's not a threat, it's friendly advice," he countered with a smug look.

Nick attempted to bring him back on track, "So you're saying it's him we should be talking to?"

"As we already agreed, there were no charges brought and the girl was fired. He instructed me to pay her one hundred thousand Baht, which I did, and so that was the last that I thought about the matter."

"Apart from when you billed him for your time, no doubt."

"Of course," Again the smile and smug look.

"I'm sure you know the name Mongkon Ngaan-dee." Marky said as a statement of fact.

Huangsap shifted in his chair and folded his arms across his chest before replying, "It doesn't ring a bell." He held his pose, but a single trickle of sweat ran down his left temple.

"Officer Ngaan-dee is in a cell just along the corridor from here. He's been busy filling us in on everything he knows."

Huangsap took off his glasses, polished them using his tie, the carefully replaced and adjusted them. He appeared unconcerned and leaned in again to speak softly, almost conspiratorially, "Look, officers. I'm just a simple lawyer, a flunky if you like, for those that pay me. Mr. Mee-sombat paid me for the matter you're referring to, so it's probably best you speak to him. But as I said, be careful."

Marky and Nick realised they had gained nothing and did not have anything more to put to him other than claiming false confessions from the two men in the cells. They had agreed they would only try that if they felt they were getting somewhere, as otherwise it could bring them badly unstuck.

"Thank you for your time. We'll be in touch if we need to speak to you again," she said, standing. Nick was nearest the door, so stood to open it.

"Any time, officers, any time."

Marky thought she would love to knock that buttery smile off his face.

❖

"Well, that was a bust," Marky said once they were back in the training room. Yu's laptop and printer were gone, so she'd already relocated to her new assignment along the corridor.

"Let's be honest with ourselves, we never really expected to get anything from him."

"No, but now he knows exactly what we know, and what's more, he's now talking to the two on the motorcycle yesterday. He probably knows already that they haven't said anything."

"We need to go back to Mee-sombat, or better still, call him in here for questioning," Nick suggested.

"I'd need to clear it with the chief to bring in somebody as high-profile as that, and I don't have enough to convince him yet. We'll just have to see him on his own turf again. We'll do that after lunch, which I'm choosing and paying for today, okay?"

"Yes, ma'am," he said and again resisted the urge to offer a mock salute.

❖

After a lunch of fried noodles at a roadside shop just a short walk from headquarters, they drove to Patong in the Jeep.

"What did your dad say about the damage to the car?" she asked.

"I don't think he was ever really going to buy a Jeep, so he'll just pay for the repair when he gives it back. I've no doubt he selected the most hideous vehicle he could find on the dealer's forecourt because he has a weird sense of humour."

"Funnily enough, it's grown on me, especially now I've perfected my technique for entry and exit. Besides, it saved us yesterday," she said, patting the side of her door.

"It did, didn't it," he agreed.

Nick parked in the underground car park at the shopping mall again and they walked the short distance to Bangla Road and Amnesia. Traffic was still running through the street as it was not yet six o'clock, but some of the bars were already open for the early crowd.

They didn't even bother looking to see if the main door was open upstairs but made their way through the maze of small bars under the nightclub until they reached the access door at the back. It was unlocked so they went straight in and headed for the offices. Marky knocked and opened the door to see the same girl sitting at her desk. She jumped when she saw them.

"Hello again," offered Marky with a friendly smile, "We need another word with your boss."

Knowing that it was futile to say no, she said, "I'll tell him you're here," and made for the adjoining door.

She knocked and entered, closing the door almost fully behind her, but was back out in a matter of seconds to beckon them inside. Anutin Mee-sombat looked like he hadn't moved since the last time they'd been here. The desk was still empty bar the blotter and phone, and he was wearing another white Lacoste polo shirt with the chain and amulets around his neck. It was a mystery what he did to keep himself occupied in an empty room.

"Please sit officers," he said, steepling his fingers, and no doubt wondering why they were back in his office. "What brings you back here?" he asked pleasantly.

They sat as instructed and took their time to open up and consult their notebooks. It was only for show; they had already decided what they would say.

"The last time we were here, you said you didn't remember anything about an attack on one of your employees right here in the club," she began.

He did not speak nor react, waiting for a question.

"We now have three independent witnesses who tell us differently. One is the ex-employee herself who was raped by one of your guests, the second is a serving police officer and the third is your own lawyer, Mr. Jirayu Huangsap."

Still no response.

"Would you like to explain why three people seem

to have a better memory of the event than you?"

He placed his hands flat on the desk in front of him and leaned forward slightly, "I regularly have friends and business associates stay late in the club for drinks. They often have their own guests with them. It's not illegal as no alcohol is sold. It's strictly a private get-together." Having felt the need to explain that, he continued, "that night I remember there being quite a number of people after hours, some of them were youngsters who had just graduated high school and were having a blowout before going off to university. They sat separately from my group of older men." He stopped, perhaps thinking how much he could safely tell them. "One of the girls came and told me a waitress had been hurt in the locker room and that she'd already called the police. I called Huangsap, then went to check on the girl. I looked in but didn't enter. From what I'd been told had happened, I figured she wouldn't want another man coming in. The police and lawyer arrived not long after. Now you know exactly what I know."

"It would have saved a lot of time if you'd been this forthcoming on our previous visit," Marky said, "what happened after that?"

"I just told you, you now know as much as me."

"The girl was fired. You must know about that."

He looked at them both, then sighed and added, "Huangsap called a couple of days later and said it would be better if she no longer worked here. I didn't want to know the details. He suggested a payment, so I gave him two-hundred and fifty thousand Baht and her account details. And that really is all of it."

"Then you might be surprised to know that he only paid her one hundred thousand Baht," Nick took great pleasure in telling him.

Mee-sombat shook his head, "I'm not, actually. The man is a snake. He coils himself around people and squeezes them. You pay him and think he's working for you, but in reality, he only ever does what is best for him. I wish I'd never met him." All this was said with little show of emotion.

"And how did you meet him?"

"One of the guests that night suggested I call him. It hadn't occurred to me to call anyone other than the police, but it was pointed out to me that it could look bad for the club, so that's what I did, much to my continuing regret."

"Do you remember the guest's name?" pressed Nick.

"Yes, he was sitting right beside me. It was Apisit Wattana."

"The public prosecutor?" asked Marky, trying and failing to hide her surprise.

"Yes, that's him. I think some of the young lads were his guests. He also made sure everyone left before the police arrived."

Marky closed her notebook and looked directly at Mee-sombat, "Thank you for being frank with us, even if a little belated."

"Officers, let me explain something to you and you can choose to believe it or not, as you wish. I'm not a gangster, nor a monster, nor a villain. I'm a simple businessman operating a nightclub. You may have heard people refer to me as the 'crocodile'?"

Marky nodded; she had heard this before and assumed it was a nickname he had somehow earned.

Mee-sombat chuckled and told them, "My wife started calling me crocodile because I took to wearing Lacoste shirts." He pointed at the crocodile logo on his polo shirt. "Others picked up on it and it stuck. It's not as sinister as it sounds and neither am I."

"Thank you again for being direct Mr. Mee-sombat. I don't think we'll have to bother you again," she said to conclude the interview.

They needed to get back to the office to put all this information together and work out what it meant, but there was a Starbucks in between them and the car, and coffee could not be ignored.

❖

Driving back to headquarters they had discussed the conversation with Mee-sombat. Did they believe him or was he an excellent liar? Both agreed that he was sincere and had not been disingenuous to whitewash himself. He was not the dangerous gangster Huangsap had painted him as, so all they could do now was work with what he had told them.

Back in the office, Marky got busy updating her association board with the new information. They now knew enough of the details of the story that started with Tida Yemyim being attacked and ended with the deaths of Townsend, the reporter and the police captain. Everything they had learned led back to the lawyer.

She moved the girl and the three deceased to one side, then rearranged Huangsap to the top of the board and drew connections from him down to officer Ngaan-dee, the club owner Mee-sombat, and the two unknown assailants on the motorbike. She had used her laptop to source a photo online of the public prosecutor, Apisit Wattana, and had added him to the lower line, but so far with only a dotted connection and a question mark.

Finally, she added one of her male head silhouettes and wrote 'rapist' underneath it. There were no lines to connect him to anyone yet. When they had first spoken to Tida it had seemed unlikely if not impossible that they would ever identify the culprit, but she now had a good feeling that they were getting ever closer to revealing his identity. She stood back to take in the entire board, then sat on the edge of the desk and folded her arms, thinking.

Nick had also been busy making his lists while she worked. Looking up when he saw she'd finished, he saw the facts he'd listed told the same story as Marky's board. He'd already put to one side the attack on the girl and the resulting deaths, knowing they would get no further investigating those. He'd come to a similar conclusion; Huangsap was at the centre of the web and the killers worked solely for him.

Marky turned to him and asked, "Do you remember when we met Huangsap at your grandfather's party?"

"Yes, Beum was with his son, and he introduced

us."

"He seemed very cosy with the prosecutor and they spent the entire evening together. It might be something or it might be nothing."

"You think his meddling goes beyond bribing police offers?" Nick asked, quickly understanding what she was getting at.

"Hey, I'm not ruling anything out where Huangsap's concerned."

"I've been trying to see where we go next, but I've got nothing," he told her gloomily.

"Me too," she agreed, "neither Huangsap nor his lackeys are going to tell us anything, and Ngaan-dee and Mee-sombat have told us as much as they know."

"Want to give it a rest over the weekend and look at it anew on Monday?" he proposed.

"Sounds better than twiddling our thumbs here," she conceded.

"Do you have plans for Sunday lunchtime?"

"Nothing but laundry and housework that I'd be more than happy to put off," she laughed.

"Mum and dad are having a few people round for lunch if you'd like to join us. It's strictly casual and you'll need a swimsuit."

"Sounds great, but don't feel you need to include me. You must have friends you'd like to catch up with?"

"Not really. Most of my school friends weren't from Phuket, they were boarders. The few that were are all now married with kids, so we have little in common," he explained, "and besides, I don't ask because feel I need to include you, I simply enjoy your company."

"Okay, then I'm in, when and where?" Marky had no fear of mixing with Nick's family now and was delighted at his answer.

"I'll send the car for you at noon."

"Wow, how am I ever going to return to living my poor-girl life when you go back to the UK?" she asked, amused.

❖

This was Marky's first real date since returning to Phuket from university more than four years ago. Although she'd been out in mixed groups, she'd never felt the pressure that comes from being scrutinised by one person for an entire evening. She would have loved to have worn the Jaspal dress again, but Beum had already seen her in that, so she had no choice but to dig through her wardrobe for something else suitable for a first date; attractive yet demure, sexy but not slutty, and above all comfortable.

She settled on a peach coloured pencil skirt with a slit up the side; it showed some leg, but not too much. This was matched with off-white court shoes and a flowery blouse. She buttoned the blouse just far enough to invite interest without showing too much bosom. The court shoes were chosen for their low heel, as she remembered that Beum was not very tall. With a final check in the mirror, she picked up her evening bag and took the lift to the ground floor.

Beum pulled up at the front of Marky's condo

punctually at seven in a white Mercedes SLC. He had the top down and Thai rap music playing, but not too loudly. She opened the door to go outside as he jumped out and ran around the car to open the passenger door for her. Having almost fallen into the low-slung seat, she lifted both legs in together in as ladylike a manner as she could. She did not bother looking up to see if he was checking out her legs; she knew he would be.

He was dressed in a similar style to the last time they'd met, with a plain white shirt over dark Dockers and a pair of loafers. She saw he also had a jacket slung over the headrest of the driver's seat. Beum smiled at her as he closed her door, then all but ran back to his own seat. "Would you like the roof up?" he asked.

"No, it's fine."

"I ask because I know the wind messes with ladies' hair."

"You often have ladies in your car?"

"What?! No! ... I just meant ..." He looked over in panic to see her grinning and realised she was winding him up. He grinned too and put the car in gear. "I thought we'd go to Dark and Light. Is that okay?"

Marky knew the place but had never been there as it was well beyond her means and therefore off her radar. The restaurant was spread over two floors of a new building in one of the older parts of town. It had been designed to resemble a New York brick warehouse complete with black-painted steel stairs down the front facade and matching steel-framed windows. She also knew it was the latest hotspot in Phuket Town for the in-crowd to gather. "Great, I've never been," she confessed.

Beum pulled up at the front door ten minutes later, put the roof up, then handed his car key to a valet for parking. Coming round behind the car to join her at the entrance, he offered his arm to take her inside. A greeter opened the door for them and led them to a table for four near the bar. To one side was a green leather upholstered bench the length of the wall, to the other side were two matching chairs. Beum waited until she was seated on the bench, then took a chair opposite her with his back to the bar. The waitress removed the 'reserved' sign from the table and handed Marky a menu. She gave Beum a menu and wine list and said she would be back shortly to take their order.

Marky looked around to take in her new surroundings; she probably wouldn't be back here again she thought. The bar had stools arrayed along it, all with large leather-covered seats to match the benches and chairs. The bartop was a mass of brass piping showing labels of various imported drink brands. The wall behind covered two storeys and was filled with bottles of liqueurs and spirits. A rolling ladder was waiting if they needed to be retrieved. She could not make out much more from this corner but resolved to take a look around and get a selfie when she was able to excuse herself to go to the ladies' room.

Beum suggested a bottle of wine and a selection of cold starters, which she went along with. Flicking through the menu, she saw they at least had some dishes she knew, albeit priced ten times higher than she would want to pay for them. She chose her own main dish and Beum placed their orders with the waitress.

A wine waiter was at the table not two minutes later with a bottle of chilled prosecco and two flutes. He made a big show of opening it, then poured them a glass each and placed the bottle in an ice bucket and draped a towel over it.

Beum raised his glass to offer a toast, so she clinked glasses with him. "To our first evening together," he said, with an irresistible smile.

Marky smiled in answer, looking directly at him. She had to admit, he was very handsome and looked elegant despite the casual clothes he wore. He was certainly very easy on the eye.

The restaurant was busy, being Friday night, so the service was leisurely. By the time their starter plates were being cleared, it was eight o'clock and a duet had taken to the tiny stage in the corner. They greeted the crowd and introduced themselves in English; they were from the Philippines. He played the guitar and she had a keyboard. When the main courses arrived the couple were already into their third western classic.

Beum leaned in to be heard over the music, "I reserved this table so we'd be near the band, but we can move if it's too loud."

"It's fine," she said, twirling her spaghetti aglio olio and thinking it hadn't been a great choice for a first date. There was no way to eat this in a refined manner.

"So, tell me what it's like working with the farang," he went on.

"Why do you call him that?" she asked, disapprovingly.

"Oh, don't worry. I've been calling him that since we were toddlers and he's always called me 'coolie', you know? A Chinese labourer?"

"But he looks as Asian as we do," she objected.

"All kids get a nickname, and Nick's the only half-child amongst all our family. I'll stick to 'Nick' if you prefer."

"Please. It just makes me uncomfortable."

Beum was quiet for several minutes after that exchange and Marky did not answer his original question. By the time she had finished her spaghetti, she had begun to feel sorry for making him feel bad, especially as that had been his first attempt at conversation.

"What do you do for work?" she asked, despite having been told he was a deadbeat — Nick's word.

"Oh, a bit of this and a bit of that. I have a finger in a few pies, hoping one of them will bear fruit, you know?" he answered, smoothly responding to her question without answering.

"Any of them interesting?" she persisted.

"Nothing I want to bore you with," he smiled and reached for the wine to top up their glasses. He shared the last of it between their glasses and asked if she would like a second bottle.

"Thanks, but half a bottle of wine is already more than I normally drink." She did not feel at all the worse for it, but her head would no doubt hurt in the morning.

"What do you do when you're not detecting?" he asked, leaning in close enough that she could smell his cologne.

"I guess you mean hobbies, not keeping up with housework and the thousand other personal jobs I never find time for?" she joked.

"Yes, any sports?"

She shook her head, no. "It feels like I've had to give up everything since joining the police. I used to jog every other morning and go to a Thai boxing class on the weekends. Somehow, they just fell by the wayside as I got promoted and took on more work. I was also a member of an ecological group called Trash Warriors that did beach and forest cleanups. We'd meet at a different place around the island once a month to spend a morning collecting rubbish."

"That sounds like something worthwhile. And you don't do that anymore?" He sounded genuinely interested.

"No, and the rubbish collecting ended not just because I'm busy. I became disillusioned with individuals taking on responsibility for saving the planet. The amount of trash we collected every month started to depress me. I realised that our small effort could never make a difference. It needs governments, global leaders and major companies like Google, Shell, Facebook and ICI to lead the charge. That's the only way things will ever change," she explained with passion.

He nodded his understanding without comment

and she realised he was as shallow as Nick had said he was lazy. Such a shame that an attractive man had no ambition or drive, but she knew most Thai men aspired to the playboy lifestyle that Beum enjoyed.

"Would you like to go on to a club?" he suggested.

"I don't think so, it's late already." It was in fact just past ten, but there being no decent clubs in town, it would mean a drive to Patong and back. That would add an hour to however long they spent there, and she'd have no hope of being in bed before midnight. She saw the disappointment on his face and said, "Maybe next time?"

❖

He drove her home with the roof down. It was cool at this time of night, so she enjoyed the breeze. Pulling up outside the condo entrance, he pushed the gear change forward into park but didn't switch off the engine.

Marky had already decided she wouldn't ask him up. From the experience of this one evening together, she knew she wouldn't go out with him again, so had momentarily considered the idea of a one-night stand. The idea of no-strings sex with this handsome man was quite exciting, but the thought of Nick finding out made it impossible. For reasons she couldn't explain, she wanted Nick to keep a good opinion of her.

Beum made no attempt to kiss her, perhaps sensing her mood. If he had, she wasn't sure she would be strong enough not to be tempted, so quickly thanked him for a lovely evening, opened the door and went inside without looking back.

# Chapter 11

Saturday was spent writing another report for the chief superintendent after breakfast. Nick guessed he would be called home now that it was clear they had probably come as far as they could with the Townsend case. A trip to Mrs. Townsend to bring her up to date and hopefully give her some closure would also be needed. He hoped she would be satisfied knowing the men who had almost certainly shot her husband had been caught and would serve time, albeit not for his killing. Like Nick, she would probably be disappointed that Huangsap would likely get away with it. He could only hope the colonel's investigation would turn up something more.

Nick's mother wanted every family member at home all day Sunday, to ensure they were all there to greet guests when they arrived. This was the reason he had told Marky he would send a car for her. Chaw's husband had been tasked with driving the red behemoth; Nick spied him grinning as he climbed in.

The car returned by twelve-fifteen and Nick met Marky on the front steps. "Come on in," he told her, admiring her long, bronze legs. She was wearing white cotton shorts, which only just peeked out below a long pink Levi's T-shirt. Large-lensed sunglasses were pushed up into her hair, and an Adidas shoulder sack with drawstring was slung over one shoulder. Reaching the door, Marky stopped to kick her flip-flops off.

"Oh, don't worry, we're not inside yet. Keep your shoes on for now." He led her through the door and she saw it was an open courtyard with a sand-washed floor, interspersed with terracotta tiles. The house formed a C shape around the courtyard, and today all the doors around it were wide open to provide easy access in and out of the downstairs rooms. A long dining table of nine seats had been set up down the centre of the courtyard, four chairs to each side and one at the head. The table was complete with a red and white gingham tablecloth, floral centrepiece and full place settings. With a water glass, a red wine glass and a white wine glass per person, it was as far removed from a casual lunch as Marky could imagine. Beyond the table she could see steps down to a garden level and a swimming pool beyond.

"Come and say hello," he told her and continued past the table and down two steps to the garden. Tom and Wanpen Foster were sitting on rattan furniture under square sunshades, glasses of iced drinks on a table in front of them. She was pleased to see they were dressed as casually as her because she'd had no idea what would be appropriate. Thankfully, she seemed to have got it right. She offered a 'wai' greeting to both. Tom nodded and smiled.

"Hello again, Marisa. Please come and sit," Wanpen offered, patting the chair next to her. Mrs. Foster had clearly put her behaviour at their last lunch meeting well behind her. Today she was all charm. Marky did as instructed, dropping her bag on the floor beside her.

"I'll get you a drink," Nick said and went back the way they had just come.

Nick's sister Jane shouted hello and Marky looked up to see her waving from an upper terrace. She appeared a moment later from one of the ground floor doors and hurried over to join them, taking the chair on the other side of Marky.

"Hi, it's good to see you again!" she told her, a genuine smile of pleasure on her face. Jane was barefoot and wearing only a red bikini top and a tropical print sarong around her waist, covering the bottom half. Her skin was pale next to Marky, but she was equally tall and had a full figure.

"It's very nice of you all to invite me," she answered courteously.

Jane smiled and jumped up again. "I'll be back in a minute. My friends are just arriving." She skipped back up the steps and made for the front door. Marky heard childish screams from outside and guessed this was the aforementioned friends saying hello. When Jane came back inside trailing two girls behind her,

Marky was relieved to see she wouldn't be the only Thai here today. She didn't feel awkward and knew her English was up to the task, but she'd never spent a day entirely in the company of foreigners. It was the unexpected she was scared of, and the potential to make a mistake. It's just a family lunch with friends, she reminded herself. Relax and enjoy it.

The two new arrivals came over to say hello just as Nick returned with a drink in each hand. Clearly, they all knew one another already, as the girls each took one of his arms to accompany him back down to the garden level.

"Hello Tom, hello Pen," they said almost as a chorus. Marky marvelled at how readily they used first names for their elders and did not bother to 'wai'. It was obviously acceptable because Mr. and Mrs. Foster smiled and welcomed them.

Jane arrived with drinks for her friends and began the introductions. "Ay and Bee, this is Marky, Nick's colleague." They both turned to her and automatically chose to 'wai' and greet her in Thai.

She didn't return the 'wai', but instead said, "It's a pleasure to meet you both," in her best English.

Jane continued, "We're old schoolmates that don't see enough of one another anymore. These two are far too busy," she mocked them.

Marky saw an opportunity to enter the conversation and so asked them both, "What do you do?"

Ay was first to answer, pushing her long hair behind an ear, "I help daddy in his business. He's in real estate."

Marky nodded that she understood but in fact had no more idea than before she had asked. 'Real estate' could be anything from a lowly condo rental agent to a property developer. She assumed it was more likely nearer the latter.

Bee followed with her own answer, "I do interior design. I have a studio on the bypass with a coffee shop to showcase my work. Perhaps you've seen it or been in for a drink?"

"Oh, is that Blue Plum?" she asked.

"That's right! You know it," she beamed, clearly delighted.

"I'm quite a regular customer as it's just along the road from my condo. I love your coffee."

"Thank you. You must say hi next time you're in."

"I will," Marky assured her but knew she wouldn't.

"Volleyball time!" Jane announced, "Marky, you can make up a four with us girls." This was said as an order rather than a suggestion.

Ay and Bee stood, slipped off their shoes, and followed Jane toward the pool, shedding T-shirts and shorts as they went, to reveal they too were already wearing bikinis. Their clothes were left on a plastic garden chair. Another chair was stacked with fluffy white beach towels at the ready.

Marky turned to Nick to ask, "Is there somewhere I can get changed?"

"Sure, follow me." He led her back up the steps and through the door Jane had appeared from. They climbed a wide flight of stairs that led up to the wrap-around veranda, then Nick opened another door.

"This is my room, you can change in here."

She went inside and he closed the door behind her. Nick's bedroom and en-suite bathroom was bigger than her entire studio condo. It was definitely a man's room, with masculine touches everywhere. The furniture was modern and sleek, in grey and burgundy with hints of chrome. The king-size bed would have filled her own room. On the walls were framed pictures; she looked more closely to confirm they were painted and not printed. There was no theme to them, one was a view down the river Thames and another looked like a copy of something she recognised as being by somebody famous, but the name escaped her.

All this was taken in as she took off her clothes, feeling strange to be standing totally naked in Nick's bedroom. Opening her bag she selected a black bikini she had bought the previous day and slipped it on, arranging it to cover what it could. The old, modest one-piece stayed in the bag; it wouldn't see any use today. She put her shorts back on and had a quick look in a mirror for a final check before returning downstairs.

The girls were already in the water, splashing one another and giggling like teenagers. She saw Nick looking as she approached and was pleased he didn't look away when she noticed. He was clearly enjoying the view. Removing her shorts in as ladylike fashion as she could, she left them on the chair with the other girls' clothes, then asked, "Which end do you want me in?"

Jane said she should join her in the deeper end as

they were both taller, so Marky took a breath, braced herself and jumped in. The water was cool on her skin but warmer than she'd expected. Ay served the first ball and the game began. It soon became clear that pride was at stake here, as they were all very competitive.

After five games that ended three-two in Jane and Marky's favour, Nick and his father offered to take on the winners. Ay and Bee climbed up to sit on the edge at the shallow end of the pool where they could cheer the girls' team, so Jane suggested she and Marky should move down to that end. The men would take the disadvantaged deeper end.

Tom had already ditched his top and dived in, but as Marky turned to face the deep end Nick was just lifting his T-shirt over his head. She had seen his muscular arms before, but now she knew his shoulders, chest and stomach were equally well developed. There was whistling and cheering from behind her. Ay and Bee were enjoying the show too and were not at all shy about showing admiration for a great body.

Nick seemed unconcerned by the cheers, simply smiled and dived in. Despite Jane and Marky's best efforts, they were no competition for two taller men with a greater reach. After three losses they let Ay and Bee have a go, but they too retired without a win. Nick suggested that to balance things up he would partner Marky against one of the girls and his father. Jane volunteered, hoping to be on a winning side for once and beat her brother.

An older, foreign couple arrived while they were

playing, and Nick told her they were his parents' best friends. They finished the game with a win, then climbed out of the pool to dry off. The other girls either put their shorts back on or wrapped a sarong around their waist, so Marky followed suit and left her T-shirt off. She felt as naked sitting here in just a bikini top as she had in his room fully naked earlier.

Wine was opened and they all found a chair to chat and drink before lunch. The conversation was easy and everyone was included. Nick's parents' friends were thrilled to discover she was a policewoman and peppered her with questions about her work. At two o'clock an older woman came and whispered in Mrs. Foster's ear, who then clapped her hands and announced lunch was ready.

Everyone made their way up to the courtyard and Marky waited to see where everyone else sat before taking a chair. She found herself between Nick and Bee, and opposite Jane.

Lunch was salad and seafood with the nicest white wine Marky had ever tasted, which she had to admit wasn't a long list. Nobody was in a hurry, this lunch was more about friendship and company than eating she realised.

When the meal was over, the two older couples said they were going to sit inside away from the heat. Jane and her friends had plans to go out together that evening, so they left to shower and change. Nick and Marky were the last two left sitting at the table.

"I hope that wasn't a hardship?" he asked.

"Not at all. I really enjoyed myself."

"I'm really glad you came, and particularly as you

wore that bikini," he told her with a grin, and she was sure he was only jesting.

"You made a splash yourself, judging by the girls' reactions," she said in return.

"Hah, they've never grown up. They still act like they're in high school. I bet that's why they're still single."

"Hey, I'm single too, remember!"

"Only because the right man hasn't come along yet."

"I hope I recognise him when he does," she told him, "is it okay if I get changed? I should be going too."

"Sure, you know the way."

Marky was back down in just a few minutes and Nick was waiting with his car keys, "I'll drop you off myself."

Arriving home, she was thankful Nick hadn't asked about her date with Beum. It would have put a dampener on what had been a lovely day for her.

❖

The white SLC pulled up outside Nick's parents' house at dusk and was left there with its roof down, there being no threat of rain. Beum climbed the front steps slowly, rang the doorbell and let himself into the courtyard.

"Hello?! Anyone home?" he shouted. The dog heard him first and came running, followed by his aunt Wanpen from the direction of the kitchen.

"Tang-ju, what a surprise. We don't see you often

enough. Please come inside." She stepped back through the door she'd appeared from and stood waiting for him to follow. He kicked off his loafers and went inside.

She led him through to the lounge where Tom and Nick were playing nine-ball pool on a full-size table. Nick looked up from taking his shot, "Beum, thank goodness you're here, we need a referee to prevent any further cheating."

"I wasn't cheating!" insisted his father, arms apart in appeal.

Beum forced a smile and asked, "What's the score?"

"Fourteen games to eleven in my favour, but it ought to be a lot more," Nick told him, "what brings you by?"

"I was hoping to have a chat with you if you've time?"

"Sure, let me win this one and I'll be right with you."

Wanpen returned from the kitchen with iced teas for everyone, and Beum took a stool to sit and watch the game. Nick won as promised, then suggested they retire to his father's study. While playing the final frame, he'd been thinking what Beum could possibly want to speak to him about. It could only be something to do with business or money and he prepared himself to politely decline an investment or loan.

Beum took a seat on the small sofa and looked Nick in the eye. After a moment's hesitation he said, "I know what you've been investigating."

He didn't continue, so Nick asked, "Did Marky tell you about it?" already knowing that couldn't possibly be true. She was far too discreet to talk about a case with an outsider.

"No, from Wayu actually, and I'm here on his behalf as well as mine." He looked down. Again, he was in no hurry to begin to explain, and Nick knew better than to push him.

Nick wondered how Wayu would know what they were investigating just from their short visit to Huangsap's office. They hadn't told him why they were there. Surely his boss didn't confide in him? He waited for Beum to continue in his own time.

"I was there the night that girl was attacked in Amnesia," he finally said and looked Nick straight in the eye, "and before you think it, it wasn't me that did it."

"That wasn't the first thing that came to mind, I assure you," Nick told him honestly. He already had a pretty good idea where this was going.

Beum continued, "A few of us had gone out to celebrate graduating high school. It would be our last night together before we split up to go off to different unis in different places. We'd met up to eat in town then gone drinking in Patong. After going in and out of a few go-go bars down Bangla, we ended up in the club after midnight. It's an easy place to pick up the good stuff, you know?"

Knowing he meant they had bought drugs, Nick told him to go on with his story.

"Anyway, we'd all been hanging around the dance floor when Wayu said his father was upstairs in the

VIP area with the owner, and we could join if we wanted. We were drunken eighteen-year-olds, so that was like an invitation to the inner circle, you know?" He paused again. "We went upstairs, I think there were six or seven of us by this time. Some had bailed already. We took the booth next to his father and a bottle of whisky appeared. We carried on drinking and some carried on snorting, especially Wayu, he was wrecked."

Beum stopped to drink some tea, then put the glass down on a side table and resumed his story. "We were up and down the stairs to the dance floor with the hostesses until the club closed, then Wayu said we should just sit where we were. He seemed to know what would happen, like he'd been there before. The DJ stopped playing and announced the club was closing, but he left some music on at a lower volume as people left the club. The lights came up a bit, but it was still quite dark. Eventually, it was all pretty quiet and our group and Wayu's father's group were the only people in the place. Other than a few hostesses and waitresses of course." He picked up his glass again and took a large swallow. "There was this one waitress that Wayu had his eye on, a really pretty girl not much older than us. He kept groping her whenever she came close and the rest of us were cheering him on, like idiots. Looking back I can see how unfair it was, but we were young and drunk. Finally, he pulled her onto his lap and held her there despite her wriggling to get free. Everybody was laughing, but I could see she was angry. She slapped him really hard and he let her go, I think through surprise. I doubt anybody had ever slapped him before."

Beum looked at his empty glass, not comprehending when he had finished it. He put it down again. "I don't remember him getting up from the table, honestly. The next thing I knew, his father was at our booth telling us to leave right away. He didn't make a fuss or anything, just said we needed to go. We caught up with Wayu at the back door as we left. The minibus we'd gone over in was waiting and took us back to town and dropped us off one by one. This is the first time I've thought about it since, and all I've told you is all I know." He looked imploringly at Nick, "Tell me I haven't done anything wrong!"

Nick took a deep breath before answering. "It doesn't sound like it. If you genuinely didn't know what had happened, then you didn't fail to report a crime."

"I didn't, I swear!"

"But I'm sure you guessed he'd done something, and you could've asked. Any time from then until now. Ignorance isn't innocence, Beum." Nick knew from experience that people's capacity for self-delusion had no limit.

"I know, I know," he said, almost in tears now.

"You said you were here on Wayu's behalf too. What did you mean by that?"

"He didn't say outright, but he's suddenly become very scared and I think he wants to confess."

"He can't make a statement to me, I'm not a Thai police officer."

"But you can make sure it's Marky that deals with

him, can't you?"

"There's no need to. It's her case, so it will definitely be her, but don't think for a minute she'll be soft on him."

"He doesn't want sympathy, he wants to do the right thing."

"It's a bit late for that," said Nick, taking his phone out and dialling Marky's number.

❖

Beum called Wayu and agreed to bring him to meet them at the police station at eight that evening. Nick drove back into town, collected Marky, and the two of them were waiting in the stuffy ground floor interview room by the time the two younger men arrived. One of the reception officers showed them through. Marky told Beum he would have to wait outside and sent him back to sit next to reception. She invited Wayu in and pointed at the single chair opposite them.

He looked dishevelled and distressed, and was wearing only a plain white tee shirt, shorts and flip-flops. Marky had set up a miniature action camera on a tripod and asked him if he agreed to her recording the interview. He simply nodded in reply. She started the camera recording, then took out her phone, started the audio recorder and placed it on the table between them.

After stating the time, date and names of everyone present, she looked sideways at Nick, then began. "You have something you want to tell us?" she asked Wayu gently, almost sympathetically, although that was not what she felt. They didn't yet know how willing he was to confess, so had agreed to begin slowly in an attempt to draw him out, rather than frighten him from the outset.

"Yes, but I don't really know where to start."

"Wherever you like. We can always go back and forth if you remember something else," she urged him.

He nodded and sat up straight. "Uncle Ji is truly a horrible man. He forced me into working for him after I graduated from law school. He's never trained me or let me do any legal work, just keeps me in the office doing menial jobs."

Marky didn't want to hear how he felt sorry for himself but saw an opportunity to get to the point, so asked, "How did he force you to work for him?"

"He threatened me."

"With what?"

"With what happened that night at the club."

"Do you want to tell us about that?"

While speaking, he had been staring fixedly at Marky's phone on the table, but now looked at her to say, "I need some assurances."

"Of what?"

"I don't know really. I just, well, I kind of hoped that if I came forward to confess it would go better for me."

"A confession will always go in your favour, yes, but I can't make any promises. If you've done something illegal, then there will be a fitting punishment determined by the court. A confession may mean the judge will be more lenient." Marky had to be honest, even at the risk of him clamming up. Besides, they now knew what he had done and had agreed they would charge him one way or another, regardless.

"What will happen to me?" he asked.

"That's for the court to decide."

"No, I mean tonight. If I tell you what happened?"

"Well, if you've committed a crime, then I will arrest you and you'll be detained while we investigate."

"I won't have to go home?"

"No, you wouldn't be going anywhere."

His shoulders relaxed as she said this. He was obviously scared and had every reason to be if he knew the three recent deaths were connected to Huangsap.

He looked from one to the other of them, reached a decision and began talking, "The girl in the club — I don't know her name — made me look stupid. I'd been drinking all evening, then we had some blow when we got to Amnesia."

Marky interrupted him to ask, "You mean cocaine?"

"Yeah, we all had a snort. I'd just been messing with the girl, but she slapped me very hard. I couldn't accept the loss of face in front of my friends, so I followed her. I didn't know what I was going to do, but I had to do something."

Marky badly wanted to tell him he needn't have done anything, just let it go, but she did not want to stop his flow now he'd started.

"She went to a staff room and I followed her in. I slapped her like she'd slapped me, and she fell. Up to that moment, that was all I was going to do, hit her just like she'd hit me," he paused again, then went on more quietly, "but when she fell face down her skirt came up and I could see her panties. From then I couldn't control myself. I don't know what happened, whether it was the drink or drugs, or what."

Neither Marky nor Nick spoke, not wanting to break the spell of the moment. Wayu started sniffling and ran the back of his hand across his nose. He put his hands in his lap and sat there shaking as he sobbed quietly.

"What did you do?" Marky asked, wanting his own words on the video and audio.

He did not look up, but said "I raped her."

Nobody spoke. Marky's and Nick's minds were racing with what this meant. After a full two minutes of silence, Marky asked "What happened after?"

He raised his head slowly, as if it had suddenly become heavy, his eyes now wet with self-pity. "I left the room but couldn't face anyone after what I'd done. I sat on the floor just outside the door, then another girl appeared and went inside. I knew I should move, but I couldn't. She came back out after a couple of minutes and swore at me as she went past. That made me snap out of it and I went downstairs looking for a way out of the club. After a few more minutes everybody else came down, we got in the minibus and it took us home. I put it behind me, tried to forget about it, and was relieved when the police didn't come calling."

There was nothing more they needed him to say. He had explained how it had happened and confirmed what he'd done, so further details were pointless right now.

"Why are you coming forward now, after six years of silence?" Nick asked.

"I already said, my life is shit. He treats me like a slave and there's nothing I can do about it. It could go on forever if I don't do something to make it end, and this is the only way out I can see."

This made Marky livid. "So you're confessing for yourself? Not for the sake of the girl whose life you destroyed or the families of the people that were killed covering up this crime?" she berated him angrily, visibly trembling.

"Yes, yes, all of that, but mostly to make it all stop. When I think about what happened, I can't believe it was me that did it, that I lost control so badly. I'm so sorry." He dropped his head into his hands.

Sorry for yourself, thought Marky. She exchanged a glance with Nick.

"What has Huangsap said to you about that night since it happened?" Nick continued, worried that Marky would not be able to control her anger if the man gave more thoughtless answers.

"My parents had a going-away party for me at home before I went off to uni in Bangkok. He came. He made a point of getting me alone and said that a job was waiting for me when I graduated. It wasn't some generous, benevolent offer he was making, it was a threat. He didn't say it outright, but the implication was that he owned me. He's never mentioned it again since, until yesterday."

"What did he say yesterday?"

"He said people had died because of this, so I must remember to keep my mouth shut. I took that to be another threat that I could be next."

Marky asked, "Who else knows about what happened that night?"

"Nobody, as far as I know."

"Not even your father? He was there that night."

Wayu looked up, obviously surprised they knew this, then it must have occurred to him that Beum had told them. "He's never talked about it, so I've always assumed he doesn't know. He knew something had happened that night, but I don't think he knew I was responsible. I couldn't bring myself to tell him or ask him if he knew. The disappointment would be too much for my parents, and the shame was too much for me."

They'd got what they needed for the moment, and they could always interview him again if they had more questions, so Marky called a halt. "Okay, Wayu, here's what's going to happen next. I'm going to bring in a custody officer and he'll be present while I charge you. He'll book you in and you'll be taken to a cell, where you'll be held alone. I don't want anyone else talking to you, so I'm going to give an order that you are to have no visitors, and that includes not seeing a lawyer or any family. Do you understand?"

"Yes."

Nick left her to it and went to tell Beum what had happened. Beum wasn't surprised his friend had been arrested so Nick showed him out then went upstairs to wait in their office. The police station was dark and mostly deserted at this time on a Sunday evening, but he saw a light from under the door of the meeting room. Curious, he went farther along the corridor, knocked and opened the door. Yu looked up from her laptop and smiled broadly when she saw who it was. There was no one else with her. She was wearing casual clothes, jeans and a blouse, and looked very attractive compared to the usual dull uniform he'd seen her in every day.

"Hello there!" she said, clearly pleased to see him.

"Hello to you too. Why are you working so late alone on a Sunday?"

"I promised to have all these cases summarised for Monday morning. I stayed late today because I didn't want to work yesterday. This is the last one though, so I'm almost done."

"I see. We've just finished too. I'll be off once Captain Pondee comes up. Anyway, it was nice to see you."

"You too," she smiled up at him, positively beaming.

He began to close the door, then thought again and opened it back up, "I know it's late, but I don't suppose you'd like to join me for a drink or something to eat?"

"You mean now?" she asked. Her cheeks visibly reddened and her smile grew even wider

"Yes, unless you need to get home?"

"No, no, I'd love to. I'll wait here until you're done if that's okay?"

"Great, I'll see you shortly," he told her and closed

the door, now smiling himself.

If he could have seen through the door to inside the meeting room, he'd have seen the young constable dancing in her chair, punching her arms over her head.

❖

It had taken Marky almost another half hour to get Wayu charged and in a cell alone, so it was now almost ten. The smaller cells had filled up quickly the last couple of days, but there was no longer any need to segregate the two amateur assassins now that Huangsap had spoken to them. Ngaan-dee was in the third cell and Wayu was placed in the first one. They were too far apart to speak, but Marky doubted they were aware of one another's existence or involvement anyway.

She looked jubilant and relieved when she returned to their office. Falling into her chair, she looked at Nick and said, "Whoever else gets caught for whatever else in this investigation is just a bonus. Wayu is the guy we never thought we'd identify, never mind be able to convict. I'm going to call Tida tomorrow and try to convince her to come to court for his trial."

"Will she need to be there?" Nick wondered aloud.

"With a confession, it's possible to get a rape conviction without the victim present, but it will go much easier if the court can put a face to a name. I doubt she'd have to testify."

"Where do we go from here though?"

"I still want Huangsap, so I rather think we need a search warrant for his home and office. There's got to be some evidence to connect him to something."

"Doesn't that overlap with the colonel's new inquiry?" Nick counselled.

"Perhaps, but they don't have cause; we do," she smiled gleefully, "anyway, that's enough for today. Take me home please and I think I'll celebrate with a beer."

"Certainly, ma'am," he told her, then added "oh, Yu will be coming along. We're going for a drink together."

"Oh, okay," she said and he could have sworn he saw a touch of disappointment or jealousy. It was only there for a fleeting moment, but he was sure he'd seen it before she recovered herself. She smiled, collected her things and said "Shall we?"

❖

Nick drove to Dive bar in the centre of town once they'd dropped Marky off at home. Yu was now in the front seat of the Jeep, still unable to stop smiling. The streets were quiet, with little traffic this late on a Sunday and plenty of places to park. Nick found a spot in the road near the bar and parked with the passenger side nearest the footpath. He went round to help her climb out, but she already had the door open and was halfway out by the time he got there.

The bar was quite busy, even at this time, and a number of people were still eating. Nick ordered beers for them both, as well as fried chicken wings and a bowl of spicy 'som tam' salad to share.

Yu turned out to be great company, being easy on the eye and interesting and funny to chat with. Originally from Hatyai, she'd been posted to Phuket nearly two years ago when she graduated from cadet school aged twenty-one. With the plates cleared away and their second beers almost drunk, Nick reluctantly suggested he take her home. It was almost midnight and they both had to start at eight the following morning.

Directing him to the rented room she shared, he felt she emphasised the fact that her nurse roommate was on night shift. It could not be his imagination; why else would she say that if not to let him know she had the place to herself?

"How long do you think you'll be staying in Phuket?" she asked.

"Probably just a few more days. This case is all but wrapped up."

He hadn't driven far from the centre of town when Yu directed him into a narrow side street. She pointed at an apartment building ahead and told him to stop just after it. He pulled up, put the car in park and turned to look at her. The street was dark, but he could see she was still smiling.

She didn't make a move to get out, just returned his gaze. She wanted him to kiss her, that was obvious. But if he did, would she take it to mean more than it did? That he wanted to see her again?

She laughed, "One of us has to speak eventually."

He laughed too, "Sorry, my mind was drifting."

"You are coming up, aren't you?" she said, daring

him to refuse.

He switched the engine off in answer.

❖

The apartment building had four floors with six rooms on each. There was no lift, but thankfully she lived on the second floor. She unlocked the door, reached in to switch on the light, then stood aside to let him enter first.

The room was small but tidy. Most of the limited space was taken with a double bed, and a hanging rail served as a wardrobe in a corner. He slipped off his shoes as she excused herself and went into the bathroom. Unsure of himself, he sat on the bed.

When she came back out two minutes later, she went to the headboard and switched on a small recessed light, then walked back again to switch off the ceiling light. She stepped to stand in front of him now and was so close he could smell her. He put his hands on her hips, she lifted one knee onto the bed, then the other, straddling him, then pushed him backwards until he was lying flat. She sat astride him, unbuttoning and removing her blouse, never taking her eyes off him. Nick pulled his tee-shirt over his head.

It had been a while since he'd been with a woman, so Nick hoped he wouldn't get overexcited and it be over too quickly. As she slowly removed her bra to reveal small, but perfect breasts, he realised he was hoping in vain.

# Chapter 12

By the time Nick arrived with coffees at half-past eight, Marky had already listed her reasons for the request of a search warrant and had then prepared the application for the court. All she needed was the boss's approval.

Marky went directly to the colonel as soon as he arrived to ask permission to apply for a search warrant for Huangsap's home and office. After bringing him up to date with events over the weekend, she assured him that anything found relating to other cases would be passed on to the inquiry team. Anything and everything would be usable for prosecution if it had been legally gained under a court-issued search warrant. He signed off on her request and she hurried back to the office.

"Let's go!" she yelled, more excited than he'd ever

279

seen her. They grabbed their belongings and went down to the Jeep. Phuket Provincial Court was now in a new building on the other side of town since earlier in the year. The Phuket provincial authorities had been busy building a new court, provincial hall, and other administrative offices for the last few years, and some of them were just now coming in to use. Like most government-led projects, the buildings were all long overdue and way over budget.

Nick had never seen the old court building but had to admit the new one was impressive. In keeping with the island's heritage, all the new government structures were in the Sino-Portuguese style. The court building had steps leading up to a portico supported by six massive pillars the full height of the facade. Inside they had to pass through security checks, despite Marky's police ID and uniform.

He knew she had been here before for a warrant as she had explained the procedure for him on the way over. She led the way into the administration offices, then a clerk opened a door to allow them access to the corridor leading to the judges' chambers.

Stopping outside the third door, she stood erect, straightened her uniform, took a breath and knocked twice, loudly. Nick noted the name on the brass plaque 'His Honour Pattapong Yod-panya'. They heard 'come' from inside and Marky opened the door. Nick followed her in.

They stepped into the large room and walked the few paces that would bring them in front of the judge's desk. Stopping a polite distance away, Marky didn't 'wai' today, but bowed her head low and said "Good morning, judge, thank you for seeing us." Nick followed suit, having been briefed on the protocol. She had also told him that if they were invited to sit, he must not cross his arms or legs, should sit up straight and keep his feet on the floor. Nick was trying hard not to stare, but Marky had told him to maintain eye contact when they were speaking.

The judge put down his pen and looked at them in turn. "My secretary tells me you have a request for a search warrant." He held out his hand, palm flat. Marky stepped forward, handed over her documents, then stepped smartly backwards to her previous spot. She didn't speak.

The judge looked through the paperwork. It consisted of four typed pages, but Nick knew only one of them contained details of the person whose property would be searched, the reason for the search and the addresses. The others were formal legalese. Clearly, the judge also knew the other pages were redundant because he went directly to the relevant page.

"Well, this is very unusual," he said, placing the sheets on the desk in front of him and looking up at Marky, "you want to search the offices of a prominent member of the Phuket legal profession. You've included his office address in here, so I assume you understand a search will provide access to all his case files too?"

"Yes, your honour."

"There could very well be files relating to ongoing cases, and I can't see how it would be fair to allow the police to be privy to them while they're still being investigated. I'm inclined to allow your request, but there must be some limit as to the search of the office."

"I understand your honour. I will amend the paperwork to reflect that."

"There's no need to take more of your time and mine. I'll make a note on here that any files relating to open cases are to be excluded from the search." He picked up his pen and began writing, speaking as he wrote, "I really do hope this comes to something, otherwise you'll have unnecessarily damaged the reputation of one of Phuket's most successful and respected lawyers." He finished writing and looked up at Marky, offering the signed and stamped documents back to her. She stepped forward to retrieve them, making the odd flick of the wrist that Nick had seen before when students collected their degrees on graduation.

Marky bowed her head again, so Nick did the same, then she took two steps backwards before turning to leave the room.

"Well done. You're really very impressive," he said once she had closed the door.

"Thank you. It's more difficult to impress a man while wearing a uniform than a bikini, I'll admit," she joked as they headed back outside.

❖

Being granted a search warrant had not been a foregone conclusion, but Marky had prepared a search team nevertheless. She had two female constables, a lance corporal and two forensics officers. They all squashed into the small training room to be briefed before setting off. Marky tasked the lance corporal and one of the constables to go to the office. If Huangsap was not there, then they would have to force access, because Wayu was in custody. Marky, Nick, and the others would go to Huangsap's house, where she expected they would make any important finds.

They set off in three vehicles, one to the office and two to the house. Marky had told the others to wait in their car until she had gained access, then join them once they were inside. The same maid opened the door to them, Marky held the warrant in front of her by its top and bottom, and said, "Police, we have a warrant to search these premises." The maid took a step back, her hands flying to her open mouth. Marky stepped inside and Nick followed once he had checked the others were exiting their car to join them.

"Who is in the house other than you?" Marky asked the maid, who was frozen with fear. She didn't answer but pointed behind her to a door. They set off in that direction, Marky opened the door and they entered into a glass-walled orangery. Huangsap and his wife were seated at a dining table with cups and plates of food before them.

He shot to his feet, dropping his napkin from his lap as he did so, then shouted, "What the hell is the meaning of this?"

Once more, Marky displayed the search warrant,

but the lawyer snatched it from her hands.

"I need you to remain seated while we search your house. If we require your assistance we will come for you. If you interfere in any way you will be arrested for obstruction. Do you understand?"

"This is ..."

"Do you understand?!" she shouted to shut him off.

Deflated, Huangsap sat down and glared at them.

"Good. This constable will remain with you while we execute the warrant," she told them, indicating the young officer standing to one side. She nodded to Nick and he followed her back out to the hallway where the others were waiting.

"Do the likeliest rooms first. See if there's a study. If there is, begin there. The sergeant and I will clear the easier rooms down here, starting with the kitchen." she told them, and the two forensic officers made for the other doors to see what rooms they hid. "Here you go," she said, grinning and offering Nick a plastic bag, "you get rubber gloves today."

Working methodically, it did not take the two of them long to go through the kitchen, pantry, living room, toilet, and storeroom. They left the orangery for now, where the Huangsaps and the maid were waiting. One of the officers was in the ground floor study but shook his head when Marky looked in. They went upstairs in search of the other officer, who likewise had nothing to report.

Going back to the study, she asked the officer, "Is there a safe or lockbox in here?" He shook his head again, no.

Nick followed her back to the dining room. "Mr. Huangsap, do you have a safe in the house?" No response.

"If you are helpful and tell us where it is, we can avoid ripping your house apart looking for it," she told him. Still nothing.

"I'll show you," said the wife, standing. Huangsap made to grab her arm, but she shook him off. "I don't want these people in my house a moment longer than necessary,' she spat at him.

The woman took a moment to gather her dignity, then walked unhurriedly through the hallway to the storeroom under the stairs. The ceiling and stairs were so high it had a full-height door and she could easily stand inside. There was a shoe cupboard against the wall. She pushed it and it slid easily aside to reveal a safe built into the wall.

"Can you open it, please?" Marky asked.

"Sorry, no. He's the only one who knows the combination."

Marky followed Mrs. Huangsap back through to the orangery, where she sat down again. "My offer still stands. If you open the safe we won't have to pull it out of the wall and take it away to force it open."

His wife glared at him. The lawyer knew Marky had the power to do as she threatened and believed she was serious, so he reluctantly stood up and walked through to the hallway. Marky stood aside while he entered the code on the keypad, then took his place once the safe door was open.

There was a small bundle of thousand Baht notes, some land titles in an envelope, but the item which got her attention was a clear ziplock bag. She removed a plastic evidence bag from her pocket, held the first bag up for Nick to see, then dropped it into the other bag.

It contained a pair of ladies' white cotton panties.

❖

Marky called up for a police vehicle. She could not bring Huangsap in using the Jeep, although it would be rather fitting that he met his end in it when they had not, she thought. Feeling nothing but disgust for the man and not wanting to get any closer to him than she had to, Marky allowed the newly arrived officers to cuff Huangsap and take him in, with the strict instruction to park at the front door of the station and enter through reception in full view of public and police.

Promising to meet them at the station, she then thanked Mrs. Huangsap for her cooperation and they left. The woman seemed neither surprised nor saddened that her husband had been arrested. She calmly went back to her interrupted meal.

The officers had Huangsap in the same interview room they'd used before. He was still cuffed when Marky and Nick entered.

"I don't know what you think you've got. The underwear means nothing," he said even before they had sat down.

"At the very least it means you're some kind of pervert," she told him and heard Nick cough to smother a laugh, "I'll tell you what we *have* got, not what we think. I doubt there's any of Wayu's DNA on that underwear because they were removed before he raped her. And she never put them back on, because you stole them." If Huangsap was surprised to hear her claim Wayu was the rapist, he didn't show it. He gazed steadily at her. "The girl's DNA will be on them, though. Once we confirm they're hers, Wayu's confession means he'll certainly be convicted of rape and assault."

He reacted this time, hearing about the confession. It changed everything. "So charge him. That doesn't connect to me."

"Oh, but it does. Your possession of the underwear proves you were there that night. We also have the confession of one of the police officers who attended the callout. An officer who you bribed into covering it up. At the very least we'll charge you with perverting the course of justice and bribing a police officer. With a bit more digging, I'm sure we'll come up with some more to add to the list."

His bluster and confidence were shot through. He sagged in the chair and said nothing.

"Would you like to call a lawyer?" Marky asked sweetly.

❖

The phone rang several times before the girl finally picked up.

"Tida? This is officer Pondee."

There was nothing but silence for a few seconds, then, "I was hoping you wouldn't call."

Marky tried to be upbeat, but it was difficult given the subject, "I have good news, Tida. The man who attacked you has confessed and been charged. He's in a cell right now."

"I told you before, it makes no difference to me."

This was exactly what Marky had feared. As likely as it was that he would be convicted anyway, Tida's presence, or better still testimony, would ensure it and result in a longer sentence.

"Tida, I know it's difficult, but please help us put this man away."

"You said he's confessed. Isn't that enough?"

"Maybe, probably, but if you come to court it will be a big help. You don't have to testify, if you don't want to, just be present. I believe seeing him sent to prison for what he did will give you some closure and help you get on with your life. Will you trust me?"

"I'll think about it." She clearly didn't want to talk about it any longer than necessary.

"Okay, fair enough." She'd now reached the point she couldn't avoid any longer, "Just one more thing. Can I send you a photo of him to confirm he's the right person?"

Silence for a beat, then "okay."

"Thank you Tida."

❖

Huangsap had been turned over to the custody of the court, which meant he was being held on remand in prison. Marky didn't want him in the cells next to Ngaan-dee, Wayu and the assassins, for fear he could threaten them.

Now in their office, they watched the video of the interview through again with the colonel, who shook his head and asked, "I don't understand why Huangsap kept the girl's underwear. Why not just get rid of it?"

"He's sharp, sir. He probably grabbed them thinking they could have DNA evidence on them from the attack. Taking the girl to the hospital and having her seen by a friendly nurse meant there was no rape test kit or swab done either. He was covering tracks."

"That part I understand, but keeping them in his safe for six years?" He shook his head again.

"More than one person has told us he's opportunistic and controlling, sir, working only for himself. He was able to use them to coerce Wayu. He effectively made him his slave."

The colonel rubbed his cheeks, thinking, "Surely the boy knew he'd taken them off before he did it, so they couldn't possibly have his DNA on them."

"Wayu told us he was high on drink and drugs, and how confused he was afterwards. He also didn't know she hadn't put them back on, so he wouldn't know there would be no DNA. He fell for Huangsap's bluff."

Nick interrupted to ask, "When he took the underwear, did he even know who'd done it at that point? Wayu had already gone to the back door by the time the lawyer arrived. He told us that himself, so there's no way Huangsap saw him."

"Then somebody else must have told him. If he

already knew when he got there, then somebody had called him. If it was after he arrived, it could only be Wayu."

They all knew the club owner didn't know who had done it, so it hadn't been him who had told Huangsap when he'd called him in to help; he only knew there had been an incident because the other girl came to tell him. He probably didn't even know who Wayu was.

"Or his father," Nick added, "it was him who suggested the club owner call Huangsap after all. If he'd seen Wayu follow the girl, he could quite easily have spoken to Huangsap himself as well."

The colonel held his hands up, "Slow down a bit. I can see what this is leading up to and we need to be cautious here. It was one thing to search Huangsap's house on not much more than a hunch, but interviewing a public prosecutor is a whole different ball game. Does he even know his son is in custody?"

"I don't think so sir," Marky was impressed that the colonel had arrived at the same conclusion as she and Nick. She continued, "I don't see any option other than speaking to him sir. We could do it informally at his home or office. If he's known nothing about it all this time, then he's got nothing to be concerned about."

"Alright, but he's one of the most senior civil servants in the province, so I'll be there too. You can interview him in my presence, and you can be sure I'll stop you if you go too far."

"Sir."

❖

The public prosecutor for Phuket province ran an office of six assistant prosecutors, four deputies, several legal experts, plus administration and support staff. With the office being near the employment office and land transport department, it was already located in the area which was now becoming the civil administration centre for Phuket. The new court and provincial office were now just along the road, rather than the other side of town. As Nick parked the car, Marky wondered if police headquarters would ever be moved here too. The colonel had travelled separately and they saw his driver drop him off at the front door.

It was not every day that the chief of police for Phuket province called by, so the prosecutor's senior assistant was ready and waiting in the lobby to receive him. Marky and Nick followed a respectful distance behind.

The assistant took them to the third floor in the lift and directed them to a small conference room. Once they were seated along one side of the long table, she left to organise coffees.

When the door next opened it was the prosecutor who entered, followed closely by a woman wearing an apron and carrying a tray of coffees. She placed it on the table and left, closing the door behind her.

They all stood to greet him and introduce themselves, then the prosecutor took a seat on the other side of the table. Marky sat in the middle directly opposite him, with Nick to her left and the colonel to her right.

"Mr. Prosecutor, may I call you Mr. Wattana?" she began.

"Please do, we're not in court." His office dealt with the police on a daily basis, preparing cases or moderating, so it was not unusual to have officers in the building. It was unusual, however, for the chief of police to request to see him personally.

"Are you aware, sir, that your son is in custody, charged with assault and rape?" Marky had decided to hit him hard from the first question. If he already knew about it, it would have little effect; if he was ignorant of what Wayu had done it would put him off balance. From the shock on his face, she immediately knew he was unaware of the arrest.

"What? Why ... how ...?" He was unable to form a question, but stopped, cleared his throat, and tried again, "please explain."

"Your son, Wayu Wattana, came to Phuket police headquarters yesterday evening to confess to the assault and rape of a twenty-one-year-old waitress in a Patong club in 2015. His confession was recorded on video and audio."

He had quickly recovered his composure. "Thank you, officer. It's very good of you to come down here to let me know personally. I appreciate it. Now if you'll excuse me, I need to let his mother know what's happened and arrange to visit him. Where is he being held?" he asked, beginning to rise from his chair.

"If you don't mind sir, we have a few questions for

you first, then we'll leave you to attend to your family."

He sat back down and waved a hand to indicate she should continue.

"Witnesses have confirmed you too were in the club on the night of the attack. Is that correct?"

"I'm sorry, I don't remember."

"We have also been informed that you advised the club owner, Mr. Anutin Mee-sombat, to call Mr. Jirayu Huangsap, a lawyer, to assist with the incident. Is that correct?"

"I'm sorry, I don't remember." He added a shake of the head for emphasis this time but continued to gaze steadily at Marky.

"Can you tell us what your relationship is with Mr. Huangsap?"

Apisit continued to look Marky in the eye but did not reply. She could see he was thinking hard. Finally, when it was clear no answer would be forthcoming, the colonel spoke, "Thank you for seeing us, prosecutor. We'll leave you to attend to your son."

Clearly relieved at being let off the hook, he nodded, stood and left the room without another word. Marky badly wanted to tell him he'd cut her off too soon but knew better than to question the boss.

The tray of coffee remained untouched on the table.

❖

It was not often he got some time to himself, so

after the meeting with the prosecutor Colonel Orntong decided to go for a bite to eat before returning to his office. A small cafe run by a retired police sergeant and his wife was much frequented by police officers, and it was there he went to sit alone over a plate of chicken rice.

The young officer Pondee was very impressive, he thought and wished some of his other officers were as capable and dedicated. Too many of them did little real investigative work, just pushed paperwork around until they could justify closing a case and forgetting it. It wasn't about training, it was more to do with attitude. If they weren't dedicated to solving crime and helping the public, why did they ever become policemen in the first place?

He knew the public opinion of the police wouldn't improve in his lifetime, but he at least wanted to do what he could toward that end, and he knew there were enough similarly minded officers on the force to get it done. With luck, Pondee would stick it out and become one of them.

Back in his office, his secretary put his coffee down in front of him and left the room. It was about time for the local news, he realised, so pointed the remote at the TV standing on a side cabinet. It came to life just as the opening credits were running. Two newsreaders appeared, sitting behind a long counter, with a backdrop of Promthep cape behind them.

"Good afternoon, welcome to the five o'clock news on channel three," the first one began, then looked sideways to his colleague.

She picked up as if they were playing tennis, "Our

lead story this evening is the shock resignation of the Phuket public prosecutor, more on that in a moment."

"What the fuck?!" spluttered the colonel, spitting out his coffee. He reached for his desk phone and dialled the meeting room along the corridor, "Pondee, my office, now!"

Marky was in the room within thirty seconds, the foreigner in tow as always, he noted. "Sir?"

"Sit, sit!" he waved at the chairs and returned his attention to the TV, raising the volume.

"... now back to our lead story. The public prosecutor for Phuket province called a surprise press conference just an hour ago to announce his immediate resignation. Mr. Apisit Wattana gave a short statement citing family issues and the need for privacy but declined to answer questions or give any further details. He will stand down as of today and his duties will be taken over by his deputy ..."

The colonel switched the woman off mid-sentence and turned back to his two guests. He didn't ask a question, just raised his eyebrows to invite opinions.

Marky thought a moment, then offered, "It could simply be he knows the rape case against his son will become public knowledge and overshadow everything he does. He won't be able to work without being asked about it. Looking at it in that respect, it's not an unexpected move."

Nick was more forthright, "Either that or there's more to be found, and he's quit to protect the office of the prosecutor."

"The man can't be separated from the office. If

he's done something he shouldn't while in office, it's irrelevant if he quits," Marky pointed out.

"Your can of worms is still wriggling, captain. Stay with it," the colonel told her, "there's more here, I'm sure. I can feel it in my bones."

"Sir." They stood and left him alone to ponder.

❖

Marky's Line messenger pinged as they sat down. She opened the app to see that Tida had confirmed Wayu as her attacker. That's another box ticked she thought and stood back up to update her board with this new detail.

"I really must thank you for telling me about these boards. They're a huge help in visualising the bigger picture," she told him. She had printed a photo of the prosecutor, Apisit Wattana, and added him to her association chart. Lines now connected Tida down to Wayu, then sideways from him to Huangsap and Ngaan-dee. From the lawyer, they led to the two unnamed motorbike assassins and the club owner Mee-sombat. She now drew new two lines from Apisit, one to his son, Wayu, and the other to the lawyer, Huangsap. She tapped the final line she had drawn and said, "This is the connection we need to make."

"Agreed, but I'm all out of ideas."

"Well, there's one thing we can confirm right away." Marky dialled a number from a business card and waited for an answer which took some time in coming, "Mr. Mee-sombat, thank you for taking my call."

She spoke for less than a minute, then hung up and told Nick, "As I suspected, Mee-sombat never told Huangsap who the attacker was, because he doesn't know, not even now. So, if it wasn't Wayu, then it had to be his father. He's known what happened all along."

"If that's correct, and I'm inclined to agree it is, then there's a very good chance he's been manipulated by Huangsap too."

"Which brings us back to where we usually find ourselves — with no evidence or means to prove our theory. We already had one lucky break with Wayu. I doubt we'll get another."

"Hmmm, another thing occurred to me while you were on the phone. Mee-sombat's hands aren't entirely clean of all this, in fact it all started with him. He did the right thing having the police brought in, but then he made the mistake of listening to Apisit and making the call to Huangsap. From that moment on he expected it to be dealt with and hushed up. He even paid for Tida's silence."

"The other girl had already called the police remember — he didn't tell her to do it."

"You're right. Does this sit well with you?"

"Not really, but he's the least of our concerns at present. I'll put him back on the board as a 'follow-up' for later."

Marky sat back down and the two of them sat quietly, hoping the other would have a flash of inspiration. Nothing came, so Marky suggested they call it a day.

# Chapter 13

With nothing to go on that would move their inquiry forward, Marky was updating the case file and completing interview reports for Wayu and Huangsap. As a captain, she could easily have got another constable in to help, but right now she needed a distraction.

Nick sat opposite, alternately playing Scrabble and Sudoku on his phone. He'd told her it helped him think because concentrating on the game cleared his mind.

They both turned to the door when they heard a soft knock. It opened and Yu put her head in. She looked at Nick, smiled and reddened, then turned to Marky to ask if they had a few minutes.

"Of course, come in."

Yu was carrying several A4 cardboard files of

different colours. She sat down next to Marky and put them on the desk in front of them. "The material recovered from the search of Huangsap's office is keeping four people busy, there's just so much paperwork. We have to read everything because we don't know what might be important and what isn't."

"And these are ...'"" asked Marky, pointing to the files.

"Important," said Yu. She opened the first one, "this is a land dispute that the prosecutor's office decided not to forward to the court. After just a brief review of the fraud claim, it's obvious the case has merit, and when you look at the details and documentary evidence, it should have been easily found in favour of the plaintiff. Huangsap represented the defendant."

"Okay, give us the short version," Marky told her, not in the mood for a trip down a legal rabbit hole.

"Mr. 'A' died and left a large parcel of undeveloped seafront land to his adult children Mr. 'B' and Mrs. 'C'. They agreed to sell it and split the proceeds. As Mr. 'B' lived in Bangkok, he signed a power of attorney for his sister, a Phuket resident, to sell on his behalf. She sold the property and neither informed him nor gave him his half of the money. When he later found out it had been sold and asked her to pay, she referred him to the document he'd signed. He did that and found he'd given up all rights to the property or proceeds, so he sued. The power of attorney had been drawn up by Huangsap and the charge of fraud was later signed off as 'no grounds for prosecution' by Mr. Apisit Wattana himself. As the case had been kept out of court, Mr. 'B' also had no right of appeal. And, without a criminal conviction for fraud, there was no way to force a civil case."

Nick asked, "Just out of interest, how much are we talking about here?"

"Two hundred and twenty-six million Baht."

"Wow. Why have you brought this to us?" Marky asked her.

"I heard you went to see the prosecutor yesterday. It was all round the station, then he resigned, and the news went round again. I already knew he was Wayu's father, so I put two and two together. I thought these might help."

Marky looked across at Nick and said, "Who said we wouldn't get another break?" She was beaming again. "This is good work, Yu. Take us through the rest of them," she told the constable, closing the first file and pushing it aside.

Yu opened the second file and summarised what she'd found. File after file demonstrated possible collusion between the prosecutor's office and Huangsap. Most cases had never gone to court, and all the others had been prosecuted in such a poor way that the court never found against Huangsap's clients. They needed to show these to the colonel and they needed to bring Apisit Wattana in for questioning.

❖

Marky got time with the colonel just before lunch. Nick didn't join her as the new information did not relate in any way to the investigation of Townsend's death. She hadn't been gone more than fifteen minutes before she was back in the office dropping the files back on the desk with a thud.

Nick saw the defeated look on her face and asked, "Not the answer you wanted then?"

"No. The colonel doesn't think this is enough to warrant an interview. I feel he's more interested in using Huangsap's cases to weed out dirty officers than he is to take on the prosecutor. That inquiry now has several people working on it and everyone in the station knows what it's about."

"I bet there are a few nervous officers about then."

"That's for sure. I wouldn't be surprised to hear of transfer requests or resignations any time soon. That doesn't help us though."

Nick had been giving it some thought while she was out of the office, and now offered his idea, "Remember Wayu said he had everything well organised in the computer?"

"Yeeees," she said, looking up at last.

"The other inquiry is going through the hardcopy case files. Nobody has looked at the computer yet, have they?"

"I don't think so. I didn't see it set up anywhere. Let me check," and with that she went straight back out of the room, to return a few minutes later carrying a desktop computer case. Another trip along the corridor provided the monitor, keyboard and mouse, then they worked together to connect it up.

Once it was powered on, Marky looked through

the directories and quickly found a very large Excel file titled 'cases'. Clicking on it, it opened to reveal a massive spreadsheet of cases going back several years. Wayu must have entered older cases that had been completed long before he even worked for Huangsap. The level of detail was extraordinary; parties to the case, dates, events, notes, actions, outcomes, even links to photos and scanned documents stored on the computer. Wayu was no doubt oblivious that he'd created the perfect record for bringing his boss down.

"This is a goldmine," Marky whispered, reading through line after line of case information.

"Let's make sure it's a goldmine for us before we're told to pass it on to the other inquiry. There's got to be something here we can use to get Wattana in for questioning," Nick advised and Marky nodded in agreement, scrolling down the enormously long sheet.

By the end of the afternoon, their backs were aching and their eyes strained from staring at the small monitor, but they had a list of four cases that they were sure could bring down Wattana by showing clear collusion with Hungsap. Marky began typing up a summary of the cases to present to the colonel in the morning while Nick printed out all the supporting materials that had been linked.

With it all stacked and stapled, they headed home at a reasonable hour, confident that tomorrow would see them near the end of their inquiry.

# Chapter 14

Impatient to conclude her case, Marky had been desperate to see the colonel as early as possible, but he was tied up with prearranged meetings. His secretary eventually called at ten to say he would be free by half-past. Marky was now waiting outside his office for the last visitors to leave.

Entering his office as the final person left, Marky saluted and said good morning. The colonel looked up and sighed when he saw she was back again, but she placed four sets of stapled sheets in front of him on the desk and stood back without a word. Intrigued, he picked up the first one and began reading. He replaced it after two minutes of quiet consideration and moved on to the second. Nothing was said as he worked his way through the summaries until the last one was back on the desk and he sat back.

"Well, Pondee. I did say I admired your dedication. These are yet another example," he said, indicating the four piles.

"Thank you sir."

"Based on these, I agree we can proceed to interview the ex-prosecutor. He's now a private person, but as a courtesy, we'll do it at his home if he prefers. Once again, I wish to be present, but I'll leave it to you to make the arrangements. Liaise with my secretary to find a suitable time."

The last statement was a dismissal, so Marky thanked him again, closed the door as she left and waited until she was out of sight of the secretary before punching the air in celebration.

❖

A call to the prosecutor's office was all it took to get Wattana's home address and mobile number, then a second call to him to agree to a meeting at his home at one o'clock. The colonel went in his own vehicle as always, with Nick and Marky leading the way in the Jeep.

Arriving at his home, it was clear that civil service legal jobs didn't pay as well as private practice. The house was detached, but barely half the size of Huangsap's. Some of the neighbouring properties were in need of repair and the entire estate looked dowdy and poorly maintained.

Wattana himself opened the door when they knocked and led them through to what was clearly his study. He sat behind his desk and they each took one of the three seats opposite, Marky in the centre.

"Please, tell me how I can help," he began.

"Have you been able to visit your son, sir?" Marky asked, in no rush to get to the meat of the visit.

"I have, thank you. My wife is too distressed to go, but I've spoken with him." He turned to the colonel, "I'd appreciate it if he can be kept at the station lockup for as long as possible. He's a sensitive young man and won't do well in prison."

The colonel nodded noncommittally.

Wattana turned back to Marky, understanding it would be she who asked the questions.

"May I record our conversation?" she asked.

"I've no objection," he agreed, but she detected a moment of doubt in his expression as if he had not expected this to be anything more than further questions about his son.

"Please tell us about your relationship with Mr. Jirayu Huangsap," she went on.

After a moment's hesitation, he shrugged and replied, "We had the same relationship I had with all the lawyers who defended cases in Phuket courts. He's a very busy man, so all the prosecutors will know him." So he was admitting to knowing the man, but not on any personal level.

"Unlike your son, he is now on remand in Phuket prison," Marky revealed and waited for his reaction. He maintained the poker face, but she saw the subtle change in his eyes at this shocking news.

"May I ask on what charge?"

"It's quite a list, but some of the charges have led

to us making further inquiries. For example, could you tell us more about these cases?" she said, dropping the same four stapled sets of sheets side by side on his desk facing him.

Not picking them up, he looked slowly at the typed headings from the first to the last, clearly knowing the details of each well enough that he did not need to read them in full. Marky waited. This was no time to interrupt. He would either cave or clam up. Thankfully, after a long silence, he chose the former.

Wattana turned to the colonel and said, "I want you to know that whatever I did was to protect my son. Unfortunately, the hole got deeper and deeper as the years went by." His shoulders sank and he shook his head as if he now realised it was finally over.

The room had gone so quiet, Marky could hear the man breathing. "Tell us how it started," she prompted before he changed his mind.

"It was the night Wayu attacked that girl. I saw him get up and follow her, but never dreamed he would do such a thing as he did. He's always been a shy, quiet lad. One of the other girls came to tell Anutin, that's the owner ..."

"We know who he is," Marky confirmed.

"Right, well anyway, one of the girls came to tell him that she'd called the police because a waitress had been attacked. The music wasn't so loud by this time, so I overheard what she said. She didn't say anything about rape, otherwise I might have acted differently. I knew it was my idiot son, so I suggested

Anutin should call Huangsap. I didn't know him well, but I'd heard he had connections and was considered something of a 'fixer'. All I could think was that I had to help my son."

Marky wanted to say he ought to have thought of the poor girl first, but didn't want to interrupt him now he'd started.

The colonel leaned in to ask, "Why didn't you simply call Huangsap yourself?"

"I thought it would look better if someone else called, just in case it eventually got out. Anutin readily agreed because he didn't want the publicity, so it suited both of us. When I found out it wasn't just an assault and that Wayu had raped her, I called Huangsap myself to tell him because I was desparate by then. He turned up and it all went away. I tried to forget about it and we got on with our lives."

"Until?" Marky asked.

"Until a few months later when he called and insisted on seeing me away from the office. It didn't occur to me that he'd blackmail me, so I went along and met him."

"When was this?"

"Just after new year of 2016."

"Surely you expected there must be a quid pro quo?"

He shook his head, no, "Anutin had paid him generously, so I thought it was all done with. Then when I met him he said he had a case he needed me to steer away from court. I told him I couldn't do such a thing, and that's when he revealed he had the girl's underwear and a nurse as a witness. He said it was a one-off case he needed help with, which I foolishly believed. Besides, there was no way out. I had no doubt he'd carry out his threat to have Wayu arrested."

"You're an experienced lawyer yourself. Didn't it occur to you that he'd be in trouble too if he produced the evidence months after the crime?"

"I did think that, but it wasn't a risk I could take. He had the underwear and the nurse was a credible witness that the girl had been raped. There had been no police report, so he could easily have woven some story to explain the delay."

"So you did as he asked?" Marky pushed.

Wattana's head dropped and he nodded. "Yes. And then he came back again and again like all blackmailers do. It's been going on ever since. Once I'd started there was no way out. I'm a fool."

The colonel interrupted again to ask, "Did you ever accept a payment?"

Wattana looked up at him right away to answer "No, never. I wouldn't do such a thing." He turned to Nick then Marky, pleading with his eyes that they believe him.

Marky decided to deliver the final blow, "There is no DNA from Wayu on the girl's underwear, so it was all for nothing."

Colonel Orntong stood up and Wattana slowly did the same, knowing what was coming.

"Apisit Wattana, I'm arresting you for corruption in public office and for perverting the course of justice. You have the right to make a statement or to remain silent. Anything you do say may be used as evidence against you in court. You have the right to consult a lawyer and to inform a relative or trusted person. Do you understand the charges against you?"

Wattana only nodded, head down.

"You'll travel to the station in my vehicle, without cuffs, but I can't promise you any special consideration beyond that."

"I understand, thank you."

❖

Their list of arrests and charges was growing fast, so Marky decided to rearrange her board yet again. Photos of those arrested had their name and list of charges below them.

Wayu was still being held in the cell downstairs on the charge of assault and rape. Beum had agreed to act as a witness, as had Ngaan-dee after more threats from the colonel. Tida also now planned to come to Phuket for the trial, and Marky hoped she might yet agree to testify. The girl sounded more confident each time they spoke, so knowing her attacker was facing punishment was clearly helping her recovery and slow return to a normal life.

Huangsap had been charged with conspiracy to murder on three counts, conspiracy to attempted murder, blackmail, perverting the course of justice, interfering with evidence and bribing a police officer. Neither of the killers would speak against him, but the motorbike driver's phone had revealed calls between the two of them, as had Huangsap's own phone. Marky was confident the evidence was sufficient to see him put away for many years. He would certainly never work as a lawyer again.

Ngaan-dee was also charged with corruption in public office, perverting the course of justice for all the cases he had interfered with, conspiracy to murder and attempted murder. The colonel had doubts that the murder charges would stick, but he'd agreed they should try.

The two killers had still not been identified and steadfastly refused to give their names, but they'd been charged anonymously with three counts of murder and attempted murder all the same. Even though their faces were partially covered on the CCTV from the reporter's condo in Bangkok, the video quality was good enough to still identify them as his assailants. The driver's mobile phone also gave away their location in Bangkok on the date and time of his death.

Apisit Wattana was charged with multiple counts of corruption in public office, made bail the same day and immediately went to ground. Being such a high-profile public figure, he'd been hounded by the press ever since, but not a single news station or newspaper had spoken to him or managed to get a photo.

Once Marky completed all the necessary reports, all that would remain would be the work of the prosecutor's office grinding its way on the long road toward the courtroom.

Marky had proposed charges against the club owner, but the colonel had shut the idea down right away, telling her to be pleased with the success she had. He would still be around to be arrested another day anyway, he assured her.

Nick had been busy writing up his own action list while Marky was doing her board. His first priority was to let the chief back home know the Townsend case was resolved and that he would be travelling back very soon. The two wives needed personal visits; perhaps Marky could visit Wanchai's wife while he saw Townsend's. Finally, but not least important, he had to take Marky to lunch with grandfather as he had promised. Another item he didn't write down but made a mental note of was to ask Yu for another date before he left. An encore would be fun.

"I'll leave you to it if that's all right?" he asked when he saw she'd finished.

"Sure, I've got a ton of paperwork to do anyway. Will you be in again at all?"

Nick wasn't blind to the disappointment evident on her face while asking this. They both knew the case was over and their time working together was ending.

"I'll be here tomorrow morning with coffee and croissants as usual," he assured her, "and then we'll have lunch with grandfather if you like."

This cheered her up enormously and she beamed her usual smile. "I'll look forward to it."

❖

Marky had happily agreed to them visiting the wives separately, and so Nick had gone to Mrs. Townsend's house on the way home. Although glad to

313

hear her husband's killers had been caught, she was distraught to find out he had been killed for something he had nothing to do with. He'd been a good man and too keen to help anyone that asked. Her grief had turned to anger, but Nick knew it was just one of the phases she needed to go through before she could get on with her life. Townsend had left her well off and she was an intelligent woman, so she would have no money worries at least.

Nick knew Marky's job of telling Captain Gerdpon's wife he had been killed, as she had suspected, was going to be more difficult. There was no real evidence to confirm it beyond doubt, but hopefully Marky could reassure her it was true based on all they had learned. He hoped it would be enough for the woman.

Yu was still working out of the meeting room on the chief's major inquiry, so he had dropped by on his way out of the station to ask for another date, a proper one this time. She was as keen as he had hoped and expected, and they'd settled on Friday night at seven.

With his parents urging him to stay a little longer now he was free of the case, Nick agreed to book a flight for the following week. That would give him a few more days with them, and a few days to acclimatise to London time and weather before going back to work on Monday the first. He'd emailed the chief with a summary and to confirm his return already, so there was little left to do other than relax and enjoy the time off.

A family dinner and a quiet evening at home were

very welcome. Watching and listening to his parents and sister chat over the meal made him think about how life would be if he moved back to Phuket, but in his heart he knew he wasn't ready yet.

Something would have to change before that became possible. He didn't know what that might be, but for the moment he was happy with things just as they were.

# Chapter 15

As promised, Nick had turned up early with coffees and croissants. The morning had dragged on for him, as Marky had been busy with all the paperwork that needed to be completed. With so many people in custody and so many charges, it wasn't going to be a quick job. He'd suggested getting in another constable to help, but she insisted it was quicker to do it herself than have to explain it all anew to someone else.

"I'm really looking forward to this," she told him, as he parked the car at the rear of his grandfather's house.

"Me too. I don't see the old fella as much as I'd like. He's quite a character, you know."

Chun-hiang Ying-jareun-paisan was seated alone at the dining table in his regular spot waiting for

317

them. He smiled as they entered and nodded slightly to acknowledge Marky's 'wai'. Nick gave his grandfather a kiss on the cheek and a hug before indicating Marky should sit next to him. Once she was seated he took the chair on the other side of his grandfather,

"It's a delight to meet you again Miss Pondee," he told her, turning his steel-blue eyes and smile on her. Despite his age, Marky could see how he had charmed so many wives and mistresses when he was younger.

"It's very kind of you to have me for lunch."

"Pretty young ladies are a rarity in this house nowadays, so it's very pleasing to an old man's eyes to have you here. Let me get us some drinks," he said, reaching for a sash hanging against the wall beside him. He gave it a single pull, but Marky heard no sound. A middle-aged woman in a black and white servant's uniform soon appeared with a tray bearing three glasses. She set it down on the table, then moved the glasses to coasters in front of each guest.

"Iced chrysanthemum tea is my preferred drink nowadays. I hope that is alright?"

"Perfect, ah-gong, thank you." Thai manners dictated that she address the older man using the same word for grandfather as the family used, despite the two of them not being related. He smiled at her courtesy. Marky saw Nick watching them with an interested and amused expression and cocked an eyebrow in enquiry.

Nick leaned forward, "Ah-gong. I will have to tell you myself because Marky is far too modest. She has successfully concluded the case I was sent here to observe and has single-handedly brought down two killers, a rapist, a police officer, a lawyer and the public prosecutor."

The old man had turned to listen to Nick, but now returned his full attention to Marky, "Good heavens, young lady, you have been busy!"

"Please don't listen to Nick when he tells you it was all my work. He contributed a lot and we had another competent young officer helping too." She had coloured visibly at the attention.

"Nevertheless, it's quite an accomplishment."

The cook returned with another uniformed helper who Marky guessed was the maid Nick had referred to. They carried a tray apiece and quickly transferred plates of steaming food from the trays to the rotating platter in the centre of the table. Marky saw it was all Chinese fare, a steamboat fish, some pork dumplings, rice and a vegetable dish. Plates and cutlery were already laid out.

"Please begin," grandfather instructed, "and if you wish to speak as we eat, that's quite alright with me."

Nick spun the rotating platter to serve his grandfather some rice and a little food from each plate, then waited while Marky did the same.

"Nick tells me you have some interest in Phuket history."

Marky was surprised, first that Nick would tell his grandfather that piece of information, and secondly that he'd even mentioned her.

"I have, but as I'm sure you know, what they teach in school is either incomplete or wholly false. We can only understand our present and plan for the future if we learn from our past, don't you agree?"

Grandfather tipped his head in praise of this last remark, "I do. Please, ask away if you have some questions I can answer. As you know, I've lived a long life and experienced much."

Marky didn't waste the opportunity. For the next hour, she and the old man chatted and laughed as if they'd known one another for years, with Nick barely speaking. Eventually, with the dessert long finished, he said he needed to have a rest.

"Oh, I'm sorry. I've been going on and didn't think."

"Don't apologise, my dear. I've thoroughly enjoyed our chat. It's just this old body demands a nap after lunch."

Nick stood to help his grandfather up and Marky did the same. The old man took his grandson's arm and allowed him to lead him out of the room. Nick looked over his shoulder to indicate she should follow. They crossed the corridor and entered through the door opposite into what was clearly the private living room. It was huge.

This room was completely at odds with the rest of the house she'd seen. There was no Chinese furniture evident here; it was very grand in the style of a Victorian English country home. The room was four times as long as it was wide, with six tall windows along one wall. Heavy blood-red curtains hung to the sides of the windows, with decorated cornices above running around the ceiling. Two chandeliers hung down and wall lights dotted the walls above framed paintings.

Nick led his grandfather to a large wing-back armchair standing alone in the farthest corner of the room and helped him settle. It was next to a window with a good view of the front gardens and had a side table with silver framed photographs standing next to it. On closer inspection Marky could see that they were all old black and white prints of four different women. Judging by the fashion of their clothes and that none of them appeared to be Nick's mother when she was younger, Marky assumed these were the four 'wives' his grandfather had once loved. She was surprised, but pleased to see he gave them equal standing.

Marky approached to say goodbye, "Thank you again for having me ah-gong. I really enjoyed talking with you today."

"As did I young lady. If you don't mind, I shall have Nick send me your number and we'll do it again soon."

"I don't mind at all. I shall look forward to it."

Marky was secretly thrilled to be invited back by this lovely old man and hoped it would not be too long before he got in touch.

They left him to his nap and made their way back outside to the car.

"Well, you certainly made an impression," Nick told her as he started the engine.

"I was surprised he'd like to see me again, I'll admit."

"Don't be surprised. You're interesting to talk to and good company, and that's something he's short of."

"But your family is so big!"

"Half of them don't make an effort at all, many more only visit when they need something, and younger people don't have time for the elderly. Besides family, all his other visitors are after something from him, so you can see why he enjoyed chatting with you."

"That's so sad."

"Don't feel sorry for him. Mum comes almost every day, and Jane and dad visit regularly. They have him over for dinner at the house at least once a month because he doesn't like eating out. He's not very high-tech, but I manage to video call with him at least once a week."

The comment about not eating out made Marky laugh. "He's not at all like you then! You do nothing but eat out."

They had arrived back at the station and Nick pulled up at the front door to drop her off.

"You're not coming in?" she asked.

"No, I promised mum I'd stay home this afternoon. I'm trying to keep her happy before I leave." Marky hesitated to get out of the car, uncertain if or when they would meet again. Nick knew what she was thinking and said, "I'll give you a call. We must have a night out to celebrate before I head home."

This cheered her instantly and she said, "That sounds great. See you!" and jumped out.

❖

Sitting with his eyes closed, grandfather knew he would soon fall asleep. He never lasted long after lunch, especially after so much conversation. The young woman had been quite remarkable he thought, comfortable jumping from one subject to another and having a solid opinion on everything they discussed. It was particularly pleasing to find she had an interest in local history, as most youngsters nowadays seemed concerned only for the future and what it offered them.

This long life had taught him many things; he had lived through boom and bust managing several companies and hundreds of employees, had endured through the second world war, the Thai revolution, numerous depressions and recessions, and far too many military coups to count.

Even now, despite his advanced age and lack of mobility, he still had some influence and could make things happen when he chose to. He chose to do so now and reached for his mobile, his elderly fingers fumbling with the buttons to wake it up.

❖

"Call for you on line one, sir." his secretary told him when he answered. He pressed the button that would connect him without thanking her.

"Colonel Orntong speaking."

"Good afternoon colonel. Do you have a moment to speak?"

The colonel reacted to the voice on the line by sitting up straight, "Of course, Mr. Ying-jareun-paisan. What can I do for you sir?"

"I've had the pleasure of entertaining one of your officers at my home this lunchtime. I just wanted to let you know I believe Miss Pondee makes an excellent police captain."

"Thank you for letting me know sir."

"I'm glad we understand one another colonel."

The line went dead and the colonel looked blankly at the useless instrument in his hand, aware he had just received an order.

❖

"Have you seen the notice that's gone up?" Yu asked, poking her head around the door of the training room.

"No. What's it about?" Marky asked, looking up from the report she was typing.

Yu came fully inside and closed the door silently behind her, "The colonel has called a full station meeting for next Tuesday morning at nine, exceptions given only for those on night-shift below the rank of sergeant. Everyone else to attend," she explained in a quiet voice.

"Wow. What do you think that's about? I've never heard of such a thing before."

"Me neither. I've got no idea, but he's been in and out of our inquiry room asking the officers about progress, and I heard he's also interviewed Ngaan-dee alone a couple of times."

324

"That's all quite curious. Let me know if you hear anything more about it."

"Will do ma'am," she agreed as she pulled the door open to leave.

# Chapter 16

Marky was surprised but pleased to find Nick leaning against the wall outside the meeting room with their usual morning fare when she arrived.

"This is a nice surprise! Have you been waiting long?" she asked, unlocking the door.

"Just a couple of minutes," he said, following her inside. Looking around at the charmless, windowless room he told her, "I'll miss this place, you know."

"Just the place?" she challenged.

"You too, of course, that goes without saying."

They sat facing one another and opened the bag of croissants.

"So what brings you here today?"

"I got a call from the colonel's secretary asking me to be here for a staff meeting and the press conference that will follow."

327

"I see," she said, but didn't really. What on earth was the colonel up to?

❖

There being no formal room large enough to accommodate all the station staff, the meeting was being held in the canteen, where all the tables and chairs had been pushed back against the walls to make space. By the time Marky and Nick arrived at five to nine, the room was nearing capacity. They found a space to stand just inside the door and waited for the colonel to appear. Listening to the chatter around the room, it was clear no one yet knew the reason for this unusual gathering.

The colonel appeared right on time, carrying some document folders and his hat. Those in the room stopped talking immediately. He waited until the doors were closed then took up position in the corner of the room; everyone moving aside to give him space. He did not hurry but took his time to look around first.

"Good morning, everyone. I'm sure you're all wondering why I've called this extraordinary meeting, so I'll get right to it. There are some good news items to announce and sadly some unpleasant ones too. So, to the first. Sergeant Nick Foster."

Nick was shocked to hear his name called out but automatically stepped forward. The colonel selected one of the folders he was carrying and withdrew an envelope from inside.

Handing it over he said, "A letter of

commendation with our sincere gratitude for a job very well done, sergeant."

Nick was too shocked to know what to say, so mumbled a thank you, remembered to 'wai', then stepped back. The gathered crowd offered some muted applause.

"Acting Captain Marisa Pondee," he called next. Marky stepped forward, stood at attention and saluted. The colonel selected a second envelope, passed it over and said, "Your confirmation of promotion, Captain Pondee." This brought a little more applause than Nick's had, as the crowd now sensed this was a straightforward awards ceremony.

"The final item of good news for today is for Constable Mayuree Jai-ngaam." He waited and Yu came forward from the opposite side of the room, saluted and accepted the proffered envelope. "Your promotion to lance corporal and transfer to Ta Chatchai police station to join the inquiry team under Major Sirikant."

Marky enthusiastically joined in the clapping and cheering as Yu made her way back to her place, now red in the face from the attention.

The colonel held up a hand and the room went quiet once more. Two officers lifted a table down from atop another at the side of the room and stood it in front of the colonel, "Now to the unpleasant news," he said, "come forward when I call your name." He removed a sheet of paper from his final folder and began reading off a list of names, senior ranks first. Each man stepped forward until there were six of them at attention in front of the table. The colonel put away his list then looked each of them in the eye, before saying "Place your weapons on the table."

The men were momentarily confused by this order. Four of them complied immediately, as they would to any order from a senior officer. A sub-lieutenant did not move, as he carried no sidearm. The last man, a corporal, opened his mouth to ask what this was about, but the colonel shut him down and repeated his order. This time the man reluctantly complied. The colonel waved a hand and six officers came quickly forward with handcuffs ready to cuff a man apiece.

With the men shackled, the colonel turned, opened the door himself and left the room without another word. Everyone else stood silently, not comprehending what they'd just witnessed. The six officers began walking their charges out of the canteen. The chatter started up as soon as they had left, as everyone offered their own idea for what had just transpired. Nick and Marky were in no doubt at all about what had happened.

❖

Being in a windowless room meant they had no idea how big a press conference it was going to be until they came downstairs. They were expecting the local newspapers and maybe a local TV crew to cover the announcement of the Townsend case and its aftermath, so they were surprised to find both national and local TV crews and newspaper reporters and photographers filling the steps at the front of the station, jostling for the best position.

The colonel came downstairs with his hat already on his head, so Marky put hers on before they went out. A podium had been set up to hold the microphones, and the colonel stepped up to it. Marky stood behind and to his left, Nick to the right. He felt naked standing there in civvies amongst the brown uniforms. Once the photographers had got all the shots they needed, the colonel began.

"I'm pleased to announce the conclusion of a very complex case today, which began as an inquiry into a single shooting death. Captain Marisa Pondee led the inquiry, assisted by Sergeant Nick Foster of the London Metropolitan Police." He indicated left and right as he mentioned their names. "Several conspirators are now in custody, and Captain Pondee will answer your questions relating to that investigation shortly. Furthermore, discoveries made in that case led to the opening of a new, large-scale inquiry by outside officers into corruption within Phuket Police Headquarters. This has already led to the arrest of seven serving police officers and two retired officers." That last part was news to Marky and Nick. "Four more officers have been suspended pending further investigation. A full review of all cases investigated by this police station over the last five years is now underway, but you will appreciate this will take some time to complete. I have nothing more for you just now, so I'll pass you over to Captain Pondee."

The reporters began shouting questions as the

colonel turned away, but he had no intention of answering. Marky stepped up to the podium and waited until they had given up and settled down once more.

"Firstly, I'd like to say we're very pleased that we've been able to bring closure for the victim of a historic sexual assault. The attacker ..."

❖

The final few days in Phuket had flown by, being busy with his parents and joining his sister on-site at the new construction project. Jane had walked him all round the muddy site in the midday heat, explaining at length where everything would be built and what it would look like when finished. He marvelled at her enthusiasm and nodded in all the right places.

He'd kept his promise to Marky and taken her out for dinner. Razzle rooftop restaurant to the south of Patong had been the perfect setting for their farewell. They had promised one another to keep in touch and he was sure they would. It was rare to come across somebody he could get along with so well, so quickly, and so he would make an extra effort to keep their friendship alive despite the distance.

With Yu he'd gone back once more to Cape Yamu, which she'd found suitably impressive. He'd been presumptuous and booked them a sea view suite for the night, but she hadn't minded at all. As Yu didn't have to work the following day, they'd slept late and made love again before he'd dropped her at home. No promises were made or expected either way, but Nick hoped their paths would cross again one day. Even if nothing more serious ever came of their relationship, she at least provided a good reason to visit Phuket more often.

As he opened the door to enter his team's shared office at Scotland Yard, he caught sight of the boss just taking his coat off in his glass-walled office at the other end of the long room. Nick smiled, raised one hand in greeting, then the other to show the tray of coffees and bag of pastries he had brought. This was met with the boss's usual curt nod.

Sitting down at his desk he saw a yellow sticky note he had left for himself on his desk telephone. It read 'Call Emily Brown ext. 2122'.

Feeling quite at home already, he sat down and smiled in anticipation.

Lightning Source UK Ltd.
Milton Keynes UK
UKHW042053210622
404768UK00002B/425

9 786165 932899